THE MAD WITCH'S ORC

VICTORIA DOVE

VESTRAHORN MOUNTAINS
OLD SHALIMAR RUINS
ETTERA
HELIOS
TAYBE
IHO
LACRA

BEAR LAKE
SILVER FOREST
SOLAR CITY
SANOGRAD
RAVA

Book Cover by Feyspeaker

Editing: A Taylor(ed) Edit

Paperback ISBN: 979-8-9946998-0-5

CONTENT WARNING

Please see author's website for detailed list of all content warnings

www.authorvictoriadove.com

CHAPTER ONE

CALYPSO

"**B**urn the witch!"

Calypso watched from the shadows of an alley a scene that she'd witnessed a hundred times prior. Every corner of Shalimar contained the same townsfolk spewing vitriol, callous guards dragging the accused women, and unoriginal threats. It was either "burn the witch" or "drown the witch." She wished that once someone would shout something interesting, like "bake the witch into a cake."

The guards passed the alley in which she was waiting with Nyx. There were so many guards, Calypso could hardly make out the woman they were leading.

Someone threw a pint glass from the tavern next door, and it shattered on the ground before the envoy. One of the guards yelled in the direction from which the glass was thrown, but they didn't slow their pace. Bloody footprints emerged from the broken glass. They hadn't even let the woman wear shoes.

Black smoke swirled around Calypso's legs as loose embers bit at her hands. She took one step forward, itching to leave the alley.

"Not yet." Nyx's stern voice grabbed her attention.

Calypso studied her sister, who'd insisted on conducting this rescue. For a moment, she considered ignoring her warnings and ambushing the guards.

It would be so much easier if her sisters would just let her lean into her power the way she wanted.

She cannot stop you. Your power exceeds hers.

The intruding voice hissed in her head. Her hallucinations were worsening and becoming harder to ignore. It wasn't hearing the voice that worried Calypso, but the moments when she felt herself agreeing with its sentiments.

She forced a nod and stepped back to Nyx's side. The black fog that had surrounded her a moment ago was nowhere to be found. Calypso almost asked Nyx if she had seen it, but she wasn't ready for her answer.

Instead, she stayed silent and watched the accused woman finally reach the platform at the center of the town.

The town magistrate wobbled up the steps to stand at the front, his black robes tightly stretched over his rotund belly. He looked over the crowd with an inflated sense of self-importance.

"We gather today for the trial and sentencing of Marianna Clairmont," he bellowed. "This woman stands accused of witchcraft!"

The crowd erupted.

The sudden onslaught of noise caused Marianna to flinch. Even from a distance, her tremors were visible as she stood at the center of the wooden platform. Dark, grimy hair stuck to her face, and her eyes were wide with fear. They searched the crowd for even a hint of compassion, but none was there.

Calypso would give her something better than compassion. She would give her *revenge*.

"For your first offense," the magistrate continued, "you were seen gathering plants on the outskirts of town."

"That's true! I saw her!" yelled a woman in the crowd.

The magistrate frowned at the interruption but resumed. "As I was saying. These plants were later used to create poisons, causing harm to your fellow townsfolk."

Calypso resisted the urge to tap her foot in annoyance. She hated when these sham trials were drawn out. It was clear they would find her guilty regardless of the truth.

"Second, you summoned your witch's strength to break the nose of the merchant's son."

Everyone's glance flew toward an indignant-looking young man with a dark bruise coloring his face. Calypso snorted in disbelief, sensing the true reason Marianna was targeted.

"Are you sure she is even a witch?" Calypso whispered to Nyx. "Sounds like she's just some poor girl who rejected the wrong boy."

The agreement had been to rescue witches, not meddle in the plights of humans.

"I am sure," was all Nyx responded.

Calypso returned her attention to the trial, noting the eagerness of the growing crowd.

"Finally, there is the undeniable evidence of these accusations." The magistrate dramatically paused before continuing. "You possess the mark of witchkind."

The magistrate waved his hand at one of the guards, who ripped the woman's thin dress from shoulder to thigh. Her breast, belly, and hip became exposed for the village to leer at as the magistrate triumphantly pointed at the black mark of magic. The upside-down triangle with a single line running horizontal through it branded her as an earth witch.

Given the size of the mark, Calypso guessed the witch had likely come into her power only a year or two prior.

Murmurs and exclamations spread through the crowd.

"For these three signs, you have been deemed a witch," the magistrate concluded. "And for this crime, you are sentenced to burn at the stake!"

Several of the guards climbed down the platform to grab torches while the other guards tied the poor woman to a large wooden stake. She struggled helplessly against their hold.

"Have at them, Calypso." Nyx quickly moved toward the ladder, her bow at her back. "I'm headed for the rooftop."

Anticipation spread through her as Calypso stepped out of the shadows toward the unsuspecting crowd.

"It's in poor taste to start the festivities before the main guest arrives." Calypso's mocking voice rang out loudly.

There was confusion followed by gasps.

She had purposefully worn a black dress with transparent sleeves to highlight her numerous marks of magic, and with her untamed red hair, it was a striking sight.

"Who dares interrupt?!" the magistrate called out, adjusting his spectacles.

"I'm wounded that you don't recognize me." Calypso strode down the middle of the crowd, which had now parted, not wishing to touch her. "After Lacra, I thought my name would've traveled here."

Whispers spread among the folk. "It's the mad witch!"

"I will not tolerate this intrusion! If we are going to burn one witch, we might as well make it two." The magistrate waved the guard forward. "Guards, seize her!"

Before the command finished, a faint whizzing sound pierced the air. Then two guards wordlessly dropped to the ground, each with an arrow through their eye. Nyx's shots never missed.

The other guards stood stunned for a second before recovering and hurtling down the platform toward her.

Calypso reveled in the feel of her hands setting ablaze with that living fire that always burned inside her. The flames mercilessly struck the guards, searing their skin and melting their eyes.

The townsfolk screamed and scattered. Few tried to help but quickly fled as they saw how pointless it was.

It was a gruesome sight to behold, and Calypso made no effort to hold back. Burning was not a pleasant way to die, yet this crowd was so quick to inflict that on someone else.

Her worst wouldn't make up for a fraction of the deaths that had occurred over the last ten years. The regent king's decree banning witchcraft had triggered a violence so brutal that the soil surrounding past coven houses was still stained red.

With the guards charred and smoking at her feet, Calypso turned toward the magistrate.

She loved saving them for last. Something about their look of disbelief that their plans had fallen apart was so delicious.

"I think we should switch it up and burn a lawman instead." She took slow, predatory steps in his direction.

The man stumbled to the ground, scrambling to get away. In his pathetic fear, he dropped his torch, which rolled toward the bound witch. The hay at her feet instantly caught fire.

"Damn it!" Calypso cursed and raced toward the platform.

She reached the woman quickly, but the fire was already spreading rapidly. Unfazed by the flames, which would not hurt her, Calypso grabbed a knife from her boot and sliced at the rope.

Once released, Marianna sagged forward from weakness and shock. Calypso picked her up, one arm under her knees and one at her shoulders, and jumped off the platform.

She glanced over her shoulder to see the magistrate running down the cobblestone road.

Then he fell. An arrow stuck out of his neck.

This was one instance where she would prefer Nyx to be a little less accurate and let the man suffer.

She turned her attention back to the shivering witch.

"I need to see your feet." Calypso set her down gently on the stones and looked at her bloodied and blistering feet. The burns only went up to her ankles, but they were severe.

Whatever rush had been keeping the pain away was slowly dissipating, and the woman began to scream.

"Look at me." Calypso grabbed the woman's face, forcing her to meet her eyes. "I will help you, but you need to calm down."

At first, Marianna didn't respond, and Calypso worried she was too far in her own mind, but then the woman nodded.

Calypso used her knife to cut her palm, letting the deep red blood coat her hand like a glove. She reached out toward the other witch, who reared back, horror scattered over her features.

"It will heal your feet." Calypso's explanation wasn't reassuring enough as Marianna continued to hold herself stiffly away. "If you think your pain is excruciating now, this is nothing compared to the agony that will come later."

A wave of pain must've hit right then because Marianna's features went pale. Desperation set in, and she nodded, leaning forward toward Calypso.

It took only a handful of seconds for Calypso to leave the bloody inscriptions upon Marianna's skin. They emitted a soft glow before disappearing, and Marianna's body absorbed her black magic.

Marianna was still shivering but calmer. The magic would heal her burns and protect her from fire, never to be set aflame again.

Calypso picked up the small witch, who was losing consciousness from exhaustion, and began her march toward the meeting point.

Her steps were brisk with irritation at her sisters—Nyx and Astra—for the delay this detour caused. She wanted to leave these tiny villages and head to the northern district. She wanted to burn her mark onto the realm and spit in the face of its nobility.

Most of all, she wanted vengeance.

Thomas Haworth. Ker Beck. Hugh Davinger.

Calypso's finger slid across the sharp edge of her dagger, drawing a bead of blood.

Thomas Haworth. Ker Beck. Hugh Davinger.

The names of her nightmares had become a comforting chant throughout the years. She repeated it over and over in her head until it was all she heard. It kept her focused. It kept her mad.

The list had been longer when she and her sisters had initially formed their pact, but they'd been busy throughout the years and names had fallen off in delightful ways. Infuriatingly, those three powerful men still lived, their names an echoing reminder.

"She seems to be recovering well."

Astra's voice broke through her thoughts. Calypso turned to find her golden-haired sister walking up to her. In a different life, Astra Katsaros would be hosting a ball and raising a drove of babes to honor her noble name. Instead, the fickleness of magic had marked Astra's hands when she came of age and branded her a witch.

"Who?"

"Marianna." Astra glanced toward the other witches near the caravan. "The witch we rescued a few days ago."

Calypso resumed sharpening her dagger. "I would imagine not being actively persecuted is an improvement in her situation."

"No argument here. Do you have your things ready?" Astra asked, insisting on continuing the conversation with her.

"I have been ready every time you've asked these past two days."

"You know we need to wait for Nyx to return."

Of course, Calypso knew that. She was the one who sent her in the first place.

"Unless you are here to tell me Nyx is hiding behind you, this conversation has started to bore me."

"Let me know if you plan on being an ass the entire journey or just until we set out."

Calypso scowled at her but bit back a retort. "I am eager for the next step. Yet, I find myself . . ." She paused, uncertain how to describe what she felt.

"Anxious?" Astra finished for her with a small grin of amusement.

She glared at her and corrected through gritted teeth. "Unsettled."

"I believe most would find it normal to be *unsettled* before murdering a district lord," Astra said. "Don't worry. It will go well."

"I am not worried about Thomas Haworth," she snapped, her efforts to contain her annoyance clearly pointless. "I just don't understand why we need to take the others with us. It should only be me, you, and Nyx."

The others in question were the witches that they had rescued over the past couple of years. It wasn't part of their pact to stop trials and break free witches about to be burned. However, Nyx and Astra kept finding these tragic cases, and it served as an outlet for Calypso's need for violence, which had appealed to her.

Now she was stuck with a dozen witches to cart around in a caravan. Their powers awakened but not yet developed, which made her feel like she was protecting a litter of stray kittens. Irritation simmered beneath her skin, testing the already thin thread of her patience.

"They have nowhere else to go. Also, we could use their help." Astra was quick to put up her hands before Calypso could speak. "I love how you are so confident in our abilities that you believe we could storm the capital alone, but I think we may need more than three witches for this."

Astra was wrong. They needed only each other. That's the way it had been since their refuge at the Sanctuary of Mother Selene ten years ago, and that's the way it should remain.

The difference was that then they were three girls fleeing Sanograd after the regent king's decree made bearing a witch's mark a death sentence. Their magic was weak then, barely a couple of years from their awakening. But what they didn't have in power, they made up in rage for all they had lost. The trauma bound them as sisters in all ways but blood. From that pain was born their pact of revenge against the men who had hurt them.

Now ten years later, they were no longer the fearful girls they once were. They had harnessed their abilities to become things that should be feared instead.

"Let me know when Nyx returns," Calypso said before walking away from the conversation.

Questions of how long Astra would tolerate her volatile moods crept at the back of her mind. The black magic Calypso had infused herself with had transformed her into something more reactive and less in control.

Like a mocking reminder, the black tattoos along her forearms tingled. Her fingers automatically went to them as her eyes skirted to the women sitting together. Their expressions were light, their voices cheerful as they spoke to one another.

They should not be here.

She couldn't tell if that was her own voice or the voice of the madness that was slowly seeping in. The voice had been very distinct when it first spoke several years ago. Gravely and deep, like the rumblings of a beast. It worried her that the voice was becoming indistinguishable from her own. It also worried her whether there would be a day when this wouldn't bother her.

Unsettled by her thoughts, she rushed away from camp, heading deep into the woods until they were out of sight.

The vise around her lungs released a fraction when she spotted the river ahead. For whatever reason, she'd discovered water settled the voices.

Without wasting a moment, she shed her clothes and stepped into the cool water. With a rapid plunge, she immersed herself underneath, allowing the cold to take her senses. She stayed under until the burn in her lungs was too much, and she broke the surface once more. Then she exited the river, choosing to remain naked for the moment. Her internal fire never left her cold.

She looked down at her body. Right above her belly button was the mark of magic she gained at puberty, three black lines forming a triangle—the alchemical sign of fire. The interlacing knots that ran up both her forearms and covered her upper chest, she had inflicted on herself.

As a witch's power grew, their markings expanded as well. There was once a time a witch would display her vastly marked skin with pride in their mastery of witchcraft. Now, such a display was a death sentence.

Their markings developed with time and study, and only the practice of black magic could hasten this process, but not without its cost. Black magic required a sacrifice of life, with the blood of the victim used to tattoo more markings and forcibly gain more power.

Truthfully, she both loved and hated the evidence of her black magic. The power she gained was intoxicating, and, most importantly, it would allow her to get her revenge. What she hated were the intruding voices, the hallucinations, and the feeling that she wasn't always the one in control. But it was a price she was willing to pay.

"Just one more year," she muttered to herself.

All she had to do was last one more year. If everything went according to their plans, the three men she hated most in the world would be dead, and she didn't care what happened to her after that.

It was hours before Calypso felt in control again. Deep purple streaks crossed the sky, and the forest was darkening.

She dressed once more and walked back into the clearing. Spotting Nyx's sleek raven hair in the distance, she cursed herself for being gone so long.

With a quick step toward camp, she passed Astra and gruffly asked, "Why didn't you tell me Nyx had returned?"

"I didn't want to disturb you," Astra responded, heavy with connotation. Calypso's ventures into black magic were not a secret amongst them, but her sister preferred not to witness it.

"I was just bathing," Calypso snapped back before reaching into a basket of food and snatching an apple.

Catching Nyx's eye, Calypso gestured toward the firepit. "Let's speak."

The three of them stepped aside, heading toward an empty spot by the fire to talk separately.

"Please tell me you have good news," Calypso implored, unwilling to be camped out here a moment longer.

Nyx nodded briskly as she took off her cloak. "Things are moving along as planned. The orcs travel southeast toward Helios."

"And Captain Von Ahlen?"

"Currently being debriefed by his guard about the oncoming attack. I would imagine they will be up in arms by tomorrow night."

"Pity for the captain." Calypso took a bite out of her apple. Everyone knew nightfall gave orcs an advantage. "I trust our tracks are covered?"

Nyx's exhausted face turned incredulous at the offense. "Of course. Gemma took on the face of one of the captain's newest guardsmen when she gave the report. Some young man by the name of Rupert."

"And what is the actual young Rupert doing at this time?"

A rare smile broke the porcelain features of Nyx's face. "He is at a brothel outside of Helios, being handed drink after drink. He will wake up with a massive headache, no recollection of the night before, and a story about how he spotted the oncoming orc horde."

"Perfect."

The Orc Wars had been going on for as long as Calypso could remember. While she normally didn't care to involve herself in other troubles, they served as useful distractions.

Johann Von Ahlen was the captain of the guard in the northern district, responsible for keeping the peace, and for answering the beck and call of the district lords. She had no personal grudge against him. But she did need him far away from Taybe.

The bitter captain would not be able to resist the temptation of fighting the orcs and gaining some ground after having had several humiliating months. She didn't doubt that he would gather his guard and head over to Helios.

Finishing her apple, seeds and all, Calypso faced her sisters with an eager grin. "We should get some rest. There is a lord whose head needs removed from his body."

Chapter Two

VIDORAK

"You can either unlock the door, or I will slice you open and feast on your insides," Vidorak threatened the human man he was holding up by the neck. Orcs didn't eat human entrails, but the man didn't know that.

The man panicked at the threat, legs kicking out helplessly. Vidorak had already come to the raid on edge, and this was just worsening his mood. He was ready to toss the human to the ground and break open the door to the granary with his axe, abandoning his intention to do things the less destructive way.

Before he could act, Nazghor came over and bent down to the human's eye level, trying to make his large orc form appear less threatening.

"Don't mind him. He's just grumpy because his braids got tangled. Now, if you open the door, we will let you go."

Vidorak glared at his friend, but the words calmed the human, who nodded vigorously. He unceremoniously dropped the man, who scrambled up and fumbled to retrieve a key from his pockets.

With shaking hands, he started to unlock the door. "You won't kill me, right?"

"Hurry before I change my mind," Vidorak snarled impatiently.

The lock clicked, and the door to the granary opened. As the orcs made to enter, Vidorak briefly registered the man dashing away into the night.

Nazghor tsked. "He's heading straight toward the others. If he had waited a moment, I would've told him to head to the river."

"You can't save everyone from their poor decisions," Vidorak mumbled, the human already forgotten, as he entered the building.

"But can I save myself from your bad mood?" Nazghor responded, unfazed by Vidorak's surly demeanor.

Vidorak ignored his friend as they grabbed bags of flour and wheat, loading them onto a cart for transport back to the mountain. He moved quickly, wanting to be done with this so they could begin returning. He didn't have a good feeling about this raid.

As if on cue, tiny glowing dots appeared in the distance.

Vidorak cursed. "He has done it again."

"Maybe that's just a torch," Nazghor commented, following his eyeline. Then several more lights popped up and spread. "Maybe not."

"His bloodthirst will be the end of us all," Vidorak spat out.

Nazghor grabbed him by the neck and brought him closer, his jovial tone gone. "Be careful what you say, brother. This is not the place."

Those discussions needed to remain private to avoid the wrong orc overhearing. For the past several years, Vidorak had been working with those he trusted to break down the chieftain's influence. Challenging him when so many jarls still supported his uncle's brutal regime would make a power shift unachievable.

Due to the war, the Crown banned the human towns from trading with orcs, limiting their options. The clan was suffering in the desolate mountains. It was raid or starve.

But the destruction of homes and murder were gratuitous. His uncle's orders bred wanton violence, harsher than necessary for gathering resources.

From a young age, Vidorak learned to remain cold and emotionless during the needlessly violent raids as he planned for change in the background. There was still more to be done before he could officially challenge his uncle for control of the clan, but remaining quiet was becoming increasingly difficult. Nazghor's words were another reminder of how his control was fracturing.

"I will be back." Vidorak stepped out of Nazghor's hold, heading toward the fires.

Nazghor cursed. "Grushag, go with him and make sure he doesn't end up dead. I will finish up here."

The scarred orc nodded and stepped into the shadows, following silently behind. Vidorak paid him no mind as he made his way toward the center of Helios.

The bell tower rang, alerting the small town to the invasion. A symphony of screams and terror that was all too familiar echoed in the streets.

A townsman desperately ran down the road in his nightshirt only to come to an abrupt stop. He fell to the ground with an axe sticking out of his back. His orc attacker came forward, laughing as he pulled the axe away.

The smell of ash burned Vidorak's nostrils as he roamed the once lively streets of Helios. Watching the violence unfold, the thrum of rage in his veins beat at the wall he'd built inside him.

Amid the chaos, Vidorak spotted a stocky orc with short-cropped hair and bone piercings in his ears entering one of the homes off a side street.

Mabanok's loyal to his uncle was absolute, and he never hesitated to carry out every ruthless command. The brutal orc wished to become clan jarl by any means necessary, even harming his own kind.

Vidorak changed course and headed in Mabanok's direction. Muted by the sounds of the town burning, he could pick up on the cries of small children as he approached the home.

The door was wide open, and despite the darkness, Vidorak could see clearly. Mabanok was facing away from him, his large orc frame taking up most of the room. From the sounds of it, he had a female pinned to the table in front of him.

Vidorak slipped into the house quietly, his hand tightening on the handle of his axe. In a swift motion, he slammed the blunt end of the axe over Mabanok's head, causing a loud crack. The looming orc fell backward without even realizing what had happened. Vidorak stared down at him, noting how his chest unfortunately still moved.

He turned his attention to the human female, who was trembling as she held onto her torn dress and looked at him, likely wondering if he was going to take her next.

The sound of soft crying in the corner drew his attention, and he spotted two small children huddled near the bed.

"Please don't!" the woman cried out. "I will do what you want, just don't hurt my children."

His uncle didn't care if his orcs raped the human women. In fact, if an orc had been particularly vicious during a raid, his uncle might even reward him with a human pleasure slave at the mountain.

"I will not hurt you."

Unfortunately, he couldn't say the same for any other orc who came by and saw her vulnerable.

He noticed a dresser in the corner and went over to it. With a swift tug, he pulled it out a couple of feet. "Hide behind here."

After a moment of hesitation, the woman got to her feet and grabbed her two children, taking them behind the moved furniture. She crouched down, her small ones huddled by her, still sobbing.

"This will keep you out of sight, but you need to stop the crying," Vidorak said and placed a blanket over the top and side of the dresser to hide the gap.

He returned to the unconscious body of Mabanok and glanced back, satisfied that from the entrance of the home they weren't visible.

He grabbed the orc and dragged him out onto the street. Grushag was close by, watching what unfolded.

"Take him somewhere further away and dump him. If we are lucky, wild dogs will finish the job for us."

Without even a nod, the scarred orc heaved Mabanok over one shoulder and disappeared. Vidorak continued toward the governor's house, shouting and destruction picking up with every step. The home was at the top of a hill, overlooking the valley below.

A dark, booming laugh broke through the chaos, and Vidorak followed the sound until he spotted his uncle. Three guards wearing chain mail and carrying swords surrounded him. His uncle carried a war hammer but didn't reach for it, instead attacking the guards with his brute strength.

Despite his age, Urim still fought like a wild boar, crushing his enemies to dust. Broken bones didn't instantly kill someone, so screams of pain permeated the air as his uncle left his enemies fallen and writhing.

Urim was bloodied and grinning at the sight when Vidorak approached.

"Uncle, what happened?"

The raid was meant to retrieve resources only—grabbing flour from the granary, meats and cheeses from the cellar of the governor's house. They had not discussed burning and pillaging the entire village.

"Our plans have changed, nephew." Urim pointed to the south. "It seems the captain wants to play."

From above, Vidorak spotted the unmistakable coloring of Captain Von Ahlen's guard on the circular wooden shields of the soldiers. Scanning quickly, he calculated the captain must've brought at least one hundred men while they had less than half of that in orcs.

While favor was still on their side with their positioning and strength, it would be a bloodbath and the casualties severe.

"The losses are not worth this loot."

"You suggest we let him chase us off?" Urim stared with thirsty hatred at the approaching army. "I will not yield to the man who murdered my brother."

Despite everything his uncle put him through, Vidorak understood that hatred. While Urim's rage burned hot, Vidorak's was cold and measured.

It was almost twenty years ago that Johann Von Ahlen murdered his father, causing Urim to become chieftain and throwing the clan into an endless war.

Vidorak was just an orcling at the time, unable to do much besides hide his grief. One day the captain would answer for his crimes. But first, Vidorak needed to make sure the clan didn't break under its own brutality.

"I suggest we retreat and approach him on our terms at a different time." Vidorak spoke as if unbothered either way.

There was silence as they watched the guard approach. His uncle's hand twitched, clearly aching to grab his axe. A few other orcs joined them as others noticed the oncoming assault.

One orc asked, "Chieftain, what shall we do?"

With a last hard glance, his uncle commanded, "Finish grabbing the loot and retreat north through the forest."

The orcs nodded and left to follow his orders and inform the others.

His uncle put a hand on his shoulder. "I need you to find out how the captain came to know we'd raid here. But first let's have some fun."

Vidorak remained silent, waiting to find out in what way Urim would add more stains to his soul.

"Let's have a little competition. I want to circle behind the soldiers and pick them off until they notice. Whoever gets the most kills can take first pick of the loot."

With silent acceptance, they disappeared into the shadows of the woods and broke away from the rest of the raiding party.

When the hunt begins, turn your knife on him instead.

The voice in his head begging to end his uncle's reign had become more persistent. If it were only him, he would've tried long ago. But his failure would be a price his mother and his allies would pay.

A price one friend had paid already. Orif had bravely made a statement opposing Urim's allowance of abuse toward the human females. His uncle subsequently sent him on a mission with Mabanok, but Orif never returned. The message was clear: anything less than unquestioning loyalty was intolerable.

They stalked through the woods, and Vidorak leaned into the beastly part of him. The part that fed off death and destruction. Orcs were prone to violence, their brute strength giving them a predisposition in that focus. But too much bloodshed and they could lose themselves to a berserker frenzy, killing everything in sight, no matter if friend or foe.

They stepped behind the guards, and his body moved on instinct, its only goal to bring death. One by one, dark hands twisted necks, silent cracks ending lives. He sliced the arteries of the men who had the misfortune to walk in the back, their warm blood spilling onto his hands.

"I heard their tusks are so large they can't close their mouths. Can you imagine, Jon?" said a human soldier up ahead. "Jon?"

The soldier looked back, searching for his friend, only to see a pile of bodies littered behind and two demons stalking forward.

"Behind us! Orcs!" he managed to shout before Urim pushed a knife through his chest. The rest of the noise came out as gurgles.

The seconds it took for the soldiers to turn and take in the change in circumstance was all the time they needed to vanish into the night, leaving the soldiers to count their dead. There was a feeble attempt to follow them into the woods, but they were long gone, the distance too great at this point. With the competition over, the orcs circled north, heading to meet with the raiding party once more.

"You won. Seems I've taught you well," Urim grumbled.

Vidorak felt no joy in that. His hands were still coated with the warmth of their blood. It didn't matter how late they arrived at the mountain; he would wash.

"I'll take the girl," Vidorak stated, spotting a human female being brought back in one of the wagons, her slight frame shaking with silent tears. He would leave her with his gentle mother and then later return her to the town when this raid was forgotten.

"Finally taking a female to warm your bed?" his uncle said.

Vidorak didn't respond and stayed silent on the way back. He saw Mabanok in the group, a red welt coloring the back of his head. His steps were unbalanced, but his eyes looked angry.

One day when he was certain those he cared for were safe, he would challenge and depose his uncle.

Unfortunately, today was not that day.

He just hoped he wouldn't succumb to a berserker's death before that.

Chapter Three

CALYPSO

They rode into the sleepy town at dusk. It looked no different from the other farm towns that were scattered across the northern district of Shalimar. One main cobblestone street ran through the center on which sat markets and craftsman workshops. It was quiet now as most of the inhabitants had returned to their homes out in the valley.

Even though she had worn a high-collared black dress with long sleeves to hide her marks of magic, suspicious eyes still glanced their way. They were right to be suspicious because Calypso did not arrive with peace in mind. By tonight, they would understand what a witch's power truly was.

The town seemed so idyllic that no one would've thought a massacre had occurred here a decade back. After the decree had passed, Lord Haworth had dragged out the six witches of the Taybe coven, stripped them to expose their markings, whipped them until they couldn't stand, and then burned them at the stake.

"Your left eye is twitching," Astra noted, her horse walking steadily next to hers.

"I'm wondering whether to whip and burn Lord Haworth. However, the idea of stripping him naked is rather unappealing."

"I like your poetic sense of justice, but do warn me if you decide to go that route so I can avert my eyes."

It wasn't the Taybe coven massacre that brought Calypso here. It was her desire for answers about her mother's death. The story told to the realm was that ten years ago Seraphina Galanis, witch counselor to the king, had gone mad and murdered the royal couple. This left the kingdom in the hands of their eight-year-old son, Prince Isaac. Given the prince's young age, it was decided that the royal advisor, Hugh Davinger, would be appointed as regent king to serve until the prince came of age. The royal murder was so atrocious that Davinger's first action as regent king was to pass a decree outlawing witchcraft and targeting all witches as traitors.

The truth was the nobility of Shalimar was comprised of Purists who despised all the magical races. Having a witch serve in such a prominent position had been scandalous. But King Torin was no match for her mother's charm and intelligence, and eventually he'd also seen the wisdom in working together.

Deep-rooted sentiments did not die easily, and a faction had felt the need to eradicate her mother's influence. Unfortunately, Calypso had yet to confirm who truly murdered the royal couple. What she knew was that Lord Thomas Haworth had testified at the court as an eyewitness to her mother's bloodshed. The judgement had resulted in her and her mother being held in Sanograd's dungeon for days before Calypso escaped the capital and fled to the sanctuary.

Eager anticipation spread through her when she saw the Haworth manor come into view. The manor loomed over the town with its imposing towers, encircled by a stone wall with a sturdy wooden gate at the entrance.

At the sight of them, the guard at the gate sat up straight and hurriedly stuffed a glass bottle back in his pocket. He had a sword strapped to his side, but otherwise lacked any defensive armor.

Just as Calypso went to reach for her power, Astra pushed her horse forward, passing her to speak with the guard.

"Good evening, sir. Lord Haworth is expecting us. Though he did not mention employing such a handsome guard."

The flirtation was weak, but her statuesque beauty had the guard flushing. "I was not informed of any guests arriving today."

Astra kept her voice light and sweet. "As much as I'd rather stay out here with you, the lord doesn't like to be kept waiting."

Between fear of angering Haworth and Astra's easy smiles—and likely the alcohol he'd consumed prior to their arrival—the guard was convinced enough to open the gate and let them through.

Calypso glanced at the guard as they passed, wondering if he even knew how close to death he'd been.

"I could've taken care of that faster," she mumbled.

"True, but blood is so hard to remove from stone," Astra responded.

They left their horses by the stable and headed toward the manor. As much as Calypso wanted to rush to the master's suite, she knew they had to take things one step at a time. There were about a dozen guards employed on the estate that would need to be dealt with. She didn't want to risk her sisters getting hurt because of her impatience.

The servants' quarters were located in a separate building from the manor. Its windows were open to let the cool evening breeze in while the sounds of chatter emitted.

Nyx broke away, rounding the corner of the building. Then, she returned a moment later. "About half of the guards are there, along with some of the other staff."

Calypso had expected a couple of guards, but *half* were lounging around playing cards?

"It's almost too easy," Calypso said as she reached down swiftly and set fire to the grass near the edge of the building.

"The moment of no return," Astra commented as they watched the fire grow in strength.

Calypso shook her head. "That moment happened years ago. This is simply the consequence."

Once the fire had grown to a size where it emitted heat, Nyx put her hands out and gently called upon the wind to corral the smoke through the open window. The smoke entered like a snake slithering into the room, unseen and unheard.

At first, nothing changed. The men continued their conversation without worry. Then, exclaims of alarm suddenly interrupted the jovial chatter from the house.

"Where's the fire?!"

"It doesn't matter! We have to get out of here!"

The inhabitants trickled out, hurrying to escape, unaware that the real danger awaited them outside.

Silently, Astra sank to the ground and dug her fingers into the soil. Calypso wondered if Astra knew that her green eyes darkened to almost black when she used her power.

The soil vibrated softly as Astra's command spread through a network that she'd once tried to explain to her, but Calypso could never quite understand.

White roots emerged from the ground like skeletal fingers and wrapped around the guard's ankles. As the men tripped onto the ground, their torsos became restrained, their mouths covered. Not a single shout was heard as their eyes moved around in panic.

"We will leave you to it." Calypso briefly touched Astra's shoulder, who didn't acknowledge her.

She trusted Astra to restrain each person and keep them from notifying the rest. That left only those who were in the manor.

Calypso and Nyx entered through the unguarded sunroom. The manor was large, and those inhabiting it weren't expecting an attack on a random night. The men they ran into were surprised, half drunk, or asleep. It took only a quick manipulation of the wind from Nyx to knock them out. Calypso kept her fire at bay, not wanting to alert others with screams of pain.

They traversed the corridors searching for the kitchen with a plan to go up the back stairway. Rounding the corner, Calypso spotted a flurry of motion half a second before a massive blow to the head had her stumbling backward. Her vision dotted as a metallic thud continued to echo in her ears. Her fingers flew to her head, coming back sticky with blood.

Once her vision cleared, she saw an old woman standing over her with an iron pan held high. Flames burst from Calypso's hands, fueled by her quick anger.

"Stop, Calypso!" Nyx's voice snapped her out of her impending attack.

She now registered that Nyx's slight frame was holding back the arms of the elderly woman, preventing her from swinging again.

"Why?! That hag tore my head open!" Calypso snarled as she stood up, head still throbbing.

"She's just an old woman."

Calypso scoffed. "That old woman did more than any of the guards. Besides, I am not prejudiced."

"Just try to kill me, you she-devil! I won't let you take over Haworth Manor!" The old woman tried lunging again at Calypso, but Nyx held her back.

Having come to her senses, Calypso extinguished her fire and looked into the old woman's eyes. "And exactly what did Lord Thomas Haworth do to earn such loyalty?"

She was truly curious. Was there any good in the man? All she knew of him was evil. A man propped up by self-serving lies.

There was a brief flash of something across the old woman's eyes before she steeled her spine once more. "It doesn't matter. I have served the Haworth family my whole life, and I will do what I must to protect this home."

Ah, family loyalty then. In a way, it was brave. Though still incredibly stupid.

"Even in the face of death?"

The old woman nodded briefly.

"Very well then."

Calypso stepped forward, but before she could even lift a finger, Nyx whispered a few words and put a hand over the old woman's nose and mouth. In a blink, she sagged against Nyx's hold, unconscious to the world.

Calypso raised an eyebrow questioningly.

"Skullcap powder," Nyx answered simply. "Now, help me get her to the couch."

"I wasn't actually going to kill her," Calypso muttered, but took the legs and helped carry her into the next room over. "Goddess, she's still dragging that pan."

They set her on the couch, pan and all, to sleep soundly for quite some time.

With the worst attacker taken care of, they headed up the back stairway. No one else came to bother them. At the end of the hall on the second floor were two grand double doors indicating the master chamber.

Her body twitched as they approached the doors, anticipation pulsing through her veins. Her fingers closed in a tight fist, her sharp nails digging into her palms. All these years, and he was finally so close. She could practically sense him on the other side, resting peacefully, unaware of the pain she would bring.

Rip the flesh from his body and burn his insides.

The voice took advantage of her heightened emotions, but the voice was wrong. She had to remember not to kill him too quickly. Her revenge would happen, but answers would come first.

With a deep breath to gain some control, she reared back and slammed the heel of her boot forward. The force of the doors whipping open sent a thrilling jolt up her leg.

The bedchamber was overflowing with luxuries to the point of gaudiness. In its hoarded suffocation, the lord lay upon the central canopied bed.

Lord Haworth sprang naked out of his bed, his limp dick dangling as he reached for his pants. When Calypso spotted the young maid who'd been underneath him, she almost forgot her earlier goal.

"What is the meaning of this?!" Lord Haworth shouted as he sloppily buttoned his pants. "Where is my guard?"

He marched toward them, indignation marking his ruddy face. The idea of his alcohol-laced breath near her made Calypso's skin crawl, and she kicked his soft middle before he could get any closer. The force sent him crashing into the bedside table, and the maidservant's screams pierced through the room.

"Your guards will not disturb us this evening." Calypso smirked at how he gaped at her while holding his belly.

Behind her, Nyx ushered the maidservant out of the room, leaving them alone with the lord. Despite his intake of alcohol this evening, he recovered his senses quickly and scrambled to stand. Lord Howarth kept his eyes on Calypso as he stepped backward toward his fireplace. The kick must not have made her message clear because when his back hit the fireplace, he turned and drew out a sword that was mounted on the wall.

He pointed it toward her and charged forward like a bull. Calypso laughed as flames encircled her arms. Whips of fire struck out, wrapping around the lord's feet and tripping him. He screamed as the burns set in.

Too impatient to wait until he recovered, she approached him, reached down, and grabbed him by his hair. Mercilessly, she hauled him up until he was on his knees, forcing his head back so that he looked at her.

With eyes flooded in gold, she said, "Save your screams for later. You will need your voice."

"What do you want?! Money?" Lord Haworth sputtered when she released his hair, but kept him kneeling.

"Oh, I will take your money. But a confession would be nice too."

"Confession?" He had the gall to look genuinely confused, as if his wealth hadn't been gained by lies.

"I know there is a lot to choose from. But I am referring to your testimony at Seraphina Galanis's trial."

"I spoke only the truth about that witch. She burned the royal couple alive."

"It seems your memory is faulty. I will help correct that." Flames erupted from her right hand as she ran her nails against his cheek.

There was something mesmerizing about how his skin couldn't decide whether to blister or bleed more.

Do it again.

The dark voice lulled her into leaving another mark on his other side. She felt like an artist with a living canvas.

"Calypso," Nyx warned behind her.

Trance broken, she stepped away from the lord, pacing to clear her head. Her hand ached to hurt him again. For all his screams, it was nothing compared to what her mother went through in the dungeon.

"You are Seraphina's bastard daughter, aren't you? Everyone thinks you're dead."

There was no denying the relationship. In the past ten years, she'd grown to resemble her mother closely. She had the same tall and broad frame with striking copper red hair. They both carried the alchemical signs of fire, though her mother never made a show of it publicly. That is where the similarities ended. Her mother's heart had been gentle and hopeful, while Calypso's had grown cold and unforgiving.

"I don't care what everyone thinks. I want to hear only your confession."

"What does it matter? No one will believe you," he said. "You are just a raving mad witch."

"For once, you actually said something truthful." Having cleared her mind, she returned to where he was kneeling. "Joseph Collier also feigned ignorance, but by the end he was begging for death."

"Joseph? He's at his home in Lacra."

"Parts of him are, yes. He was quite talkative about the gambling debts you owed." Joseph Collier had served as treasurer for the Crown, often overlooking the illegal purchases among the nobility. Most interestingly, he had told her of how a certain northern district lord had his debts completely cleared right after her mother's trial.

Calypso didn't regret killing Joseph. Nor did she regret using his blood for black magic afterward to increase her power. "Now, answer my question. What did you do in exchange for having your debts cleared by the Crown?"

He must've seen the truth in her eyes because his face went pale. "I was told to testify against Seraphina Galanis. To say I'd seen her enter the chambers of the royal couple and set their room ablaze."

Hearing him confirm her suspicions calmed something in her. It wasn't all just in her head; there truly had been a coordinated attack against her mother.

"Who asked you to do this?"

"I don't know." He shook his head vehemently. "It was done through notes passed by a messenger."

"The thing is, I don't believe you." She circled him slowly. "I think you know something more."

"I don't, I swear."

"A man like you wouldn't take such a risky deal. You would want a guarantee."

His hesitation was all the confirmation she needed. "If I tell you, will you let me go?"

"I will set you free," she promised.

He latched onto her words. "Like I said, I never spoke with anyone except a messenger. I was being asked to do a lot. I wanted to know I wouldn't get betrayed. After our last exchange, I followed the messenger. I wanted to know with whom I dealt."

"Go on. Who was it?"

"I don't know. The messenger entered a guarded building, but never came out."

Calypso was done with the scheming lord holding back information. She gripped him around the throat and pulled him to his feet before slamming him back into the wall.

"Who paid you off?" she repeated through gritted teeth.

When he wouldn't speak, she squeezed his throat, letting the flames dance on her skin before allowing him to breathe once more.

"I said I don't know!" Lord Haworth coughed as he caught his breath. "But the building was owned by Hugh Davinger."

There it was—another piece of the conspiracy. Hugh Davinger deserved to die for his decree against the witches of the realm. At first, Calypso had thought it a brutal political move to appease the nobility when he grabbed power. Throughout the years, she began to suspect he was involved in what had happened to her mother. The evidence was never strong enough to know for certain. Just like the information Haworth now provided, it was merely enough to raise suspicions.

"Seraphina Galanis deserved what she got."

Calypso glanced back at Lord Haworth to see him staring at her with vitriol despite the sweat dripping down his ashen face.

"All she ever did was try to better the realm. She never hurt anyone. She was an innocent witch who burned because of your lies." There was no sense in wasting breath trying to convince him of reality. It didn't matter that her mother had strived to build a connection between the magical races and humans. In the minds of the Purists, those who held the marks of magic would always be a threat to the prosperity of the unmarked.

"The truth is your mother killed the king and queen." He cleared his raspy voice with a deep cough. "If it wasn't ten years ago, it would've been later. King Torin was too lenient and listened to her advice too often. Ridding our realm of witchcraft was the only way forward."

He paused, and a look of pure disgust went over his features before gritting out, "Because, you abomination, there are no innocent witches."

There was a crunch, followed by an uneven gurgle, and finally silence.

Calypso's stare didn't leave his face until death glazed over Thomas Haworth. Then she allowed herself to look down at her hand, which was wrist deep in his chest. With a jerk, she pulled out his dark heart.

CHAPTER FOUR

VIDORAK

Unplanned meetings were never a good thing. In Vidorak's experience, it either meant they would discuss another raid, or punishment would be doled out. Their pillaging of Helios was recent, making Vidorak guarded. He was not the only one. Jarl Bruk sat stiff-backed in the war council chambers. The other jarls and their seconds remained at ease as they faced his uncle, who occupied the chieftain's chair.

"I received an interesting letter." Urim slid the parchment across the circular wooden table toward the others.

Only Jarls Bruk and Kinar read as their seconds hung back, not knowing the written language. Vidorak's mother had taught him how to read as an orcling, but he kept his eyes on his uncle. Urim wore the ruby amulet proudly as a satisfied grin spread over his face. He was infrequently without the dragon's eye amulet since the raid at the sanctuary many years back.

While they read, Urim continued. "Captain Von Ahlen wants to meet in Ettera. It seems the Crown is waving the white flag."

Jarl Bruk was the first to speak. "This could be a trap."

It was definitely a trap.

Urim waved away this concern. "And if it is, you will kill him."

"I agree with the chieftain," Jarl Kinar interjected. "We have won every battle against the captain this last season. He surely seeks peace."

They had several wins recently, but winter was on the horizon and their food stores would suffer. The lack of food made their warriors weak, and the captain won more during that time of year. Peace talks were not needed when all Von Ahlen had to do was wait them out.

"I don't care about peace," Urim said. "I want to know about payment. What he offers for a truce."

Vidorak knew his uncle would never honor any peace agreement. As the jarls discussed terms, Urim's dark gaze shone with hungry greed.

"Jarl Kinar, I want you to go with two of your orcs. Mabanok, you will join." With a final touch to his amulet, he added, "This is just the beginning. Soon our reach will spread past the Ihoi River."

The amulet's legend completely consumed Urim. Legend stated the amulet had been around since the beginning of time, when magic was feral and potent. Those who possessed the amulet were destined for greatness, accumulating unimaginable wealth.

As the orcs left the war council chamber to ready themselves for the road, Urim stopped Vidorak. "I want you to go as well. But I want you to watch Jarl Kinar closely. There are those who whisper against our family, nephew. But don't worry, I will find them, and I will kill them."

Meeting his eyes, Vidorak wondered if his uncle suspected him, but quickly threw out the thought. Urim preferred his punishments direct and savage; psychological games were not his method.

There was a time when his uncle's stare felt like he was being flayed alive. Vidorak still remembered his first kill as an orcling—a weakened human male his uncle had taken prisoner after a raid. Vidorak had gotten sick afterward, and his uncle's ire was so great, he made him kill again and again until he could hold back his stomach contents.

"I will get answers." Vidorak's voice was steady.

He left the chambers and walked through the tunnels toward his family quarters, where he resided with his mother. He gathered weapons, food, and furs for the trip. On his way out, he stopped by his mother's bedchamber, knowing she was prone to spells of melancholy since the passing of his father.

The clan shaman was treating his mother as she sat with eyes closed in her furs. Rhunga was slightly younger than Vidorak yet had served as clan shaman for longer than anyone else during his uncle's reign. He had kept this role for so long because of his ability to speak as smoothly as a Sanograd nobleman.

Rhunga's dark curly hair swayed as he danced around Mor holding a bundle of burning sage. Vidorak was convinced that Rhunga made up half of the things that he did. However, the rituals brought peace to his mother, so he held his tongue.

They made eye contact, and Rhunga gave him a quick wink before finishing his dance and setting the sage bundle in a ceramic pot to burn the rest of the way.

"Remember two drops in your water each morning." Rhunga placed a small vial in his mother's hands.

"What is that?" Vidorak asked suspiciously.

"Just essence of lavender. What else could it be?" Rhunga answered slyly, then left before Vidorak could respond.

Knowing he had limited time, Vidorak focused back on his mother, who still sat in the furs looking down at the vial as if it contained all her answers.

He had heard tales growing up about Mor the Bold and Mor the Wild. A beautiful orcess who was strong and witty and could throw daggers as well as any male orc. Occasionally, that side of her would emerge, but those striking moments were fleeting.

A part of his mother had died when his father was killed. His parents had not only loved each other, but they had been mates. One benefit of the lack of mate bonds in the last few years in the clan meant they didn't have to endure any agonizing losses. Losing a mate was akin to losing one's heart and one's mind.

"I need to leave the mountain for a bit."

"A little soon for another raid." Her eyes sharpened. While he knew she disliked Urim, Vidorak kept his plans to challenge him a secret from her.

"Uncle is sending a group to discuss peace negotiations," he said, noting the skepticism in her eyes. "Promise me you'll go to the evening meal tonight."

She nodded, but he knew better. He'd have Nazghor come and check on her later. It was the rare person who could resist Nazghor's calming manner.

He finished gathering his things and met the group at the mountain entrance. The others were visibly eager, and they set out toward Ettera right away.

It took a day's travel on horseback through the wastelands before arriving at Ettera. This was the closest settlement to the Orc Mountains. It attracted humans and other magical races who shared the desire to disappear from the eye of the law. There was no magistrate or governance house here. Even the northern guard didn't venture this far.

They left their horses at the stables and headed toward the tavern where their meeting was to be held. The noises of the tavern radiated into the street, and they entered to an energy that never slept. The patrons were all in various degrees of inebriation while they played cards, fought, danced, and even fucked in the corners.

There were elves, trolls, and even a few clanless orcs occupying the tavern. Many years back, a brutal disease had decimated nearly all the orc clans in the south, leaving them with numbers so low they simply fell apart. Those who survived traveled north for work or to join larger clans.

They were in the tavern briefly before a man led them down a side hallway toward a room in the back. He opened the door and stepped aside to let them through.

Vidorak held back as the others entered, observing the tavern one more time for signs of a trap before stepping into the office. The moment also gave him a chance to brace himself before seeing his father's murderer.

Sitting behind an uneven wooden table was Captain Johann Von Ahlen. He wore an unpleasant expression on his face as he finished his glass of whiskey in one quick movement. Behind him were three of his guardsmen and one individual who wore the golden colors of the capital.

Seeing the man from the capital didn't bode well for the meeting. In the past, the royals from Sanograd had tried to intervene in the northern war and force a treaty, but it always required the orcs to agree to serve in their human armies. The last time they'd suggested such stipulations, Urim had threatened to cross the Ihoi River and raid the southern district.

"Your chieftain didn't see it fit to join us for this?" Von Ahlen stated, observing each of the orcs.

It would only take a couple of strides to cross the room and slam his dagger into Von Ahlen's chest. Even with his guards present, Vidorak knew he was fast enough for an unexpected attack.

He wouldn't make it out alive, but he would see the life leave Von Ahlen's eyes. Despite how enticing it was, he couldn't abandon his clan while his uncle was in charge.

Jarl Kinar spoke, breaking Vidorak's thoughts. "Chieftain Urim sent us on his behalf. That should be sufficient."

Captain Von Ahlen scoffed but proceeded. "As long as it doesn't cause any delays."

One of Kinar's men, Tarnith, imprudently called out. "Quit stalling. What are your concessions?"

"I would mind your insolence," Von Ahlen snapped. "I may have requested this meeting, but don't expect things to be given easily."

"Then why exactly are we here?" Jarl Kinar grew impatient.

"I've been asked to propose a deal. You will get your peace treaty and payment. But there is a condition." Von Ahlen poured himself another glass of whiskey. "In case you haven't heard in your isolated mountain, there has been a minor problem in Taybe."

He criticized their segregation at the Vestrahorn mountains as if they had chosen it, ignoring how they were forced to wither away there.

"We are not so isolated as to have not heard of the district lord's passing," Jarl Kinar spoke.

"He passed rather quickly when his heart was ripped from his chest," Von Ahlen responded after a brief pause. "It seems a group of rogue witches has decided to make a grand, but ultimately fleeting, mark on the region. They have taken over the Haworth estate in Taybe and put up a resistance."

"Get to what you want of us," Kinar growled. "I'm sick of talking around subjects."

"What I want matters very little," Von Ahlen muttered, and Vidorak didn't miss the annoyed glance he gave toward the man from the capital. "If you want the peace treaty, you need to bring the red-haired witch, who goes by the name Calypso Galanis, to Sanograd. Upon delivery, you will receive your first payment, and the treaty becomes official."

Von Ahlen pushed forward a piece of parchment toward the jarl, who looked it over before storing it away on his person. Vidorak didn't see what was written on it, but he caught sight of the royal seal at the bottom.

"Galanis?" Jarl Kinar repeated. "Is this a common surname?"

The man wearing the capital robes spoke up. "We believe this is the daughter of Seraphina Galanis. It is of the utmost importance to stop her."

Even on the opposite side of the realm, the story had spread of the witch counselor who'd gone mad and killed the king and queen. While shocking, the happenings in the capital had no effect on the orc clans up north. They remained at war regardless of whether it was the young prince or the regent king who ruled at the helm.

Satisfied with the proposal, Jarl Kinar nodded once. "We will discuss this with our chieftain. But he will likely find the terms agreeable."

The jarl made to stand and leave, but Vidorak spoke. "Why not do this yourselves? Why sign a peace treaty when you can march your guard to Taybe?"

Kinar's look was thunderous, but Vidorak ignored him.

"You did good work in decimating our numbers."

Not a single part of him believed those words. Vidorak meticulously noted the numbers and casualties with each raid over the years. Losses were had on both sides, most notably on the humans in recent times. But nowhere near decimated.

"Not so much that one witch should scare off your entire guard."

Before Von Ahlen could say anything further, the man from the capital slammed his hands on the desk. "That witch killed a lord of this realm! That is an affront to the capital and an affront to the royal family. The regent king wants her to stand trial for this crime."

Tirade finished, Vidorak persisted. "You didn't answer my question."

The man practically vibrated with indignation. "That's because your question doesn't matter. If you want your peace treaty, you will do this."

That seemed to be a good enough answer for Jarl Kinar because he stood with finality. "We will be in touch."

He gave Vidorak a pointed look before filing out of the room with the others. Vidorak hung back, still leaning against the wall, studying the old captain.

The years of war had certainly left their mark. Around the peppered scruff of his jaw were scars, some of which Vidorak had placed himself.

Where once he had looked ferocious, now he seemed more worn and haggard.

"Do you have more commentary to add?" Von Ahlen asked, barely looking up from his drink.

"This peace treaty changes nothing. You will pay for killing my father," Vidorak swore.

Von Ahlen's bloodshot eyes sharpened at those words, but instead of fear there was confusion. Not wanting to hear any more of the captain's voice, Vidorak left the room and joined the others outside.

The promise of payment calmed Kinar's mood, and he looked to have let go of his earlier displeasure at Vidorak's interruptions. "Tarnith, I want you to ride back to the mountain and inform the chieftain of what has occurred." He turned to the rest. "We have a witch to capture."

CHAPTER FIVE

CALYPSO

*B*ile burned her throat as her empty stomach spasmed, having freed itself
of its contents long ago.

*Brutal strikes echoed in the stone dungeons, each blow cutting through her
heart. Her body flinched as if she were the one being beaten.*

*Was her mother even still alive, or were they just harming her corpse at this
point? There were no more tears to be cried, and yet her eyes ached.*

She put her hands to her ears to block out the sound.

The sounds didn't stop. The sounds never stopped.

They just grew louder and louder and louder and—

Calypso sat up in bed, nightgown soaked in sweat and her hair tangled
around her. For a moment, she was sixteen-years-old again and trapped
within the blood-smeared walls of the castle's dungeon. The week she spent
there would forever be etched in her mind.

She swung her legs over the side of her bed, needing to move and remind
herself she wasn't chained anymore. Before her feet touched the floor, she
spotted a dark figure ahead.

The lifeless black eyes of Ker Beck stared at her as the tall inquisitor stood
in the corner of her room.

She told herself it was just a hallucination even as her heart sputtered.

Ker Beck had run the dungeons of Sanograd since she'd been born. The man was tall and thin but always walked with a slight bend to his spine. His skin was pale from lack of sunlight, and his dark eyes and hair only made his lack of eyebrows that much more apparent. Many whispered about his odd demeanor, gossiped about his possible proclivities, but no one would ever dare say it to his face.

Calypso wanted to rip his face off for the torture he'd put her mother through. He'd forced Calypso to listen to it all and relished in terrorizing her with what was to come. It was almost a relief when he'd finally turned his attention away from her mother and toward her. He touched Calypso only once before her mother used the last bit of her power to help Calypso escape.

Once was enough to leave its mark.

Calypso's fingers traced the raised scar near her collarbone until she could stand it no longer and threw a ball of fire toward the hallucination. The image disappeared instantaneously, but the curtains behind it caught on fire.

"Damn it!" Calypso jumped out of bed and took a nearby vase, removing the flowers and pouring the water onto the flames to extinguish them.

With a resigned sigh, she dressed and headed downstairs to get some food. It was early in the morning, and the household would be asleep. Calypso could eat in peace before the others came and crowded her.

The plan was short-lived when she walked into the kitchen and found Paola stirring porridge on the stove. Without disguising her irritation, Calypso poured herself a cup of tea from the prepared kettle.

"I see the devil rises early." The old woman gave her a look of disdain.

The stubborn crone had refused to leave the manor after they seized it. Calypso wanted to throw her out with the rest of the staff anyway, but Nyx had apparently developed a soft spot for the old woman.

"You would know," Calypso shot back.

She took her tea into the dining room to sit in peace. A few minutes later, Paola slammed a bowl of porridge in front of her.

"If you try to poison me, I will turn you into a frog," Calypso threatened, and Paola cursed her under her breath.

She stirred the porridge and decided she was hungry enough to risk poisoning. After a few spoonfuls, a curvy, cloud-haired witch entered with her own bowl and sat down with a cheerful smile. Calypso struggled to conceal her annoyance at not having a moment alone.

"It was nice of Paola to make us breakfast," commented the chipper witch, whose name Calypso could not recall.

Calypso grunted noncommittally as she continued to eat. She was not happy to have the other witches here. The three of them—Astra, Nyx and herself alone—had made their revenge pact. The others were thankful to be rescued, but did not understand the danger that would come.

Nyx entered next, followed by someone who at first glance looked like a boy but was just a petite woman in trousers. Gemma was in her preferred appearance, with a cap of short brown hair and cerulean eyes. When they had rescued her many years back, she had taken the form of a bull-sized man and was trying to fight off a group of soldiers. It wasn't going well because while glamor magic altered the appearance, the witch's strength and skills remained the same.

At that time, Nyx had just begun building her network of spies, but struggled with consistent communication. Gemma's abilities were immeasurable in helping pass along directives and information from the capital.

"How do you like our new holdings, Gemma?" Calypso asked.

"It'll do." Gemma sat with her own food. "Ten gold coins says you won't keep it past harvest."

Calypso laughed, finding Gemma's cynicism refreshing.

The cloud-haired witch gasped in worry at those words. Nyx was unamused by their antics. "Don't worry, Clio. They are just joking."

Clio!

Calypso tried to commit it to memory, though it was a coin toss if she'd recall it by the evening.

"How long are you staying?" Calypso asked Gemma, knowing she didn't linger in one place for long.

"For two nights, then I head back to Sanograd. Now that the prince is of age, there have been discussions of change."

Prince Isaac was eighteen years old and could take the title of king, but Calypso doubted Davinger would give up power so easily.

They continued to eat as more and more witches joined them. Calypso hurried up and finished, feeling the room had become too crowded.

She took Nyx aside for a moment. "I will be gone for a few hours. If there is trouble, shoot off spark-light into the air and I'll see it."

"You are going to do that today?"

"It is as good a day as any."

Nyx's silver eyes were unhappy, but she didn't stop her either. "Be back by sundown."

Nyx didn't believe in her hunt for the amulet, and she wasn't exactly wrong. The search throughout the years had been futile.

Calypso rode off on her horse, feeling the touch of Astra's wards as she left the estate. She followed the outskirts between the woods and the farms. In the distance, she could see families working the fields, their tasks still needing done even with their district lord dead.

As the sun beat warmly on her face, she relived the satisfaction of ripping Haworth's heart out of his chest. Knowing he was no longer of this world was a comfort.

Then there were two.

Calypso knew Nyx desired to return to Sanograd and kill the inquisitor. As much as Calypso wanted to deliver Beck's killing blow, the crimes he'd committed against Nyx rivaled Calypso's own grievances.

Hugh Davinger would be a difficult one. Astra never shared why she wanted him added to their pact, but given all the recent information, he had to answer for betraying Calypso's mother as well.

Getting concrete evidence against him remained a challenge. Hugh Davinger was meticulous in his efforts. It was this ability that had motivated her mother to vouch for him to the king for the position of royal advisor.

Hugh Davinger had only been twenty-one at the time—the youngest advisor in history. More than his age, it was his heritage as a mere merchant's son that had scandalized the nobility. However, King Torin hardly denied her mother anything. He'd also enjoyed portraying the image of unity between magic and mortals with having a witch and human work side by side as advisors. It had been the picture of cooperation until, of course, it wasn't.

The top of the sanctuary came into view. Its structure was barely the size of a farmhouse, and its roof sloped sharpy on one end, speaking of a lack of upkeep that was left to fester. If it weren't for the classic golden eye motif shining bright above the wooden door, she may not have known it was a Sanctuary of Mother Selene.

She left her horse to graze outside and walked through the tall grass toward the entrance. The sanctuary that had housed her and her sisters after Sanograd had been grand and rich in appearance. No one invaded the holy sites, and they had been safe for a time, but it was a home they had never wanted. Her hand brushed the unruly vines growing on the stones. She liked the look of this sanctuary more, charmed by the way it battled with the encroaching wilderness.

She felt the wash of magic when she entered the sanctuary. How the priestesses possessed magic was unknown, as they didn't bear marks on their skin like witchkind did. Their initiation and rituals were a secret. Not just because the priestesses wouldn't say, but that they *couldn't* say.

Such a powerful entity was allowed to conduct itself freely because of the power of foresight Mother Selene had possessed. The royal family would visit the main sanctuary in Solar City in secret, but they would never give a priestess an official government title. Instead, it was an understandable partnership.

The Crown didn't regulate the sanctuary and, in turn, the sanctuary continued to provide its foresight services to the royal family. Due to this special status, the Crown overlooked the sanctuaries housing exiled witches after the decree.

Once inside the atrium, Calypso looked down the left hallway, and, as expected, the golden door was there. That was always something she found so foolish with these sanctuaries. It didn't matter what corner of Shalimar they were, they all conformed to certain expectations. Every priestess had to take the vow of secrecy, no priestess could ever leave the faith, and every sanctuary had a golden door leading to the prayer room filled with treasures for Mother Selene.

And that golden door was without a lock! Calypso tried not to smile too wide as she stalked toward it.

Before she could take another step, a familiar image formed in front of the door.

"Not again," she groaned at the sight of Priestess Olma. This morning's guest was unwanted enough. Typically, she never got more than one visual hallucination a day. Most of her hallucinations were of the dead, but Priestess Olma was very much alive. Calypso believed the woman had been around since the founding of the sanctuaries five hundred years ago; not even the devil would want the bitter old woman.

This time she showed great restraint and didn't hurl her fire at the image, instead just walked right through it. The hallucination disintegrated without trouble.

Not even the chilling image of Priestess Olma would stop her, because she *knew* the Eye of Azara was behind this door. The amulet was one of the oldest relics in the realm, formed in the time of dragons by a powerful witch. It appeared in the aid of all great conquerors, good and evil, throughout the ages. Last being spotted on Mother Selene. Once the head priestess went into hiding a hundred years ago, so did the amulet.

Like *everything* about these religious fanatics, it was secrecy and hiding. They stored it away like rats, waiting for the time their dear head priestess returned.

But Calypso had no interest in waiting; the amulet would be hers.

She put her hand on the cold door and pushed, holding her breath in eager anticipation.

Nothing. This decaying door didn't even budge.

"Open, damn it!" She slammed her hands against the immovable door.

"It's sealed with magic," a voice spoke calmly behind her.

"I *am* magic," Calypso ground out before turning to face a slightly older woman whose tanned skin stood out against the white robe wrapping around her body. Her icy blonde hair was pinned in a neat low bun. If she had to guess her age, Calypso would likely put her in her forties, but she suspected the priestesses could manipulate their appearances to a certain degree. "Open the door."

"Many would fear the repercussions of making demands in the home of the all-seeing mother."

"I thought her home was in Solar City. This is just a provincial imitation."

Even with the priestess's composed appearance, the comment caused a slight flinch.

Calypso stopped herself from growling in frustration. She did not come here to antagonize, but yet always found herself in this position. "Look, you sycophant, I do not want to be here anymore than you want me here. Just open the door and I'll be on my way."

"I am called Priestess Levorn," she snapped back. "And I know what you are here for."

"Let me guess, the Mother Selene told you herself in a dream?"

The woman rolled her blue eyes. "You are not so important for our mother to comment on. You are also not subtle. Talk of a fire witch disturbing sanctuaries across the realm in demand of the dragon's eye relic has spread even to this provincial town."

They could mock her all they wanted, as long as it ended with the amulet in her hands. "Then save me the trouble and tell me what I wish to know."

"It is not here."

Calypso waited, but the priestess walked away, lighting the candles in the atrium.

Now that she had taken her revenge on Lord Thomas Haworth, Calypso didn't want to wait any longer. Her black magic was making her madder by the day, and she still had unfinished business. Regaining their strength until they could return to Sanograd would take too long. The amulet would give her the power she needed to storm the capital unfettered.

"I am sick of waiting. Your treasury door may be magic, but I highly doubt the rest of the building is." Calypso set her hand aflame, gesturing toward the greenery planted nearby.

The priestess's eyes widened. "You wouldn't! There are ailing resting in the infirmary."

Calypso cruelly smiled. "From what you've heard of me, do you think that would change anything?"

Priestess Levorn's hesitation caused a sharp ache within Calypso's chest. She told herself she had wanted to be viewed as a monster of fury, but being thought of as someone who would harm the sick was still painful.

"I'll walk you through the prayer room," Priestess Levorn relented. "But it truly isn't here. Or any sanctuary, for that matter. The amulet was lost long ago."

Calypso wanted to believe it was lies, but even she heard the ring of truth in that statement. "Show me anyway."

Begrudgingly, the priestess led her toward the golden door and placed her palm onto the surface. The door opened smoothly under her touch, and they entered.

They barely fit into the small space, and only one person at a time could ever pray here. Its neat shelves were mostly bare. There were three metal icons depicting Mother Selene speaking to her flock and a glass container of their holy water.

For a moment, Calypso actually felt sorry for this lonely priestess. Was she any different, putting her beliefs onto something that may or may not be true?

"I see," Calypso simply said before extinguishing her fire and leaving the room.

"If you continue going as you are, you will die," the priestess called out.

Calypso sighed, but didn't turn back. She was well aware of the priestess's warning.

Chapter Six

CALYPSO

I t was on the tenth day that the town of Taybe finally responded to their lord's murder and takeover of his estate.

Astra reported back that the local militia was organizing in the town center, intending to gather what numbers it could to storm the estate.

"What does it matter?" Calypso waved her hand, focused on reviewing the spellbook for another way to locate the amulet. "Your wards will block them from entering the grounds anyway."

Astra continued pacing around the room. "First off, we only have so much black salt to reinforce those wards. And second, we can't remain isolated at the estate forever. Eventually, we will need more provisions. They will not sell to us if they hate us."

"They will sell to us, or they will die."

Nyx's sigh caught Calypso's full attention, and she looked up to see Nyx rubbing the bridge of her nose. "It will not be productive for them to fear us."

Calypso shrugged and looked back at the spellbook, continuing her fruitless search. "On the contrary. I find fear to be quite productive."

"Not if we want to re-establish a coven here."

With a scoff, Calypso shut the spellbook. She wasn't getting anywhere anyway, and clearly it was time to address serious matters.

"When exactly did re-establishing a coven become the goal? Last I remember, the plan was to kill Thomas Haworth and return to Sanograd. His estate is only as good as the money it'll provide us to bribe our way into the capital. Besides, Ker Beck is in Sanograd, and he needs to answer for his crimes." Calypso looked between the two women. "During all our years of planning, I do not recall discussing starting a coven."

"We have been talking—" Astra began before Calypso interrupted.

"Without me, it seems."

Astra's eyes fell in guilt, but Nyx met her stare without flinching. "You were more than welcome to have joined in these conversations, but you seemed to prefer occupying your time with blood magic instead."

The words they had avoided for months now hung in the air between them. Saying them out loud made it heavy, made what she did real.

Calypso knew her sisters were aware of her escalation with blood magic. Their silence felt like acceptance of her decision. Or at the very least, understanding.

"I do what I have to do for our pact. It would've taken another decade or two of training to get my fire magic to this point." Calypso slammed her hands on the table, standing up sharply. "The lust for revenge is not enough."

"You're right about one thing. Revenge is not enough," Nyx pushed. "We need to form a stronghold here."

Calypso drew back, not believing what she'd heard. "Do you not want to kill Beck?"

Nyx's silver eyes sharpened. "Beck will die by my hand. But I want more than that. I want our kind to survive. To thrive once more."

A sardonic laugh escaped Calypso. "While we are wishing for things, I would like the ability to fly. You cannot possibly be this naïve."

She didn't expect this from Nyx. If anyone, she felt Astra was one to get lost in fanciful ideas. Nyx was pragmatic, not letting her pain blind her.

Her sisters betrayed her with dreams of an impossible future. There was no future for them, only revenge. The three of them knew they likely wouldn't survive completing the pact. But as long as their demons went down with them, it would be worth it.

"You can call it naivety, if you want, Calypso. A few years ago, I agreed with you. Then, it was just the three of us. Now, we have a house full of witches who have placed their trust in us. I don't take this so lightly."

"In a way, we are already a coven," Astra added softly, as if Calypso was something made of glass that might shatter.

The sudden weight of that responsibility was too much. Calypso couldn't breathe. This was never the plan, and she didn't want it to be.

"I'm leaving," she mumbled, turning on her heel to leave the room.

"Where are you going?" Astra called.

"Into town. You wanted me to take care of that militia problem."

She stormed out and headed down the path away from the estate. She had a few minutes of peace before there was the sound of footsteps running behind her.

"Can I join? I haven't had a chance to go into town."

It wasn't one of her sisters. It was one of the witches who had joined them once they'd crossed the Ihoi River a few months back. She was dark-skinned with bright, bouncing curls that framed her face like a halo.

Calypso ran through a gamut of names before it came to her. "Aileen?"

"Got it." Her hazel eyes sparkled with amusement.

"This isn't a shopping expedition. I am going to confront whatever counts as a militia around here." This didn't scare off Aileen, so Calypso continued. "It doesn't matter to me if you join; just don't expect pleasant conversation."

With that, a comfortable silence fell between them. As they approached the town center, the twisted feeling in her gut released, and Calypso felt more at ease.

She surveyed Aileen's bare skin, looking for her mark of magic, but couldn't see anything obvious. The alchemical tattoos appeared on a woman's body around puberty, expanding as a witch advanced her powers. Most fell into one of the four major elemental marks of air, fire, water, and earth, but there were rare occasions when a witch developed one of the minor ones.

She didn't press these thoughts further as the public square came into view. A cold smile spread over Calypso's face as she observed the gathering. This was an excellent opportunity to get her frustrations out.

"Clio was right. Your pre-fight stare is unsettling. I don't think you've blinked for the last five minutes." Aileen fake shivered. "You shouldn't kill them, though."

That broke Calypso's concentration. "I would be careful telling me what I should or shouldn't do."

"This is just a militia of local farmers. I'm pretty sure that one is carrying a pitchfork."

Calypso looked back. While there were certainly strong men among them, there were a lot of young, thin faces, too. Most of them weren't even wearing any protective clothing, instead dressed in loose linen pants and plaid shirts.

"Look at it this way," Aileen continued in her easy-going tone. "It wouldn't be a satisfying kill."

Aileen was proving to be quite annoying. Though likely correct. Going hard at this group would be more embarrassing than satisfying.

The men stopped their hushed discussions and braced themselves as the two of them came forth. Calypso almost rolled her eyes, seeing the white-knuckled grip a young man had on his shovel.

Only one of the men stepped forward at her approach. Judging by the muscled arms that were crossed over his chest, she gave him the small credit of looking like he could actually land a punch. Under his thick beard, his expression was guarded but unafraid.

She put her hand out to prevent Aileen from continuing forward and then strolled up, stopping in front of their leader. "The welcome party failed to come to us, so I came to it instead. Though you'll have to excuse me, I didn't receive the announcement that I would need to bring my own pitchfork."

"This is no joking matter, witch," the man in front of her said. "You have brought violence to our town, and we mean to remove you."

Her eyes narrowed at him. "Most people would say it's rude not to introduce yourself when threatening someone."

"I am Aengus Fredrichson, the leader of the Taybe militia. And this is not your home."

"That's where you are wrong, Aengus Fredrichson." She paused, trying to recall a past conversation with Nyx about the townsfolk. "Your name sounds familiar."

Why couldn't she ever remember anyone's name?

"Leave our town, you old hag!" The boy who yelled clearly had a vision impairment, because while Calypso was used to many insults, *old hag* was completely off base.

Before she could respond, Aengus asked, "Is it true Lord Haworth is dead?"

"Yes. You are welcome."

Angry muttering spread across the group, and the men started to encircle her.

Talk seemed to be over. Nyx and the others would just have to accept that Calypso had tried her best.

Flames weaved up her arms like snakes, her vision becoming blurry as gold flooded in.

"Get her before she uses her magic!" a voice called out.

"I have the rope!"

"No, just strike her down! She'll burn the rope!"

Voices clamored on top of one another as the group argued over what to do. Calypso let the increasing disarray fuel the bloodlust that always lay just underneath the surface.

"You were the town miller, weren't you, Aengus?" Aileen's melodic voice cut through Calypso's concentration.

The men quieted as if seeing her for the first time. Their energy seemed to settle, and Calypso realized that Aileen's power lay in emotional manipulation. Although helpful, her physical defenses were limited.

"Get back," Calypso ground out.

Aengus grunted, "Aye, I was town miller."

"Why did you stop?" Aileen asked and annoyingly kept walking until she stood next to Calypso.

Calypso absorbed the flames on her left arm to keep from accidentally burning Aileen, but allowed the lick of them to remain on the right as a warning.

"It doesn't matter," Aengus answered. "That is not the problem at hand."

"I would very much disagree. You see, a working mill is the backbone of a town. Yet the one here in Taybe remains untouched. From what I've been told, that's been the case since Lord Haworth raised the rent on the mill." Aileen flung a large purse, which landed at Aengus's feet. The coins inside rattled with the impact. "Three years of wages for three years lost."

There was a moment of stunned silence as everyone stared at the coin purse. Not even the onlookers seemed to know what to do with this gesture.

Aengus broke the silence first. "I am not interested in your blood money."

"But why must you be the one bleeding?" Aileen persisted in her calm, gentle way. "A lord's responsibility is to help the town prosper. Yet the high rent resulted in a high flour tax, which the farmers couldn't pay. Come back as the town miller, Aengus. Help Taybe prosper once more."

Aengus continued to glare, leaving the coin purse untouched.

"Can they even do that?" someone whispered behind him. The crowd muttered, a divide forming from the difference of opinion.

Seeing things unravel, Aengus turned toward his militia and put up a hand. "Men, we cannot let this pass. There are laws for a reason. If they take an estate now, what is to stop them from taking your bakery next, Josiah? Or your farm, Laurence? Thomas Haworth was a bastard. No one believes that more than I, but this isn't the way."

Calypso had enough.

"Let me make it clear. Nothing is to stop me from taking your farms and shops and homes." Calypso pointedly ignored Aileen's scowl. "Just as nothing stopped Lord Haworth from taking from you. How many were left starving under his guidance? We did not come here to raze the town to the ground, though I'd say your lord was doing a pretty good job of that himself."

Much to Calypso's displeasure, Aileen stepped toward Aengus again, letting herself be close enough to be grabbed or hurt.

"You don't have to like us to see that what this town needs is a working mill. With no flour tax, your farmers wouldn't have to choose between traveling to process their grain or starving."

"No flour tax?" an older man carting a pitchfork repeated. "If you don't take that money, I'll take it and run the damned mill myself."

A pained look went over Aengus's features, but he picked up the purse. "My grandfather helped build that mill, and Thomas Haworth used it to take as much as he could from us."

"Now you can get back some of what was taken," Aileen said.

There was excited chatter between the men, their anger forgotten and replaced with eagerness to spread the news.

The crowd thinned, and only Aengus remained.

"If I had any doubts about you being witches, they are quelled. I'm not sure how you managed to turn this around." Calypso could've sworn that he sounded almost impressed. "Make no mistake though, these farmers aren't the last men to come here with weapons. Captain Von Ahlen will bring his guard."

"Great!" Calypso clapped her hands once. "Can't wait to meet them."

Aengus shook his head as if Calypso had lost her mind and walked away.

Once the farmer was out of earshot, Calypso turned toward Aileen. "So, you carry the mark of mercury."

The calm smile on her face froze, and Calypso felt a presence gently probe at her, checking her emotions. Then Aileen pulled up her sleeve and, sure enough, at her wrist was the recognizable circle with a cross below it and a semi-circle above it.

The mark of mercury was one of the three minor alchemical marks of magic, giving the ability to manipulate emotions. Gemma held the mark of salt, allowing her to manipulate vision and create a glamor that shifted her appearance. The mark of sulfur was said to give the ability to manipulate the mind and search through memories. Calypso had never encountered a witch who possessed this.

Aileen softly spoke. "I barely had to sway him. Their minds were already open to accepting us. Or at least accepting something different from their prior district lord."

Calypso had a hard time believing that but didn't argue the point.

"I don't care." Calypso turned on her heel and began walking back to the estate. "Just know, if you ever try to sway me, I will kill you."

"Understood."

They continued their walk back in silence. She wouldn't ever admit it, but Calypso was glad Aileen had come with her. Regardless of how preposterous she found the plan of building a stronghold, she could see that it benefited them not to fight against the locals.

Maybe there was something to what Nyx was saying.

Only revenge matters.

Unfortunately, the dark voice was correct. She wouldn't stray from the ultimate goal of avenging her mother.

Like a sudden awakening, Calypso felt a foreboding presence at her back. Without thinking, she pushed Aileen away just in time as several forces emerged from the shadows.

"Run back to the estate! Now!" Calypso commanded the other witch as she glared at the four giant orcs.

CHAPTER SEVEN

VIDORAK

There was no fear in the witch's eyes, only rage. Her pupils disappeared into a sea of gold, and flames erupted at her hands as she stalked angrily toward them.

The witchkind's black markings covered her arms and upper chest. While orc marks were present at birth and didn't change, he had heard the witches' marks appeared later and grew as their power developed. And she was more covered than anyone he had ever seen before.

Capturing the wanted witch wouldn't be easy, but now he wondered whether they had been purposefully set up to fail.

"Spread out!" Jarl Kinar commanded in Orcish.

The four of them encircled her, and Kinar charged forward. He was a massive orc and relied on his size and brute force when fighting. She lashed out with her fire toward the jarl, striking him across the chest. He howled as he faltered in his attack.

However, he was not a jarl because he gave up easily. He unsheathed his dagger and lunged toward her.

For a moment, Vidorak thought he'd see her death brought about by the rash reaction of the orc. But the witch moved quickly, and Kinar struck low, the dagger embedding deep into her thigh. She inhaled sharply and shot her flames at his face.

This brought her reprieve as Jarl Kinar stumbled back, blinded by her attack. Without hesitation, the witch grasped the handle of the dagger and yanked it out in one bloody motion.

"I have no business with orcs." She catapulted a ball of fire toward them, and Vidorak dove barely in time. "Leave now, or you will die."

They needed to end this quickly, or they'd lose their chance. Vidorak reached behind him and took out the magic-nullifying shackles they'd purchased in Ettera.

Her eyes sharpened. "I will melt your face before you even get close enough to shackle me."

Her fire lashed out like vipers around her, making it difficult to approach. Her weakness was the glances she took over her shoulder to confirm her friend was getting away.

"Pretend to go for the other!" Vidorak shouted in Orcish.

Mabanok feigned charging past the fire witch as if to get to her friend. Calypso hurled her flames, but he turned at the last second and targeted her instead. He threw his hands up to block her fire from his face. Going against instinct, Mabanok stepped into the blast and closed the distance between them. Then, he kicked her hard in the chest, sending her flying backward.

"Grab her!" Mabanok bellowed.

Seeing the trajectory, Vidorak rushed forward and caught her before she hit the ground. She struggled in his hold, punting her head back and slamming it into his nose.

Flames wrapped around his arms, blistering them in their path. He grimaced but persisted in restraining her. Her fury was not enough to overcome his strength, and he grabbed her wrists, yanking them back and clicking the shackles into place.

Instantaneously, the fire surrounding her extinguished. They had purchased the shackles from a trusted source of his, but one could never be too sure with goods from Ettera.

The flooded appearance of her eyes disappeared as if she'd suddenly surfaced from drowning. Now there was just a golden ring of color around her stunned pupils. Her surprise was temporary and quickly shifted to rage. She kicked him like a hellcat, ignoring her restraints.

Vidorak tugged the chain, spinning her, and her front slammed into his chest.

She tilted her head back, eyes still blazing with rage. "You will regret this."

Before he could respond, Kinar barreled forward and slammed his elbow across her head. The force was so great that Vidorak felt the impact. The small witch lost consciousness and fell limp in his arms.

One moment, he was holding her, and the next, Vidorak pressed a knife to Kinar's throat.

"You attack your jarl?" Kinar snarled. "Think about what you are doing."

The surrounding air was tense as the other two orcs cautiously observed.

Vidorak stared at the orc before him, blisters already forming across Kinar's face where the fire struck him. "I am. We were instructed to bring her back alive. You risk the treaty with your foolishness."

Kinar narrowed his eyes and grunted, "Fine. But pull a knife on me again, and I'll plunge it into your heart. Chieftain's nephew or not."

Reluctantly, Vidorak pulled back and walked away, returning to see Grorn carrying the unconscious witch over his shoulder.

When Grorn sat the woman in front of him on his horse, Vidorak felt the sudden urge to snatch her away from the other orc. "She will break your nose when she wakes. Secure her on the back of the horse."

Grorn looked at her suspiciously, then asked, "Should I tie her to your horse?"

The thought of having the feisty witch near him was unsettling.

"No," he ground out, cursing himself for not returning to the mountain after the meeting with Von Ahlen.

The fire-haired witch was now hogtied on the back of Grorn's horse and not touching the other orc. They rode into the woods, leaving the small town unimpeded. It would take a fortnight to reach Sanograd as most of their trek would avoid the commonly traveled routes.

They were deep in the woods when he felt her groan awake. To his surprise, she didn't scream or cry or yell obscenities. He begrudgingly respected her brave resolve when most would've been frightened out of their minds.

She quietly observed, and Vidorak felt the heat of her stare when it landed on him. He turned to meet her eyes. The hardness on her face promised revenge, and he was certain this docile act was just to bide her time.

When the sun disappeared from the horizon, they stopped to make camp for the night. He dismounted and watched Grorn untie the chain from around her legs and tug her off the horse. She stumbled onto the ground and snarled at the orc. "Watch it, bastard!"

Holding the chain that was connected to her shackles, Grorn led her toward a tree to tie her up.

"I need to relieve myself," she informed him.

Grorn stared at her blankly, not comprehending the common tongue she spoke in.

"I can go here, but it will be unpleasant for all of us." Then she wiggled her arms, which were still shackled behind her. "And you can't expect me to go like this."

Seeing Grorn's continued confusion, Vidorak walked over and translated, then warned in the common tongue, "If you run, I will catch you."

He removed the key from around his neck and turned her around. With the rush of the fight gone, he now picked up on her scent of embers and cloves. It took all his willpower not to lean forward and breathe in the scent.

With a click, he freed one of her wrists, but kept a tight hold on the other. As she turned to face him, her body tensed, and she swiftly threw a punch at his face. He effortlessly blocked it with one hand before it could make contact. He was about to reprimand her when she stomped hard with her boot and pain shot up his leg.

"You devil witch," he growled at her, trying not to wince from the pain.

"You only said not to run." She smirked.

Grumbling, he took her free wrist and quickly shackled her in the front before pushing her toward Grorn.

"Don't let her out of your sight," he instructed Grorn in Orcish before limping away.

Grorn nodded and led her toward the brush. Vidorak returned to his horse and started unloading his things to set up camp.

"Mad woman," he mumbled under his breath as he grabbed one of his furs and left it by the tree where Grorn would tie her when they returned. He didn't care about her comfort, but if she froze before they reached the capital, it would put the treaty at risk.

His eyes kept flickering in the direction where they'd disappeared. With each passing second, he grew increasingly agitated until finally deciding to investigate their activity. He shouldn't have trusted Grorn with her. Even with the shackles, she was not to be underestimated.

They returned before Vidorak stepped away from camp, and Grorn fastened her to the tree. The orcs gathered by the fire to eat. The meat that he'd left on the witch's furs remained untouched. That annoyed him even though he knew that's what he would do too. Poison would be the easiest way to make sure a captive was subdued for the journey, and she had no reason to trust them.

A thick layer of clouds blocked the stars, and the only light was the flicker of the campfire. Her expression remained bored, as if her capture were only a nuisance. There wasn't a hint of fear upon her features.

He would stay the night and then return to Vestrahorn in the morning. Now that they had captured her, the others could handle the rest of the trip without him.

That thought sat uncomfortably inside him.

"You took so long, I figured you had some fun with the witch," Mabanok said in Orcish to Grorn.

Vidorak froze, eyes cutting to the orc. There was a dark glint in Mabanok's eyes.

"I didn't do anything!" Grorn's eyes widened at the suggestion.

"Why not?" Mabanok pushed. "They said she is to be brought alive. Nothing about not having her prior."

Despite his initial shock, Grorn glanced at the witch with hesitant interest. Vidorak's jaw tightened as rage coursed through his veins. He felt an overwhelming urge to crush the orc's head against the ground.

"Great idea," Kinar said across the fire while staring right at him. He'd caught Vidorak's mask slip for that second. "Let's make it interesting and play for her."

With the jarl's approval, Mabanok brought out his bone dice and placed them in the center.

"Are you playing, Vidorak?" Grorn asked as he moved to sit closer.

Vidorak studied the witch he planned to abandon tomorrow. She had angered the Crown by killing a district lord and seizing his estate. She was to be tried and, likely, publicly executed.

Regardless of her crimes, he couldn't stand by and let one of the other orcs harm her like that. Nobody deserved that.

He stalked over to where they sat and joined in the game of liars.

Chapter Eight

CALYPSO

A sense of foreboding washed over her as she watched the large orcs play their games. She had not missed the lustful glances that roamed her body. The intent behind their stares was clear, leaving a nauseating feeling in her gut. She hoped that whatever reason they kidnapped her for outweighed their desires.

As the game progressed and the glances flicked more frequently in her direction, that hope dimmed. She shifted her dread to the familiar comfort of anger. Her gaze stayed steady as she memorized each of their faces. The orc with the extensive red markings across his chest initiated the game, but it was the slimmer one with the short-cropped hair that disturbed her.

Whatever happened, she knew two things—she would survive, and one day, they would die.

They continued throwing the dice until the game was over. The winner stood as others grumbled and approached her. He was the one who'd shackled her back in Taybe.

Surprisingly, he was the only one who hadn't leered at her. That didn't make his aura any less imposing. His dark eyes held a coldness she couldn't read. The red tattoo-like markings of his orc heritage ran below the center of both eyes and over his high cheekbones like drops of blood. His features were harsh with a heavy brow, two sharp tusks, and a slightly bent nose that was now puffy from when she'd head-butted him.

The sides of his head were shaved, emphasizing his pointed ears, while his hair was a thick black mane braided down his back. His body was a wall of muscle, broad-shouldered, and taller than the others. Wearing the magic-nullifying shackles, she stood no chance of stopping him.

He undid the chain from around the tree and tugged her up. Wordlessly, he dragged her away from the campfire and into the woods.

Foolish orc.

Separated from the group, there was a possibility of shifting things to her advantage.

He led her through the dark forest at a fast pace, causing her to stumble over branches and the uneven ground.

"Where are you taking me?" she asked as her eyes darted around her surroundings, looking for a way to escape.

There was no response.

When the light of the campfire disappeared behind them, he slowed down. They stopped at a small clearing, and he turned toward her.

Moonlight shone over his stern face as he coldly assessed her, and she hated the spike of fear that went through her heart.

She took a step back instinctively but caught the edge of a tree root and tripped. With her hands shackled in front, the fall took the wind out of her lungs.

He crouched down, looming over her like a demon, but didn't touch her. "You've caused me a lot of trouble, little witch."

"Let me go and I will spare you." It was a lie. She was going to kill him once she got free.

"I cannot do that." He had the gall to look remorseful.

"Tell me, what was the game you were playing at the fire?"

"It was a game to see who would take you tonight," he responded, confirming her suspicions.

"And you won?"

"Yes," he answered, his hand skimming the bottom edge of her dress. "But I'm still deciding what to do with you."

"Well, in that case." She reared back and slammed her boot into his face with all her strength.

He fell back, and she wasted no time scrambling up to run. Dashing across the clearing, she was determined to put as much distance between her and that beast as she could. The hope of escape helped to dull the pain of the stab wound in her leg. If she could make it to the end of the clearing, she'd have better coverage.

He came out of nowhere.

There were no pounding footsteps or warm breath on the back of her neck. One moment she was running and the next she was flying, embraced by his large form.

He landed on the ground first before rolling on top of her, pinning her front into the soil. The large orc crushed her with absolutely no give, forcing her to realize truly how powerless she was in this situation.

"I told you not to run," he growled in her ear. "Don't you know orcs cannot resist a chase?"

His chest lifted a fraction, allowing her to take a breath.

"Get off me!" Her voice was not as steady as she would've wished. She blamed that on the pressure on her ribcage.

"There's something else you must know about orcs. We have an excellent sense of smell. We can smell prey that's long gone. We can also smell a woman that's been recently mated. More importantly, orc males will sense that and keep their distance," he said, and she felt the pressure of his tusks at her neck. "Do you understand what I'm saying?"

"Yes," she spat out. "It's about pride. You want the others to know what you've done."

He growled, flipping her around so that she faced him. "It's about protection. The others will stay away."

"How lucky of me!" she spat out, continuing to struggle in his hold, and any hope she had of escape quickly died. It was clear she was going to be used to send some sort of message to the others in whatever Orcish political game was occurring.

"If you do not return smelling of me, the others will see it as a forfeit."

"And what exactly am I supposed to do about that?!" she yelled. "I am not fucking you."

"I don't need to enter you for you to carry my scent. You just need my seed."

"What are you saying?" she asked, frustrated.

"If my seed is on your skin, the others will think the deed done." When she remained quiet, he added, "I'm trying to help you, little witch, but I won't force you. We can return to the campsite, but know they will attempt to touch you, and I might not be there to stop them."

She hated that he made sense. The looks she'd picked up on told her plenty about their interest. It was trouble enough trying to escape without also worrying about being assaulted.

"Fine. Do it. Rub your seed on me," she said through gritted teeth.

He sat up, releasing the hold that was keeping her hands pinned above her head. She remained trapped between his thick thighs as his hands went to untie his trousers. He wasn't wearing a shirt, and her gaze traveled over his muscular green chest.

Now that she knew he would not force himself on her, she became curious about his naked form.

Nudity didn't bother her, but all her past lovers had been human. Even in this unusual situation, she wondered how he would compare.

Her eyes widened slightly when he took his cock out. He was certainly not like human males. His cock was as thick as her forearm with dark green veins and a bulbous head. As his strong, clawed hand slowly stroked along his length, Calypso felt a surprising warmth flood her center at the erotic sight.

"Enjoying what you see?" His voice was dark and husky, and she glanced up to find him looking at her with a heated stare.

"What makes you say that?"

"Orc nose, remember."

It took a moment for his meaning to sink in, and Calypso felt an indignant blush color her cheeks. She was not shy when it came to sex, but the realization that her captor knew of her arousal was unsettling.

This was supposed to be a pragmatic task, but she couldn't look away from the way the muscles of his abdomen tensed with each stroke. His head was slightly tilted back, and his jaw clenched as his eyes never left her face.

Calypso felt her own breath pick up as his strokes quickened. She should be planning his murder; instead, she wanted to reach out and help him with this task. Her mouth grew dry thinking of how he would taste, what sounds he would make if she touched him.

Even as unexpected desire coursed through her, she held back, allowing herself only to watch as his breath deepened.

"Calypso," he groaned, saying her name for the first time since they'd met, and thick white spurts of cum exploded from his cock.

She bit her lip to keep from moaning at the sight.

"Lift your skirts," he commanded in a low voice.

She awkwardly tugged up her dress until the cool air nipped at her bare thighs. He reached down, and she felt him smear his warm and wet orc seed on her thighs. She held her breath as his fingers grazed her inner thighs, knowing if he skimmed higher he'd feel her completely soaked undergarments.

Task done, he readjusted her dress and stood up to put himself away. The arousal still throbbed at her core, and she quickly grew irritated.

He gave her a hand to stand, but she struggled on her own while glaring at him. "Am I supposed to thank you? Don't think yourself noble. You still have me chained."

He took his hand back, avoiding touching her, but continued to stare down with those endless dark eyes. "I never claimed to be noble. As for the kidnapping, you are not an innocent woman. You are a witch with powerful enemies."

Her lips twisted into a sneer. "You will need to be more specific."

"Captain Von Ahlen made a deal with our chieftain for your capture."

That was unexpected. She didn't think the orcs and the northern guard could be in the same room without going at each other's throats.

"Goddamn Helios," she muttered to herself, racking her brain about how their plan had gone wrong.

The orc's eyes sharpened. "What about Helios?"

"It's nothing." She scowled and went to move past him.

He grabbed her by the shoulders and spun her around. "Did you have something to do with Von Ahlen knowing about the raid at Helios?"

She saw him connect the dots. "Don't look so outraged. I needed him far from Taybe, and you weren't exactly doing good deeds at Helios."

She braced herself for his fury, but he just let her go, his expression back to that unreadable wall.

"Considering that was news to you, it leaves the question of why he would want me?"

"Killing a district lord of the realm isn't enough reason for you?"

"I didn't just kill the dearly departed lord." She stepped forward, letting the fury burn in her eyes. "I ripped his heart from his chest. That is what I do to men who have wronged me. And you best remember that next time you play your games."

For a moment, it seemed he would ask something more, but he just bent to grab the end of the chain and turned to walk away.

"Where did you even find these?" Staring at the shackles, she willed them to unlock unsuccessfully. There were whispers of such items, but she'd never come into contact with one. Losing her power was unsettling. It left her feeling naked more than any loss of clothing would.

When the orc didn't answer and continued to lead her back toward camp, she tugged on the chain. "You are clearly willing to be more . . . reasonable than the others. However much you're getting paid, I can get you triple that amount of coin."

He looked back at her, his expression even colder than before. "Don't take my actions as a sign of negotiation or kindness. Our task is to deliver you in exchange for a peace treaty. Nothing you offer will change that."

That gave her pause. "The captain can't sign a peace treaty with you."

"No. But the Crown can. You'll be handed over to the captain outside of Sanograd, where he will take you to stand trial."

It should come as no surprise that Hugh Davinger was behind all this. She expected to receive his ire but was surprised at how swift it was.

If the orc's words were truthful, then she stood no hope of dissuading him. The decades-long war between the two groups had been brutal, and the chance to end it too significant. He may have prevented her from being touched by the other orcs, but he would not help her any more than that.

However, even in the face of unlikely success, she wouldn't give up. With a spark of amusement, she changed tactics. "Am I allowed to know the name of my captor, or have you run out of kindness?"

When he didn't respond right away, she thought he would simply ignore her. Then he answered with a rumble, "Vidorak."

They returned to the camp, and Calypso glanced at the other orcs, who were sleeping at this point. Resting easily as if they hadn't been playing a game to assault a woman just a couple of hours prior.

Vidorak took her to the tree and tied the leading chain around it once more. As he crouched to secure it, she leaned in and dropped her voice to a low whisper.

"Piece of advice, Vidorak. Never give your name to a witch, or else she can curse you."

She took great satisfaction in the flash of concern that went across his face before he retreated to his furs.

It would be beneficial to get some sleep so that she was ready to escape tomorrow. As she settled into her furs, she felt the prickling sensation of being watched. Her eyes flicked toward one of the orcs in the distance. His body hadn't moved, but she was sure he was staring at her. It was the slim orc who had leered at her throughout their game.

The heaviness of his intentions was clear, and it kept her awake longer, waiting to see what would happen. Even with the slumber of the others, he didn't make any moves toward her, and she relaxed. Before sleep overtook her, despite not wanting to admit it, she found herself a little glad Vidorak had rubbed his scent on her.

CHAPTER NINE

VIDORAK

Vidorak was grateful when dawn finally broke on the horizon. He'd hardly slept, frequently waking to monitor the witch. She'd done nothing suspicions, and instead, Vidorak had studied how the moonlight illuminated the different shades of red in her hair.

Now that she carried his scent, Grorn and Kinar were no longer interested. Vidorak suspected the jarl's intentions had only been to challenge him.

Mabanok was another story. That orc's eyes still held far too much interest for Vidorak's comfort.

He should've struck Mabanok harder in Helios and just been done with it.

Thinking of Helios, he recalled what the witch had said. He and his uncle killed many members of the northern guard that night. But how many townsfolk were spared by persuading his uncle to end the raid early?

A low body count was hardly on the witch's agenda. She'd admitted herself that she had killed the district lord brutally. But there was definitely more to the story; she'd insinuated as much. He'd barely held himself back from pressing the issue, but what did it matter? The Crown considered her such a great enemy that they would go to peace with orcs. Her fate was sealed.

Ignoring the bitter feeling in his gut, Vidorak gathered his things and readied his horse. He took out food and drink from his satchel and went to get the witch.

Now that he had claimed her, she would ride with him during the journey. That postponed his plans to return to the mountain. Like it or not, he would see the situation through.

"Eat quickly. We are leaving soon," he ordered while handing her the provisions.

She chewed slowly while studying his face. "You look tired."

Vidorak said nothing, not wanting her to think his exhaustion made him easy to take advantage of.

She then added, "Looks as though my curse worked."

Shock ripped through him, and he pushed her back against a tree with a hand around her throat.

"You will remove your curse immediately!" he growled, face inches from hers.

"Never." Her defiant stare didn't leave his. "You will be plagued with anxieties and despair the rest of your nights for all you have done to me. Your blood will forever run cold, and you will never be warm again."

His hand relaxed but didn't move away.

It wasn't anxiety or despair that plagued him last night. It had been desire. Even in the chilly night air, his blood hadn't run cold. It had been aflame with thoughts he didn't need to have. What he'd done in the woods had been to protect her from the worst of his kind, yet he couldn't deny the way he'd replayed that scene in his head. When he had sensed her sweet arousal, he had almost come immediately. The feel of her soft thighs beneath his hands was burned into his memory. Perhaps he was deluding himself into thinking he was any better than the others.

"Why are you lying?"

She wasn't bothered about how quickly her lie was discovered. "You do not deserve to know my lies from my truth, orc."

His thumb slid over the steady beat at her throat. Her golden eyes swirled with fury.

"You are right."

He let her go, quickly confirming that the shackles were indeed still unbroken. Then they mounted the horses and set out on their way. They continued riding through the woods, keeping a brutal pace to not waste time.

After several hours, they stopped to rest and give the horses a break. Vidorak practically threw himself off the mount, desperate to put space between him and the witch. He took just enough time to secure her to a nearby tree and then stalked away.

She didn't leave his sight, but he needed to breathe in something that wasn't her scent.

He splashed his face with water from his waterskin in order to clear his thoughts. While he was fairly certain she had lied about the curse, he felt as if his mind was unraveling.

"Are you okay?" Grorn came up to him.

Vidorak scowled, hating that it showed so easily on his face that Grorn could see. "I am fine."

Mabanok joined them with a sneering expression on his face. "You seem flustered. Let me take the witch off your hands."

"Touch her, and you won't be returning to the mountain."

"Very possessive over some witch whore." Mabanok continued to prod at him.

He was going to kill him. It was a long time coming for Mabanok.

"You do not talk about what is *mine!*" Vidorak's voice was low and vibrated with rage as he stepped chest to chest with the other orc. "Next time you mention her, it won't just be a strike. I will remove your head."

The confusion on Mabanok's face twisted into outrage as he realized Vidorak was referring to his injury in Helios.

Before Mabanok could respond, Kinar called out, "Back on the horses, we've wasted enough time!"

Vidorak returned to his horse feeling dazed from the interaction. While he loathed that orc, the strong possessiveness had come out of nowhere. Irrational behavior was one of the first signs before the berserker frenzy set in. With all the death on his hands, that was a fear in the back of his mind, especially given how the walls around his control were cracking.

Wordlessly, he untied the chain from the tree. He tugged more harshly than he'd meant to and saw Calypso wince in pain as she stumbled onto her left leg. He suddenly recalled how Jarl Kinar had stabbed her there. "Let me see."

"No." She stared at him with such vitriol, he had no doubt that he would be on fire if she currently possessed her powers.

"I can see the bloodstain on your dress. Let me bandage the wound."

"I do not want or need your help."

He considered throwing her over his shoulder and taking her away to check on it, whether or not she liked it. "You are being foolish."

"It bled, but now it's closed. I can tend to it myself," she firmly denied his efforts.

Vidorak wanted to snarl in frustration, but the reality of their circumstances hung over his head. If she wanted to leave it untended, that was her decision. He could bring her to the capital with one leg as long as he brought her alive.

"Fine. It's your choice."

She gave a humorless laugh. "If it was my choice, I'd be far from here."

They mounted the horse, and once more, the witch was pressed up against him. Her infuriating scent took over his senses, causing him to stiffen. He was going to lose his mind by the end of this.

As they continued riding further south, the dense forest rolled into hills and valleys. There wasn't much conversation to be had, and Vidorak could feel the occasional glare from Mabanok as they traveled.

The sun had set by the time they stopped for camp. Grorn started the fire while Kinar and Mabanok went hunting. Vidorak watched in displeasure as the witch avoided the food he'd given her. He gritted his teeth, trying to figure out exactly what she was playing at.

"Eat."

"Why? I doubt the captain will care whether or not I've been well fed. Besides, I dislike dried meat."

There was no reason for him to care. Whether she ate or whether she was sick, her fate didn't change. She was a captive that would be delivered for execution. That was the cost of a peace that had been unachievable for decades.

Needing to clear his mind, Vidorak went to Grorn and spoke in Orcish. "I'm leaving for a moment. Watch over the witch."

Grorn nodded, looking at her with an air of fear. Good. Better he fear her than lust after her like Mabanok.

Vidorak left the campsite and took out his dagger as he disappeared further into the forest. He would hunt to replenish his food supply, *not* to provide fresh meat for the witch.

On the hunt, his instincts took over, catching the scent of a rabbit. He prowled through the brush following the creature's trail. The little white fluff was cleaning itself, blissfully unaware of the danger that loomed.

Roasted rabbit was delicious, and he'd serve it to her like some final meal before execution.

Committing brutalities for the greater good had been the way Vidorak had lived for years. He killed under his uncle's command to protect those he cared for. He razed towns to feed his clan. And now he was delivering a kidnapped woman for peace.

But never were the shame and disgust so great. She may be wicked and dangerous, but she had not harmed the clan. Even with her meddling in Helios, they had been the ones to choose to raid the town.

The wall he had built inside himself to remain cold to the actions he did was breaking down. He wished he could blame the witch for it, but she just pushed him over the edge.

His destruction was happening before his eyes, and for a moment he reveled in it. If he was in freefall anyway, he might as well be true to himself. Might as well give in to the compulsion to free her and challenge his uncle. Once he returned to the mountain, he'd direct Nazghor to take his mother somewhere safe and tell Grushag to disappear.

A branch snapped, and the pointy white ears of the rabbit flew up.

In a blur, the rabbit was gone, and Vidorak sighed. There were edible berries closer to camp that he would gather. Perhaps she would eat those.

As he turned, he caught the sound of voices nearby. Crouching, he made his way silently toward the private discussion.

From around the brush, he spotted Jarl Kinar and Mabanok in a whispered conversation.

"I don't care how you do it, just kill him before we get to Sanograd," Jarl Kinar told Mabanok sternly.

"Won't Captain Von Ahlen notice that the chieftain's nephew isn't there?"

"The captain won't notice. We are all the same to him," Jarl Kinar pressed at Mabanok's hesitation. "If we wait until after the exchange, he will break away from the group."

Mabanok pondered this for a moment. "You're sure the chieftain won't find out? I don't want it traced back to me."

"Are you refusing?" Jarl Kinar growled.

"No, Vidorak deserves to rot in the ground."

"Prove your loyalty and I'll convince Urim to name you jarl."

Mabanok slowly nodded, eyes eager at the prospect. "Consider it done."

Vidorak slipped back into the shadows and made his way toward camp. He was unconcerned at Kinar's desire to have him killed. Kinar's ego was large, and he would never forget being questioned so publicly. It surprised him that Kinar would have another person carry out the act.

Either way, he wasn't worried about their plans. Vidorak looked forward to ending Mabanok. And if he couldn't take on Kinar, then he stood no chance against his uncle, so the challenge was welcome.

One problem remained. He needed the witch far away whenever the confrontation took place. He had no doubts they would try to use her against him. For all her questionable deeds, she shouldn't have to suffer the blowback.

He knew full well that releasing her would mean the end of his clan's peace treaty, and he was ready to accept the consequences of that decision. Because one thing was for certain, Calypso would not be taken to Sanograd by his hand.

Chapter Ten

CALYPSO

They had made a grave mistake leaving her with only one orc to guard her. And it was the stupid-looking one at that.

It was hard to hide her smile, and she felt like a cat who'd just caught a mouse in its sight.

The hours she'd spent trapped on the horse had given her a chance to formulate a plan of escape. As the journey continued, an ache had crept up her backside, and her thoughts of escape turned to revenge. Especially revenge on the orc who'd ridden behind her.

Vidorak.

She had tried her best to put distance between their bodies, and it came at the expense of her back. Every time her bottom felt that thick bulge, the memories from the night prior replayed in her mind. She felt like a blushing maiden at how her thoughts kept circling back to him, causing heat to blossom deep inside her.

This is what she got for being celibate for years. Her body clearly reached a breaking point, and now she lusted after her massive, stern captor.

She was not bashful about taking lovers. In truth, there had been no one who interested her enough to bed.

Pity that when she'd finally found someone that sparked an interest, she had to kill him.

Revenge would have to wait, however. First, she needed to escape and heal. The leg wound was festering, and she suspected fever would come soon if it wasn't cleaned.

After sparing one last look at the orc to confirm he was engrossed in his work, she focused on a small lump nearby. The decaying body of a crow rested at the base of the tree where he had tied her.

How ironic that she found herself here too, in a similarly precarious situation. Death was not always final, and she refused to meet her end just yet.

She scooped up the bird corpse, scattering away the bugs that had infested it, and set it before her. Facing away from the orc guarding her, she lifted her skirts until she saw the wound and gritted her teeth as she dug her fingers in. The wound rebled, gushing down her leg in rivulets. Her efforts were messy and uncoordinated, but she soaked the dead bird as thoroughly as she could.

The nullifying shackles may stop her innate fire magic from emerging, but dark magic flowed in her blood. Once it left her body, it held that charge unbound from the power of the shackles.

Carcass completely soaked, she whispered her spell.

"A mix of blood and bone, I say my pleas to the old crone. Fueled by rage, my power I will pour, for the dead to rise and serve forevermore."

It took a moment for the blood to absorb into the lifeless body, but then the empty eye sockets blinked and red light shone within them. The crow flew up with shaky movements of its reawakened wings before landing on her shoulder, awaiting her command.

"Stay hidden until the orc with the key hanging around his neck arrives. When he is asleep, bring me the key."

Once the words left her mouth, the crow disappeared into the dead of night, but Calypso continued to feel a light thread between her and the creature.

Necromancy was not something she let herself do often. There was a price for bringing back the dead. Just as the crow was connected to her, she was now connected to it. If the crow died, she would feel the vibrations of that pain herself. It wouldn't kill her, but it would be significant.

Having succeeded in raising the bird, all she had to do now was wait. The night ticked along, and soon enough, the other orcs returned.

They brought back a couple of rabbits, which they skinned and ate raw. Calypso noted her orc returned more irritated than when he'd left. Good. His irritation would make him careless.

He came back with two speared fish and set them over the fire to cook. She had said her earlier comments with the goal that he'd storm off and she could enact her plans. Food was food to her, and she didn't care about the dried meat one way or the other. But the smell of the fish was pleasant, and her stomach clenched with a reminder that she was underfed and overexerted.

Fish cooked, he removed them from the fire and strode over to sit on the edge of her fur, an arm's distance away. Then he ripped a chunk of the cooked fish and brought it toward her face.

Irritation at eating from his hand battled the hunger she was feeling. She lifted her bound hands up to take the piece, but he pulled back.

"I don't need you to feed me," she snapped.

"Either I feed you or you don't eat."

She glared at him, willing fire to erupt from her hands, but, unsurprisingly, nothing happened.

"Why? Do you think I will escape with the use of some fish bones?" She could, but he didn't know that.

"I don't know the full extent of the shackles, and I don't trust you."

He brought the meat up once more, and she relented. The lightheadedness from the repeated blood loss was making itself known. Freeing herself from the shackles would be pointless if she passed out a few feet from camp.

Her lips touched his fingers, and she could've sworn she heard him inhale. When she looked up, he was as expressionless as stone.

He handed her another slice, and they continued this way until both fish were gone. When he stood to leave, she realized he had eaten none of it.

Soon after that, the orcs extinguished the fire and laid down to rest. The minutes felt endless until they finally fell asleep, and when the snoring began, her heart started beating faster.

There was a light fluttering in the air. It was soft, but she was listening for it. The crow was following the directions she'd given.

Calypso stopped breathing, willing the world to freeze along with her. Unfortunately, the world had different plans. The slight shifting movement of a body caused her stomach to drop.

Vidorak was still awake.

This was not a good plan. She should've drawn him away from the group and then had the crow peck out his eyes.

Your foolishness has cost you your revenge.

The gravelly voice scraped at her brain, awakening as her worry mounted.

You have failed your mother.

The voice in her head knew every insecurity and brought it forth without mercy. At the moment, she didn't feel strong enough to refute the claims.

A drop of sweat rolled down her forehead as she braced for the sharp stab of pain that would signify the crow's death. The seconds that ticked by were unbearable.

Suddenly, something landed softly on her chest with a thump, and Calypso's eyes flew open. In the gentle glow of the moon, she saw the key's outline. She grabbed the key, clutching it like a lifeline.

Her little red-eyed friend landed near her head, and she examined the crow. There were no signs of harm, but she could've sworn she sensed Vidorak was awake.

When no one started shouting or running toward her, she decided not to question what had happened. What was important was that she could free herself and return to the stronghold.

Damn it, not a stronghold. The estate.

Even at a distance, Nyx's parting words echoed in her mind. She blamed the exhaustion and starvation.

Shaking away her thoughts, she maneuvered the key toward the hole in the shackles. Before she could click them open, a booming laugh broke the dead of night, startling awake all four orcs.

CHAPTER ELEVEN

VIDORAK

There was a faint scent of piss as the two human men stood frozen in fright, realizing they had stumbled upon an orc camp.

One of the men took a shaky step back. Before he could go any further, a hiss pierced the air as a dagger flew past him and embedded in the tree nearby. A thin trail of blood dripped down the man's cheek.

"Sit down, or the next dagger goes through your head," Kinar growled.

There was a brief moment of hesitation before the men swallowed and came to sit on a log near the fire.

"We didn't mean to interrupt. We were just passing through," the man with the cut sputtered out.

"What are your names?" Kinar asked, his eyes gleaming with plans.

"I'm Jacob. And this is my brother Erik," answered the brother without the cut, trying to keep his voice steady. Vidorak knew compliance wouldn't make a difference.

"It's good to have brothers. True brothers would go to great lengths to protect one another," Kinar said. "Tell me, Jacob, do you have a favorite hand?"

Jacob's eyes widened, and Erik began to chant. "Oh God, oh God."

"I'll make you a deal, Jacob. Either I take one of your hands or I take both of your brother's."

Jacob turned so white Vidorak thought he would pass out before giving any sort of answer.

Vidorak had enough.

"What do you plan on doing with them?" he said in Orcish, interrupting Kinar's game.

Irritation colored the jarl's face. "I'm just looking for some entertainment. The travel has been boring. Unless you want to share your witch."

"Are you going to kill them?" Vidorak pointedly asked.

"They have seen us. I can't have them reporting our presence and causing trouble with the exchange."

"We can tie them to a tree. By the time they are found, we will be long gone." Vidorak didn't know why he was trying to help these men when he had done almost nothing to help Calypso.

Kinar growled, causing the humans to jump up at the abrupt sound. They looked around wildly, desperate for any sign of rescue to come. Vidorak stiffened when their eyes moved over Calypso, taking in her chained state.

Jacob misinterpreted his reaction and put up his hands. "Don't worry, you'll get no protest from us. We support the witch ban."

It was undeniable that Calypso was a witch with her easily visible markings.

Erik hurried to agree. "In fact, we are headed toward a witch trial ourselves."

"A trial in the middle of the night?"

Eager to keep the focus off their hands, Jacob rushed to explain. "This isn't just any trial. Magistrate Collum likes to put on a show. There are witches, but also trolls, elves, and others. Collum says it's good for town morale to remember—"

Suddenly the human cut off, not wanting to say the rest.

"Finish your sentence," Kinar growled.

Jacob's answer was barely a whisper, but the mantra of the Purists was well known. "Remember the original order."

The theory behind the "original order" was based on a single page from one of Shalimar's ancient texts that read, "First in the realm roamed humans, then magic grew, birthing additional races." Most of the human nobility in Sanograd were Purists, whether or not they admitted it.

His brother jumped in before Kinar could say anything further. "You should've seen the witch that was caught the other day. Could change from a towering man to a small woman in the blink of an eye. I didn't even know they could shapeshift like that. Truly the devil's work."

Calypso had been casually observing the scene up until this point, but at the man's words her face snapped in his direction. Something painful and furious broke over her features.

"What is the name of this witch?" she demanded.

He shrugged. "It doesn't matter. She performed witchcraft, which means she deserves to burn."

Calypso's eyes flashed with anger. "When I get free, you will wish the orcs had snapped your necks."

The man took her threats as a joke and let out a short laugh.

Kinar stood, putting an end to their exchange. "Show us where this trail is and I'll let you live."

The brothers looked at each other hesitantly, but they realized the losing predicament they were in and nodded.

"Why?" Mabanok asked while strapping on his weapons.

"Where there are groups of humans, there are goods. While the humans are distracted, we will relieve them of the pressure of hauling those goods," Kinar said with an eager grin.

Vidorak walked over to Calypso and kneeled to her level.

While pretending to check the chain, he lowered his voice and whispered to her. "We will stay behind. Once the others leave, use the key your crow took and run."

Her red eyebrows lifted in surprise, but then her eyes hardened. "No. I want to go to the burning."

He stared at her for a moment, not understanding why she wouldn't take the chance for freedom. But there was no time to question her, so he unwound the chain and they headed after the humans.

They followed the brothers through the woods in silence. The human men looked over their shoulders nervously every few minutes as they led them. Calypso didn't reach for the key that he knew she had hidden on her.

Something about what the men had said caused her to change her plans. He hoped she wouldn't do something foolish and risk the opportunity to escape. The tension in her body increased as the sounds of a gathering crowd bled through the darkness.

"We are getting close," one brother mumbled, clearing his throat.

They walked a little further and paused at the edge of the woods, which melted into an open field. In front were several horses and wagons from those who had traveled for this trial. Throughout the field, dozens of people gathered, their distant conversations full of eager excitement.

"Here it is." Jacob pointed. "I am not sure how the others would react to orcs. But if you stay in the back, you'll be able to see."

Jarl Kinar stepped forward. "We don't plan on being seen at all."

The man didn't have time to respond before Jarl Kinar twisted his neck. A sharp crack sounded before the body slumped over.

His brother could only stare in shock as Mabanok yanked his head back and sliced across the neck, leaving him a gurgling mess.

Stepping over them as if they were nothing, Kinar commanded. "Search the wagons and bring back any goods. Kill anyone who spots you."

Grorn peeled his eyes away from the fallen humans and followed the other orcs toward the goods waiting to be stolen.

Calypso tugged on the chains in the opposite direction, her eyes glued past the wagons and horses. She walked away, unaffected by the sudden show of violence.

"Unlock the chains and leave," Vidorak snapped in a low voice, unhappy that she was lingering.

"I plan on it." She stalked around the edge of the woods with the confidence of someone not currently completely powerless.

He watched her study the roughly constructed stage in front of the crowd. The crowd erupted with excitement as a guard paraded forth three hooded figures followed by a man in black robes. Judging by the attire, it seemed the magistrate of whatever town they were at was orchestrating this event.

One by one, the hoods were ripped off the prisoners, revealing their identities to the crowd. He saw the moment she recognized one witch on trial. Her whole body froze, then her hands started to open and close, attempting to summon her power. He didn't know if she even realized what she was doing.

When her breath picked up, he pulled her attention back to him.

"Who is that?"

"It is someone I know. Someone I won't let stay up there." She pulled out the shackle key, the metal glittering in the moonlight. She awkwardly turned her fingers toward the lock but fumbled with the placement.

He reached over to take it from her and unlocked the shackles himself, noting the irony that he was the one to put them there just days prior. The metal released with a click, and the heavy chains fell to the ground.

There were red marks below her wrists from the restraints, and he couldn't help but massage the area until the heat of flames licked his fingers in warning.

He looked up to find Calypso staring daggers at him. "You're lucky that others have the focus of my ire at the moment. Do not think this erases anything."

"I wouldn't dream of being forgiven so easily." He looked over at the gathered crowd. "Not that you are asking for advice. But it would be a pity to be freed just to get captured minutes later."

"I can handle a group of villagers." She sneered.

"Would your friend want you to put yourself at risk like this?"

"She's not my friend." The statement came out quickly, but then she pursed her lips as if she hadn't meant to tell him that. "She's someone I've known for some time, who's in this mess because of me. I will not leave her. All I need is a distraction."

There was a tug of understanding with what she said. The weight of responsibility was something Vidorak was familiar with. As well as the instinct to shut out others in an effort to keep them safe.

"Stay here," he ordered.

"I am not in these shackles anymore. You don't command me."

"Just wait a moment before you create utter chaos." He put up a hand. "I will give you the distraction, then you can take your witch acquaintance and escape. Keep to the trading routes if you can. The smells will distract Kinar and the others."

Thankfully, she didn't fight him on this and nodded her agreement to the plan. "Alright, orc. Let's see what you can do."

He returned the way they had come, circling back to the wagons. There were about a dozen horses tied up, grazing by the clearing. Kinar would want to head back to camp soon, so he needed to work fast.

He carefully unhitched their ties, the horses continuing to graze peacefully. In the nearby brush, he found a couple of snakes, which he picked up. He swiftly tossed the angry serpents into the middle of where the horses gathered.

The sudden appearance of hissing tangles spooked the horses one by one, and they set off in a panic. They galloped away from the snakes and into the crowd.

In the darkness, the large animals appeared even bigger, and the humans fearfully scrambled out of the way. The group broke apart, running in all directions. Some tried to grab the horses, while others just tried to avoid being trampled.

With chaos brewing, the witch should now have no trouble rescuing her acquaintance. It was the right thing to set her free, yet he felt an ache of sadness for the end of their interactions.

He was so focused on watching the panic spread that he almost missed the way the ground started to shake under his feet. The thunder gradually grew louder and closer.

Vidorak turned his head in time to see a massive cyclops stampeding toward him and bellowing at the top of its lungs.

CHAPTER TWELVE

CALYPSO

Her bone-deep exhaustion was the only reason she hadn't imme-diately rushed into the field once Vidorak left. Having her power bound for days and forced to travel without healing had worn her down.

Seeing Gemma dragged onto the platform like so many other witches made her shake with rage. It didn't matter if she expanded every bit of energy left—she would free Gemma.

After several uneventful minutes, Calypso clenched her jaw and moved to step forward, because clearly the orc had failed her.

A rumble vibrated the ground. The sounds of horses grew louder, and she saw the beasts dash forward, scattering the crowd. She begrudgingly admitted this was an effective distraction.

Humans ran in every direction, and no one stopped twice to look at her as she pushed her way through the crowd, heading straight for the platform. An elbow slammed into her side, and she snarled at the offender, but they had already disappeared in the mayhem.

She refocused on Gemma and continued weaving her way through the onslaught. Watching his trial break down into chaos, the magistrate scrambled back and yelled at the guard, "Take them away!"

The guard dragged the witches down the platform, and they disappeared from Calypso's sight. Irritation spread through her as more people blocked her path.

"Enough of this!" Flames flickered at her palms.

She lashed out, burning the people in her way until they learned to clear the path. Unhindered, she began to close the distance toward where Gemma had disappeared.

An oncoming blur in the corner of her eye made her halt. Suddenly, Vidorak came flying through and landed in the field with a heavy thud. The ground shook with a force greater than what the horses had caused.

An enraged cyclops emerged from the woods, his single cobalt eye darting around the crowd. Their kind were near-extinct and lived in seclusion in the eastern districts, so she had only seen them in books. The cyclops was as tall as two adult men stacked on one another, and his legs were as thick as her waist.

"This orc was trying to steal the horses! I saw him!" The yell came from a stout man with a thick mustache, who walked around the cyclops with an arrogant step.

Sharp clanking of metal sounded, and she spotted the chains around the cyclops's ankle binding him to a post further back. Even extremely strong creatures were at risk of capture when their numbers declined. There were rumors of humans drugging and enslaving magical beings to host illegal exhibitions.

"Cyclops, teach that orc a lesson," the man commanded. When the cyclops didn't move right away, he took out a short whip and aimed at his legs. "Now!"

Disgust curled in Calypso's stomach at the action. Unfortunately, she couldn't stay to help. The orc would have to handle this problem himself.

Her attention returned to hunting down Gemma. Calypso might never see her again if she lost her now.

It was easier to traverse the crowd as most had stopped panicking and fixated on the new entertainment.

With the gathering now behind her, Calypso slipped between the trees, catching glimpses of the group ahead. The men hurriedly led the witches, tugging them forward by a rope tied around their waists. Through the barrier of the trees, she spotted a covered wagon hitched to a pair of horses.

"Seems you got lucky today, girls." The guard opened the back flap of the wagon. "In you go."

Near the wagon, the magistrate fumed. "What in the devil is an orc doing all the way here? I hope the cyclops crushes him."

"Sorry for your trial, Collum. Are we headed back to the jails?" the guard inquired as the women boarded the wagon.

The last woman struggled, flinging herself back, but the guard slammed a wooden club into her stomach. She collapsed, and he heaved her into the wagon with no regard.

"No, I don't have time to set up again next week." The magistrate stomped in frustration. "There was that buyer who approached me. Maybe he is still interested in purchasing."

The guard closed the flap on the wagon and faced the magistrate. "And if he's not interested?"

"Then we tie them to rocks and drown them in the river."

Calypso had heard enough.

Fire swirled up her arms like a pair of snakes, sparking and hissing in the dark. She stepped forward, branches snapping below her feet, but she no longer aimed to hide her presence.

"Who is—"

Before the guard could finish his sentence, her flames shot out and wrapped around his neck. The scream died in his throat as she shoved her fire down his gaping mouth. Burning from the inside out was a quick and gruesome death.

Self-preservation overtook the magistrate's shock, and he dashed around the wagon toward the driver's bench. He wasted no time in spurring the horses into action.

She rushed after him, her hand extended, letting the flames flicker near the periphery of the horses. She didn't hurt the animals but steered them in the direction she wanted them to go.

All attempts by the magistrate to change course were futile as the threat of the fire won, and the horses circled back around. Calypso steadied herself as the horses galloped in her direction. Just as they passed, she reached up, and pulled herself onto the bench next to the magistrate.

He let go of the reins and scrambled backward, eyes large as he took her in. She looked like a wrathful demon with her tangled hair, glowing eyes, and skin smudged with dirt from days of rough travel.

His hand closed around the club next to him, and he swung forward. Her arm shot up, absorbing the hit with a numbing shock. She wanted to send her fire down the club, but that would be a reckless move that could catch the wagon on fire.

The magistrate reared back and went to hit her with the club again. This time she caught the stick in her hand and wrenched it from his grasp. She tossed it aside, leaving him weaponless.

Survival instincts took over, and the magistrate leaped on top of her, using his size to overpower her. His hands closed around her neck and squeezed until her breathing ceased.

Through spotted vision, she reached up and dug her fingers into his eyes. Flames hungrily swirled from her fingers, bursting the organs and filling the sockets with charred remains. For a moment, Calypso heard nothing. Not the dead man's screams nor the creaking of the wagon.

Sensation rushed back in a flood, as well as the awareness that they were still galloping at full speed. She heaved the dead body off her and reached to grasp the reins. With her remaining strength, she pulled back, slowing the horses to a stop.

She bowed over and coughed as air filled her spasming lungs. After a moment to steady herself, she went to the magistrate's body and searched through his robes for something sharp.

Knife in hand, she jumped off the driver's bench and hobbled to the back of the wagon. When she lifted the back flap, three sets of frightened eyes stared back at her.

"Calypso?" Gemma's voice broke the silence.

Wordlessly, Calypso entered the wagon and immediately went to cut the rope around Gemma. The second she was free, Gemma wrapped her arms around her. Calypso froze, unsure of how she felt about this affectionate show of appreciation. The emotions were too much to handle.

"I have to free the others," Calypso muttered before stepping away from the embrace.

She cut the rope binding the other women, having difficulty looking them in the eyes when she knew what was to come. She gave them freedom, but it was a freedom she doubted would last long. Without developed power or connections, they would find themselves in a precarious position again.

Having finished, she left the wagon and walked away with Gemma close behind.

"How did you find me?" Gemma asked.

"Coincidence. I've spent the last several days dealing with an annoyance. How were you discovered?"

Gemma scowled. "Checks have increased with the prince's travel to Solar City."

This stopped Calypso in her tracks. "Why has he left the capital?"

"I'm not sure. I was trying to get more information when someone hit me, and I lost consciousness. When I came to, my glamor was gone, and I was in jail for witchcraft."

This was unsettling news. The prince had not left the capital since the death of his parents. Davinger was up to something. She would have plenty of time to mull it over on the way back to the estate.

As they moved through the woods, they passed near the clearing. From a distance, Calypso could see commotion still brewing.

"What are you doing? We need to get as far away as possible." Gemma tried to grab her, but Calypso was already walking in that direction.

It wasn't hard to spot the orc and cyclops as they loomed larger than the rest of the human crowd. They barreled against one another like a pair of giants. The cyclops grabbed Vidorak around the waist and slammed him onto the ground, shaking the earth even from a distance.

The orc moved impossibly fast for someone with blood dripping into their eyes. He kicked the cyclops's chest, sending him tumbling backward before jumping on him and pummeling his face.

She should leave. She owed him nothing. The longer she stayed here, the greater the risk to her and Gemma. Leaving would be smart and logical.

However, Calypso had long abandoned doing things the sensible way. Her unpredictable emotions were in control, and now they pulled her toward the violence in the pit.

"Give me a minute," she replied to Gemma.

She stepped toward the ring of onlookers, allowing the fire within her to claw itself out. Despite her body's wounded state, there was a wave of ecstasy whenever bloodlust took over. Normally the violence sated her for some time, but having her magic taken had done something to her. She'd gotten a taste of death and was eager to feel it at her hands once more. It didn't matter who got caught up in it. These people were here to watch the murder of witches; they all deserved what was coming to them.

Fire erupted from her and grasped the slave owner's ankles, pulling him to the ground. His scream was bloodcurdling, and the crowd turned their heads his way.

Without pause, she sauntered over to his writhing form, then crouched down to grab his hair at the roots and forced him to look at her.

"Since you like to put chains on others, why don't I put a pair on you? Mine are freshly forged and come a little hot."

The man's face reddened with indignation, and then he screamed, "Stop her!"

A crew of hired muscle came running forth, ready to protect their employer. Calypso stepped over the slaver, eager for the challenge.

The men rushed at her, aiming to overwhelm her even as she threw brutal attacks their way. One landed several blows to her head before she blinded him. Another pulled her arm back so hard her shoulder dislocated. But that didn't stop her from searing his hands.

Even as blood dripped down her face, she laughed from the exhilaration of the fight. Calypso swung a fist at the man in front of her and was surprised when it went through him like air. Scanning the surrounding men, she realized the victims of her past had decided to come play as well.

"This will be interesting," she muttered to herself and slashed out with her fire, not knowing whether she was fighting real people or hallucinations.

"What are you doing?" bellowed a voice behind her. She turned to see a muscular green form stampeding toward her. The haze cleared, and she recognized Vidorak, bloodied and bruised. "Get out of here!"

She smiled before answering. "I saw your struggle and decided to help. What can I say? I'm a giver."

Before he could comment, she sidestepped past him and unleashed the flames straight at the cyclops. More specifically, the chain at his shackles. She heated it until the metal turned almost white.

The cyclops rampaged toward them until a loud snap stopped him in his tracks. The chain shattered at the connection point, freeing him. There was a tense moment as the cyclops studied the new development. Then he scanned the arena, cobalt eye landing on the man who had kept him chained. The cyclops changed direction, and Calypso returned her attention to the other fighters, leaving the being to his revenge.

The hired muscle split between fighting Vidorak, Calypso, and now, the loose cyclops. Even with their numbers, their efforts became too scattered. It would be over soon.

Someone threw a knife at her, but Calypso easily moved aside, allowing it to pass her without a scratch. A mocking laugh escaped her. This was too easy.

She stepped forward, but a gasp behind her drew her attention. She looked over her shoulder to find Gemma bowed over, the hilt of the blade sticking out of her chest and blood dripping down her body.

Then everything went black.

CHAPTER THIRTEEN

VIDORAK

She was madness incarnate, but not in a cold and calculated way. It was the opposite. She was mad, with each emotion clearly written on her face, shining too bright for comfort. He couldn't look away and didn't want to. Vidorak felt drawn to how her smile was too wicked, and her anger too raw.

He had built such a wall within himself that even the smallest flickers of emotion suffocated him. Yet here she was, this mad witch who allowed all her emotions to flow freely.

Would her sorrow also be this intense? He had yet to see her tears, but he knew they would be gut-wrenching.

At the sight of her friend falling with a dagger in her chest, the amusement in her eyes died. Her attacks became erratic and savage. There was no strategy outside of pain. It wasn't just the thugs she struck—it was anyone that got in her way.

The onlookers trampled one another in their efforts to flee. The grass caught fire and spread rapidly across the dry field.

He saw Kinar barreling through the crowd with fury in his eyes and the shackles in his hands. Vidorak searched for Calypso, wanting to warn her or help her snap out of her state, but she had become swallowed by the smoke.

Vidorak pushed his way through the swarm of bodies but came to a halt when he spotted her fallen friend. The pull to continue his search was strong, but he couldn't leave the injured woman behind.

Even with his Orcish eyesight, it wasn't until he bent down to examine her that he saw she was still breathing. His hand went over the dagger in the center of her chest, and he pulled it out as carefully as he could. Blood immediately bubbled through, and he put pressure on the wound. She wasn't dead now, but she wouldn't last much longer.

Sensing someone approaching, he reached for his axe, but then saw it was one of the other witches who had been captured.

The woman hesitantly stepped closer. "I can help her."

"How?"

She wouldn't look directly at Vidorak, hands clenching at her skirts. "I'm a medicinal witch. I can heal her wound."

Feeling the injured witch's weak pulse, he strongly doubted that.

"What do you need from me?"

"Guard us while I work. I am not aware of my surroundings when I heal."

He picked up the wounded witch and headed deeper into the forest until he spotted a patch of dense bramble that would provide them cover. Accepting this would have to do, he laid the dying woman down.

"What is your name?" he asked the other witch as she kneeled by her patient.

"Odessa."

"I am Vidorak. I will leave you for a moment to make sure we weren't followed, but I will remain close."

She muttered her thanks and then began her healing.

True to his word, he stayed within a close radius of where he'd left the witches, guarding them from any intruders. Luckily, the other humans had fled elsewhere, and Kinar must've followed too.

Unfortunately, there wasn't any sign of Calypso. Impatience increased as he became acutely aware of each minute he wasn't hunting for her. His instincts were clawing at him to track her down.

And then what?

He had set her free, rendering the proposed treaty nullified. There was no reason to further intertwine the paths of their lives. His focus should be on returning to the mountain and challenging his uncle. And given what occurred at Taybe, she clearly had her own troubles to address.

Logically, there was no reason to spend another minute thinking about her.

Yet in a matter of days, she had burrowed herself into his mind. Taking over his focus, making him feel like he couldn't breathe unless he was breathing her scent.

His cock stiffened remembering the last time his hands were on her. There was no denying he wanted to touch her again, but he would never do it with the threat of harm hanging over her. None of that mattered, however, because she was more likely to kill him than touch him, assuming she hadn't already succumbed to her own wounds.

After doing another pass around the area to confirm no threats were approaching, he returned to where he had left the witches.

"Will she live?" He noted the paleness of her skin but saw the wound in her chest had stopped bleeding.

Odessa nodded, dark circles now present under her eyes. "It'll take time. But yes."

He reached at his side and handed her a spare dagger and most of the coins from his coin purse. "Use this to go north to Taybe. You'll find a coven of sorts there that will help you."

She took the items, gripping the weapon tightly. It would've been better to stay with them as protection, but he needed to find Calypso before she encountered more trouble.

With a final lap around the area to make sure no orcs or humans were nearby, he returned to camp to grab his horse. It set him back a bit, but now he could track Calypso at a faster pace.

Riding through the forest, he caught whiffs of her scent sporadically. There were also occasional signs that Kinar and the other orcs had passed. With the chieftain's plans resting on her delivery, he knew they would search relentlessly.

The threat of them capturing her first spurred Vidorak on to continue the search through the night. The rush in his veins stamped out any need for sleep. All he needed was her presence and knowing she was safe.

Desperation spiked as the passing hours continued to be fruitless. Once more, he wondered if this was the beginning of a berserker frenzy. Because he currently felt more beast than not. What other explanation could there be for the single-minded way he searched?

When the first rays of dawn hit, he was still searching avidly. He steadily headed north, but it'd been some time since he'd picked up her scent, and there were no signs of fire damage. Only a peaceful forest terrain and woodland critters surrounded him. One of which was currently flying around most annoyingly.

He swatted at the small black bird, shooing it away temporarily, but then the creature returned to circle his horse once more. The bird either had no sense of self-preservation or was trying to signal something.

Pulling back on the reins, he stopped his horse and waited for the crow to settle on his shoulder. Red orbs stared back at him before giving a short 'caw' and flying off.

This had to be the witch's crow who'd taken the shackle key from around his neck. Vidorak pulled the reins to the right and followed the crow through the forest. It took only a little longer after that to find what he'd spent all night searching for.

The witch was unconscious, but she was alive.

That uncurled something inside of him he didn't understand but had relinquished caring to figure out.

Seeing her shallow breathing as she defenselessly lay upon the forest floor, it became clear how poorly she was doing. He became enraged, imagining Kinar finding her so weak and dragging her to Sanograd on a journey she likely wouldn't survive.

He kneeled down and swept the hair from her pale face. He would make sure she lived and escort her back north. Then he would return to the mountain and end things once and for all.

Decision made, he picked her up gingerly and headed toward a cave he had passed not too far back. Inside, he placed her down on his furs and set to examine her closer.

Lifting the ends of her dress, he saw the heated, angry streaks from the wound on her thigh. It had worsened from lack of cleaning and the days of travel. He should've just tied her up and taken care of it the other day instead of letting her denial stop him. She clearly was not one to act rationally.

He cleaned the area and then covered it with the medicinal paste he had in his pack. He ripped one of his spare tunics into strips and wrapped them around her upper thigh, sealing in the medicine.

While undressing her, he made a note of the wounds across her body. There was purple bruising on her abdomen that he didn't like and lighter bruising along her cheekbone. Her hands and feet were littered with cuts that he cleaned and bandaged as well. It was a small mercy that she was unconscious when he fixed her dislocated shoulder.

During his inspection, he noted the extensive black markings of magic across her chest, sternum, and arms. There were more markings than her actual skin in these areas. Even on himself, his red Orcish marks were limited to under his eyes and over his cheeks, like two vertical slashes.

His finger lightly skimmed the edge of the black markings on her ribs, noting how they seemed to move at his touch. The curious thoughts turned lustful, and his fingers ached to slide further up, over the rosy peaks of her breasts. Even with her wounds, her body was soft and inviting.

Reluctantly, he peeled his eyes away and examined her dress. It was torn, dirty, and stained with blood. He took another spare tunic from his pack and dressed her in it, trying not to let his touch linger any longer than was necessary. Then he added another fur on top to ensure she remained warm.

There was no reason to linger in the cave. She would likely rest for hours, and he needed to hunt and get drinkable water. Yet, it was difficult to stop his staring, weak to the draw he felt toward her.

He refused to consider how he would react if she declined wanting to travel together. While he would never take her to Captain Von Ahlen now, there was a dark part of him that enjoyed her being shackled to his side.

The image of Jarl Kinar carrying the shackles flashed through his mind, and he cursed himself for not grabbing them. Kinar probably suspected his betrayal, and if word got back to the mountain, his mother and allies would be at risk.

Restlessly, he left the cave to gather resources. He needed to get all fascinating thoughts of that witch out of his mind. He could not afford to live his life with emotions ruling him in the careless manner she seemed to do. The only way he could keep those he loved alive was to bury all that, erase any desires and hopes he had.

CHAPTER FOURTEEN

CALYPSO

S ensation returned in flashes, hitting her all at once before pulling her under again. She surfaced first when water was brought to her lips, the cool liquid soothing her scorched throat. The next time she surfaced from the abyss, it was to the feeling of someone touching her skin. She braced, not quite having control of her movements. But when the touch continued to be clinical and not invasive, her body relaxed.

What drew her fully back to consciousness was the smell of food.

Calypso opened her eyes, blinking a few times to focus. The smell was wafting from a nearby fire, where Vidorak was cooking fish.

She remained silent as she took in her surroundings. She was in a small cave, cocooned in a pile of furs. Vidorak sat by the fire alone with no sign of the other orcs. Experimentally moving her hands, she was relieved to find the cold shackles still gone.

Her eyes flitted back to the orc to see him observing her with his dark gaze.

"Unwise decision." Her statement came out raspy. "It seems you want to die."

Instead of running away, like he should, the arrogant orc walked over and crouched within arm's reach.

She sat up and struck her hand out, wrapping around his throat. Flames licked him just enough to cause discomfort, but she didn't squeeze.

"You won't kill me." He calmly held up the waterskin.

She didn't reach for it. "You kidnapped me and took my magic. Exactly why wouldn't I kill you?"

"In your current state, it'll take Jarl Kinar a day or two to find you and drag you to Sanograd." He took a small sip from the waterskin to prove it wasn't poisoned, then he offered it again.

This time she took it, removing her hand from his throat. Her eyes didn't leave his while she drank greedily, thirsty from the fever.

"Give me the shackles," she commanded, "and I'll let you live."

His tusks twitched in amusement. "No, you won't."

"You are right. I won't. But I will give you a running head start."

"Very generous of you," Vidorak said as he returned to the fire. "And the shackles are with Jarl Kinar."

His calm manner fueled her irritability, and she considered lashing out with her flames just to teach him a lesson. But he brought back some of the cooked fish, and she resisted the urge.

He held up a piece, trying to feed her as he'd done prior. She glared at him and snatched the food, refusing to be fed by him again.

"How long has it been?"

"Two days and two nights. The infection in your thigh was extensive, and your exhaustion from the fight did not help."

She resented the accusation she heard in his statement. "Has your memory been damaged by the cyclops? That wound was caused by your clansman, and I was weakened because of the shackles you put on me."

"I remember." The words were dark, and she didn't know how to interpret that. She didn't know what to think about him letting her go when his clan's peace treaty was at stake. It was an illogical move given the years of war between the groups.

Ultimately, it didn't matter, and she didn't care. The orc's reason for his actions was his own. All that mattered was returning to Taybe to help her sisters.

The hunger turned sour in her stomach as memories of Gemma came flooding back.

"She is still living, by the way." Vidorak's words snapped her attention back to him.

"How do you know?"

"A medicinal witch healed your friend's wound. I instructed them to go north to your coven's stronghold."

She couldn't explain the immense relief she felt at hearing his words. Even so, it was only enough to soothe the sharpness of the guilt that remained. Gemma wouldn't have needed healing in the first place if they had simply left the gathering behind. But the violence had drawn Calypso in, and she selfishly allowed it to control her.

"We aren't a coven. And it's not a stronghold." The words were reflex, but there was less conviction behind them.

"Either way, that is where they were headed when we parted ways."

If she hurried, she might catch up with them. Her eyes went to the opening of the cave. Of course, she'd need to figure out exactly where she was first.

It took more effort than she cared to admit to stand. She stretched gingerly, carefully working out the aches across her body. There was still a throbbing pain in her thigh, but putting weight on it was tolerable.

She limped toward the cave entrance, too aware of him watching her movements. Her body was tense, ready to call upon her power if he tried to stop her.

The crisp morning air hit her face at the entrance, and she took in a breath. Her red-eyed creation sat on a nearby boulder, basking in the sun as much as an undead bird could bask.

"Seems you survived." She reached out to touch the crow when her hand paused, spotting her dress laid out on the boulder as well. It looked washed and mended. Areas she knew had been ripped now held black thread sewn through them, standing out against the maroon fabric.

Looking down, she took in her own attire for the first time. "You dressed me in a man's tunic?"

"In my tunic," he corrected, still sitting by the fire inside.

She raised an eyebrow, pointedly scanning his bare muscular chest. He hadn't worn a shirt the whole time together. She was surprised there were even ones his size.

"Humans don't accept nakedness too readily. I carry it with me when I'm headed into the human towns."

"Goddess forbid you're dressed improperly during a raid," she muttered as she went to run her hand over the fabric.

Maybe she would let him live. She rather liked the idea of bringing him back to the estate and letting him serve her as payback for what he'd done.

"Why does your smile give me a bad feeling?" There were twinkles of amusement in his dark eyes.

Growing frustrated with herself, she turned around too quickly, sending pain up her leg. She should be pushing a dagger through his heart, not fantasizing about ways to keep him around her. Best to part ways before her mind became further muddled.

"Why did you free me, Vidorak?" She stalked back slowly. "You cannot possibly tell me you've had a change of heart."

She walked around the fire, stopping a couple of feet from him.

He threw her a smile that looked more scary than friendly. "I never said you were free, little witch. I am simply not honoring the peace treaty anymore."

Quick as a viper, she grabbed his dagger that he'd left on the ground and lunged. She shoved him onto his back, straddled his waist, and pointed the dagger at his neck.

"What is your game?" she hissed.

Hate, greed, and indifference she could understand. Him, she could not.

He didn't answer. Instead, his rough and clawed hand moved up her thigh, sending shivers through her body. "It's time for your bandage to be changed."

She stared at him, but no further answers came. Fine, he could keep his secrets for now.

She pushed off his chest but held onto the weapon. Delicately, she unwrapped the bandage around her thigh, revealing a sticky green paste underneath.

"You mix healing herbs like a witch," she observed, palpating the area gently. "I didn't realize orcs knew such things."

"Our race is prone to fighting. An orc who cannot tend to wounds rarely survives long." He grabbed the pouch with the medicine and came over. "This is a recipe my mother taught me."

Calypso put out a hand, but when he made no move to give her the pouch, she got his intentions. "You really want to die, don't you?"

He crouched and gently cleaned off the paste, revealing the healing wound underneath. The swelling had significantly improved, and the infected drainage was gone.

Allowing him to keep treating her, Calypso studied his face. She wanted to understand him better. At its most basic, she felt he was attracted to her. Otherwise, why keep finding reasons to touch her? Beyond that, it was difficult to say.

"I'm leaving today." She watched his expression closely.

The muscles in his jaw tensed, but his hands kept working. "Where will you go?"

She inhaled sharply as the fresh salve covered her wound, but the coolness quickly offered relief. "Where do you think? Likely, the northern guard is already headed toward Taybe. There's nowhere else that takes precedence at the moment. Well, except for the Eye of Azara."

She didn't know why she had even said that last part. It had been an off-handed statement that slipped out. She certainly didn't expect to see recognition flitter across his face.

"Do you know something?" she pressed as he finished with the bandages and stood up.

"Why are you searching for a lost artifact?"

"You know something." Her statement was barely a breath. He made to walk away, but she grabbed onto his wrist, holding him back. "What do you know?"

He hesitated, clearly not wanting to answer. "I know the amulet is too dangerous to go after. Put it out of your mind."

"Too dangerous? I have a bounty on my head. I have brazenly killed a district lord of the realm. Have you considered, *I* am the danger."

"Thinking like that led to your capture."

She began to pace, needing to release the energy streaming through her somehow. "I have been searching for the dragon's eye amulet for years. Every lead I had was a dead end. Tell me what you know!"

He stubbornly stared at her, not speaking while she paced. Oh, how she wanted to threaten him with her power, but those threats would ring hollow with how badly she had shown to want his information.

"Why do you want it?"

She hesitated, hating to give up all her secrets but knowing he would sense any deception. "The amulet is the key to becoming the most powerful witch of Shalimar, and no one would ever be able to hurt me or my sisters again."

It was only a half-lie.

"I fail to see how an old amulet would achieve that."

She snarled in frustration. "I don't need to explain myself to you. I will get my hands on it no matter what it entails. I don't care what I need to do or what deal I need to make."

"Alright."

She stopped pacing and looked back at him. "Alright, what?"

"I will make a deal with you. I will tell you where the amulet is for something in return."

"What do you want?"

He didn't answer right away, staring intently at her as if trying to peer deep into her tainted soul.

Then he spoke his demand. "A kiss."

Chapter Fifteen

Vidorak

The request was a surprise to both the witch and him. He hadn't expected to say that, and was hesitant about leaning into the pull he felt toward her.

With the initial surprise worn off, her eyes narrowed suspiciously, but without repulsion, which boded well for him. "Why a kiss?"

How could he answer that when he didn't know himself?

"I want to find out something."

Her eyebrows drew together in a frown. "Have you never kissed a female before?"

"I have kissed plenty of females."

"First you heal my wounds, and now you want to kiss me. I am beginning to think you really did suffer brain damage in the fight."

No, he had felt drawn toward her since the beginning, but he was not about to tell her that.

"Do you want the information or not?"

That refocused her. "I want it. Brace yourself, orc, I don't want you to lose all ability to talk afterward."

She stepped up to him and put a hand on his chest. His heart was already beating so fast, and she'd barely touched him. There was still an inch of space between them, but immediately he picked up on her scent of embers and clove.

He stood frozen, not trusting himself to move, worried that if he reached for her, he would crush her to him. Golden speckled eyes bore into him as she lightly rose on her toes. His mind felt clouded, and—not for the first time—he wondered if she had him under a spell. The more times he asked himself that, the less he cared about the answer.

Unable to resist any further, he lowered his head, and his hand disappeared into the wild mess of red curls to cup the back of her neck.

Despite her bold words, the initial contact between them was slow. He brushed against her soft lips, not even kissing her yet, just reveling in the intimate touch. When her mouth slightly parted, he lightly drew her bottom lip into his, tasting her.

As he deepened their kiss, her hands slid up his chest to his shoulders, tugging him closer, and he felt he would lose his mind at that. She lightly nipped at his lip, prompting him to open and slipped in her soft tongue. He responded in kind, exploring, caressing, and savoring all that she would give him.

Deep inside him, a bond beautifully and irreversibly snapped taut. It was a feeling of becoming undone and simultaneously whole, as his soul became tied to this woman. Everything became clear. His sudden draw toward her, the way she chipped at the wall he'd built. Now, a primal instinct in him awakened, ready to protect her at all costs, even with his life. She was his to keep, his to care for, his to love. She was his one and only mate.

While she wasn't an orc and likely didn't feel the snap of the mate bond as he did, she didn't seem unaffected either. Her body leaned into his, her delicate curves molding into the hard planes of his chest. She moaned softly into his mouth as her nails dug at his shoulders.

It took everything not to seize her by the hips and rub her against his hard cock. Now that he recognized her as his mate, he wanted to solidify their bond completely. He wanted to give her so much pleasure that she wouldn't have any regrets about bonding with an orc like him.

Something must've slipped through the haze of their passionate kiss because she broke away, breathing heavily. "Did you figure out what you needed?"

He nodded once but didn't break their contact, with one hand still buried in her hair and the other at her back.

"Your turn." She then added, "Better not back out on me."

His hand moved to her cheek, and his thumb traced over her reddened lips. "The amulet is in the Orc Mountains, little witch."

Her eyes widened in genuine surprise. "How did the Eye of Azara end up there?"

"The way most things end up on the mountain, it was stolen. The clan raided a sanctuary in the north many years back, but I couldn't tell you which one."

She nodded and then smiled. "It seems our paths won't separate just yet."

He kept caressing her face, captivated by the way her soft lips resembled rose petals. "What makes you think I will take you there?"

She stepped out of his embrace and broke the contact. He wanted to snatch her back, hating the loss of her touch.

"I suppose I cannot expect you to lead me there out of your own goodwill." She turned her back to him and fell silent, mulling over this new information. After a few moments, she faced him again with a dark smile. "Since you have no qualms about making deals, I will pay you to take me there." Her eyes traveled down his body, spotting his not-so-subtle erection. "Unless you are interested in getting paid with something other than money."

"You would agree to that? To let me touch you and taste you however I want? To let me have my way with you in exchange for being escorted to the mountain?"

Images of licking her down to her cunt every night and fucking her out in the open against the trees flickered through his mind. It was an incredibly tempting offer—to ravish her so exhaustively, she'd forget all about her dangerous plans.

He knew enough of his little witch mate to know that even if she let him have her body, let him learn all the ways she responded (and he planned on learning it all thoroughly) her mind was a different question. He wanted it all—her mind, her trust, her fears, and her love.

"Perhaps." She gave him a sultry look, flirting with the idea. "Or perhaps I will go to Ettera and hire another orc."

Possessiveness gripped him. Under no circumstances would he allow another orc to take her to the mountains and spend those days and nights with her. She was *his* mate.

"That's not happening."

Also, she wasn't an orc. It would be unlikely that whoever she hired would be honest with her and not lead her back to Jarl Kinar.

Knowing her stubborn streak ran deep, he relented. "I will take you. But you must promise to listen to what I say. You are not familiar with orc ways."

She nodded. "Fine, I will listen and take what you say into consideration."

He growled and grabbed her by the shoulders. "Not just consideration. You will do as I ask. It is not only your life that would be at stake."

Her mouth was in a hard line, but she agreed. "I promise."

He let her go, accepting the agreement as much as he could. He turned toward the fire, running a hand over his face, wondering what his chances of success were.

"The payment?" she asked behind him.

It took him a second to remember her question. He pondered for a moment. "I will take truth as payment. I get to ask you one question every day, and you must answer honestly."

A scowl spread across her face. "That is the strangest request I have ever heard. Are you sure you don't just want to use my body?"

He grinned. "I didn't say I was not planning on doing that too. But that will not be part of our deal."

She looked him over for a moment, trying to read him with those golden eyes. "I agree to your terms of truth."

"Great. We will leave tonight."

Reassured that his witch would not run, Vidorak left the cave to go hunt, allowing her to rest again. She may be eager now, but her body was still healing, and their journey would not be easy.

The Vestrahorn mountains lay far to the north of the Shalimar realm, treacherous and looming. The land there lacked the greenery and fertile soil of the south. Instead, the mountains were rocky and barren. With the lack of farming, food was discussed as much as war. Starved and isolated, beings of all races became hard.

His mate had not interacted with orcs much, having been busy fighting her own battles with the nobility in Sanograd. Any mistake on either of their ends could be fatal. A horde of orcs could overpower anyone, even a capable witch.

There were multiple points of entry into the mountain, and he could get her in covertly enough. The true difficulty would be in obtaining the amulet. His uncle was obsessed with the amulet and rarely let it out of his sight.

They would need to discuss how to explain her presence. Human women weren't common in the mountains. Most of the ones that were there were pleasure slaves to the orcs who captured them in the raids or servants in the kitchens.

He imagined what her response would be if he suggested bringing her under the guise of his pleasure slave. He would probably end up with a black eye or a burned ass at that suggestion.

Vidorak captured a couple of rabbits and returned to the caves to find his mate sleeping. Her brows furrowed while she dreamed, and her hands clenched into fists. Even asleep, she did not stop fighting.

His hand ached to brush a red curl back from her face, to touch her once more, but he resisted. He would let her rest a while longer before waking her to eat and travel.

There was also the question of the mate bond. He didn't want to burden his witch with such knowledge when there was barely any trust between them. It was not the right time, and given the tumultuous lives they led, it might never be.

For now, he would keep that secret just as she still kept many of hers.

Chapter Sixteen

CALYPSO

They traveled primarily through the forest, wishing to avoid major roads after the incident with the witch trial. It wasn't until they got far enough north that they joined a trade route for quicker progress. Except for a few stares, nobody bothered them.

With each passing day, Calypso's strength steadily returned, invigorated by the new focus. After her mother's torture and death, something had broken within her, and was only held together by rage. Even as they rescued witches, she led each day with a deep-seated anger in her bones. For the first time, there was a tug of something else. An unfamiliar emotion had taken root—hope.

Concern that the orc could be lying crossed her mind, but he was so vehement about not taking her that she believed him. Or at least believed that he believed he knew of the amulet.

That hope was enough for her to follow him, but she still didn't trust him. Without a doubt, Vidorak had his own agenda, so she would remain cautious.

They were sitting together on his horse once more, her back to his front. Only this time instead of being bound and plotting revenge, her mind kept wandering to the hard support of his chest and the muscular arms that enveloped her.

That was another complication. Being attracted to this enormous male was clouding her judgement. It'd be easier if she found his green skin and harsh face revolting rather than wanting to kiss up his neck and bite his pointed ear.

The kiss had been unexpected. It was unsurprising that he would ask for something like that; men often negotiated with women's bodies. It was surprising how much she enjoyed it. Her lips still remembered the press of his, and they tingled to repeat the experience.

While he seemed to have enjoyed it himself, he had not wanted to negotiate bedding her. There must be something seriously wrong with her, given the disappointment she felt at that.

"It is time for my question." He suddenly broke their silence, the deep voice sending tendrils of desire through her before she could stop them. It didn't help that she had spent the last several hours just staring at his veined, rough hands.

She needed to get fucked badly. Needed to get this craving out of her system and clear her mind. Otherwise, she was prone to do something insane like run her hand up his thigh or squirm in the seat to press her bottom against his cock.

"What?" she snapped, shaking her head to physically clear her dirty thoughts.

"Our deal," he reminded her. "I want to know about the scar on your collarbone."

That was as good as cold water to wash away any lustful feelings.

She remained silent for a moment, gathering her thoughts, but ultimately answered. A deal was a deal. "That happened a decade ago. I was beaten and cut during an interrogation. That area seemed to be a particular favorite, so it scarred poorly."

Like a phantom itch, her fingers drifted to the raised scar below her left collarbone. Ker Beck had poured salt in it to slow its healing.

"Did they hurt you in any other way?" His voice was steady, but his knuckles were white where he held the reins.

"If you're asking if they raped me, no, they didn't." Instead, Ker Beck's men had raped her mother. Those thoughts were a twisted knife in her gut.

"How did you get away?"

"My mother helped me escape before she was killed." Her voice tightened as she forced the words out.

While Nyx and Astra knew her story well, the most gruesome details of her torture were something she'd not shared even with them.

There was something about telling your dark secrets to a stranger. Something addicting to spilling memories that often repeated themselves in her head without stopping.

"Who?" he asked.

"It doesn't matter at the moment."

"*Who?*" he repeated, voice a hard command.

That tone touched something in her heart, and it was too much.

He sighed when she remained silent. "Was it that lord? The one you killed in Taybe."

Calypso snorted. "Thomas Haworth couldn't have hurt me even prior to my power awakening."

"Why kill him then? For the estate?"

She shouldn't answer him. He'd already asked his question. But for some reason, she didn't want to leave him thinking she'd just killed Haworth simply for desiring his lands.

"He testified in court against my mother. But he lied." She turned her head, needing him to see the truth in her eyes. "His lies led to her death. I killed him to avenge her, just as I will the man who put that scar on my collarbone. Just as I will the man who put this all into motion."

"Your mother was Seraphina Galanis?" It wasn't really a question. He knew who she was, given the stipulations of the peace treaty, and the connection was easy to make.

"Yes," she answered and braced herself.

He stared at her briefly before asking, "Why was she framed?"

That was a step too far. It would've been easier to take him questioning her claims, to recount the gossip about Seraphina Galanis. Instead, his quick acceptance of the truth shook her to her core.

Calypso closed herself off once more. "That's all you get today, orc. I have already told you more than I needed to."

That ended the conversation, and they rode the rest of the evening in silence. Even as her back became sore, she was relieved at the distance they were covering. The sooner she got her hands on the amulet, the sooner she would part ways with the orc who saw too much of parts she'd hidden.

They arrived in Ettera late the next evening. Beyond this settlement, there was nothing until they reached the Orc Mountains. Calypso breathed a sigh of relief when they finally stopped at an inn. Even though she was recovering well, the hard travel wore her out. She wanted to wash herself, eat something that wasn't meat, and sleep in a bed.

They entered the inn, and Calypso ignored the judging stare of the innkeeper as he reached his hand under the counter, likely to a weapon. She was sure they made quite the sight, a disheveled, angry-eyed woman and a giant orc.

"Two rooms for the night," Vidorak told the innkeeper.

She felt an unexpected twinge of disappointment at his request. There was no reason to get one room. In fact, it was probably a good idea to spend some time apart.

The innkeeper looked them over before speaking. "She can have one. You can sleep in the stables."

He pointed to a sign on the counter that read, "*No Orcs.*"

Calypso pushed Vidorak to the side and glowered at the innkeeper. "That's absurd! This is the closest settlement to the mountains. How can you possibly deny orcs rooms?"

"The furniture has been broken too many times. It has become a liability issue." The innkeeper stayed firm.

Before she could grab the innkeeper's record book and clobber him over the head with it, Vidorak placed several coins on the table.

"I will see you later." The amusement in his eyes was enough to cool the righteous anger she felt on his behalf.

She snatched the key from the innkeeper. "Show me the room."

Infuriating orc. Serves him right to sleep in the stables.

The innkeeper led her to her room and then signaled toward a door at the end of the hall. "The washroom is in there. If you want to take a bath, I will bring someone up with heated water."

"That would be perfect."

Calypso headed to the washroom and sighed with delight at the presence of soap and clean towels. Not long after, a girl entered and poured warm water into the tub.

After she left, Calypso undressed and removed the bandage from her thigh. The wound was significantly smaller and practically healed. There would be no need to replace the bandage anymore, much to the orc's disappointment. He had taken a liking to touching her thigh. She hated to admit that she enjoyed it too.

One foot after the other, she stepped into the warm water, sinking down slowly. Closing her eyes, she submerged her head under the water, letting the world go silent momentarily before resurfacing.

She soaked until her aching joints felt better and the water became cool. Not ready to leave, she heated the water with her fire until it reached an almost uncomfortable temperature.

With time her body relaxed, but there remained one ache that wouldn't calm. She squeezed her thighs, remembering the feeling of his body behind her on her horse. It was absurd how massive he was. He may have taken to calling her 'little' several times, but in truth she was not a small woman. It was just that his enormous frame completely engulfed her. She doubted there was any part of him that wasn't pure muscle.

And her hands ached to touch all that strength. Her nipples tightened while imagining licking up that bulky chest and running her nails over his back. Would he like it rough? Orcs certainly didn't give the appearance of gentle lovers with soft caresses. No, a male like him would be demanding and rough.

Her lewd thoughts fed that ache, pushing her need higher. Closing her eyes, her hand skimmed down her body to her throbbing clit. She rubbed in slow circles, as images of Vidorak fucking her against a tree with the skirts of her dress around her waist flashed through her mind. He would pull her corset down, not even bothering to get fully undressed, and grip her hair as he pounded her from behind.

Her other hand went to her breast, squeezing the flesh, wishing his clawed hand was there instead. With his claws and tusks, fucking him would leave its mark, no doubt. But what she would enjoy the most would be the soreness she would have between her legs after being with him. She had seen his hard cock and knew he would completely fill her, stretching her to the brim.

Her breath picked up, and her head arched back as her movements became more hurried. She needed to come, needed to get him out of her system, needed to be clear of this desire. She had been on edge for so long that it took little to push her over.

With a moan, her orgasm hit, her heart still pounding away in her chest as she came down. She needed this to work, or she didn't know what she would do. Probably strip him and pounce.

Her heart was still beating rapidly when the sound of the washroom window being opened killed any lingering arousal.

She turned to face the window and called fire to her hand. This thief had picked the wrong inn to rob.

"It's me, little witch." Vidorak's voice came through the opening of the window. "Don't set me aflame just yet."

"What are you doing here?" she hissed and definitely did *not* extinguish her fire.

Vidorak opened the window all the way and tumbled in less than gracefully. He had the gall to frown at the fire still glowing in her hand.

"We need to talk about tomorrow. If all goes well, we will reach the mountain by dusk."

She moved the soap bubbles in the tub closer to cover her body, then scowled at her actions. She was never shy about her nudity prior and didn't want to start now. "Can we talk about this on the ride tomorrow?"

"From this point, we need to be careful about what is said. We may run into other orcs along the way."

"And if we do, how will you explain me?"

"I will say you were given to me as a reward from the last raid," he continued as she glared at him. "Human females don't just get to visit the mountain. I know you dislike it, but they are only brought back for one reason."

It got under her skin, but she would do anything to get the amulet.

"Fine." There were advantages to blending into the background as a captive. She suddenly considered something. "Do you own any human captives?"

"I don't. For pleasure or otherwise."

"Pleasure is quite a way of putting it," she responded dryly. "What will be expected of me when we get to the mountain? Am I taken to a room with all the other sex slaves?"

He shook his head. "I'll leave you with my mother in our family quarters. She will look out for you."

From her limited knowledge of orcs, their female counterparts could be just as tough and violent as their males. They raided and fought freely, which made the dynamic with the human female captives confusing to Calypso.

Ultimately, it was not her mystery to unravel. She wasn't there to understand their social hierarchies. "As long as I end up with the amulet, that's fine with me. Hand me the towel, please."

He handed her the towel, and she gave him a pointed look. "Turn around."

He obliged, and she stood, wrapping the towel around her body. After drying off, she picked up the dress she had traveled with reluctantly.

"There is a clean dress on the stool," Vidorak called behind her.

She peeked over her shoulder to ensure he was still facing away. On the stool was a neatly folded gray dress. She didn't know how to feel about him purchasing clothes for her, but the idea of putting on her old sweaty clothing was unappealing.

"You need to cover your witch marks if our story is to work," he explained, then added. "You are quite marked."

It was easier to accept pragmatism rather than kindness, though his second statement stung.

She tried forcing herself not to care if Vidorak thought her skin ugly. Moving quickly, she slipped on the dress and found it fit her well. "You can turn around."

He looked her over carefully and then nodded, seemingly satisfied with the results. "Let's meet at the stables tomorrow."

He moved toward the window, but she stepped forward, stopping him. "I am *quite* marked because I am *quite* powerful. Don't forget that, orc."

She was back to not using his name, wanting to put distance between her and this male that was pushing her boundaries too much.

Rather than leave, he studied her. "Why is that?"

"What?"

"Witches possess alchemical marks that grow, but yours are different. They change." His eyes scanned her upper body as if he could see the marks underneath the clothing.

At first, she felt the urge to tell him to fuck off. Her marks were none of his business. He knew entirely too much about her already.

"It is black magic." She wanted him to know how corrupt her heart was, wanted to push him away. "While those I hunt deserve every bit of pain I give them, they are not wrong to want to stop me. I have taken many lives for my power."

"Who's life?"

The lives of those who conspired against her mother. The lives of those she deemed unworthy.

Of course, the magic wasn't without its price. Should she tell him about the visions and the voices in her head? If he didn't think her mad before that, he would then. Certainly, he wouldn't want to touch her again if he knew.

"It doesn't matter now." She gave the coward's answer, not strong enough to state exactly how lost her mind truly was.

"Is vengeance worth it?"

"It is worth everything." Even her life. The will of the Crown was too big to stop, and witchkind was too weakened. There would be no changing their persecution. But she would take down those who wronged her in the meantime.

"I am done with this conversation. See you tomorrow." She gathered her things and made to leave.

Before she could leave, Vidorak called out. "Little witch, there is still my question for today."

"What?" she snapped, eager to be gone and back in her bed.

"What were you thinking about when you came in the bathtub?"

Chapter Seventeen

VIDORAK

Vidorak woke with a raging headache. After leaving the inn, he'd stopped by the tavern to drink. He rarely partook in alcohol, not enjoying having his senses dulled, but he couldn't stop thinking about the conversation with his witch.

He had heard of black magic before. It was a whispered topic, not pleasantly discussed amongst the magical races. It was a way for witches to gain power, but at the cost of blood and death. A price, it seems, she felt was worth it.

How many had she killed to gain the power she had? Given the blood that coated his hands, he could hardly judge her. How many times had his uncle ordered the killing of certain humans who wanted to lead militias against the orcs, sometimes in warranted revenge?

He was no different. In fact, he may even be worse. At least she had a purpose, even if a bit twisted.

While he held no judgement, his heart ached for his mate. For how she'd been wronged and hurt to the point of wanting to inflict herself with tainted powers.

Every fiber of his being wanted to fix this, fight her enemies for her, but he didn't know how. So, he let alcohol dull the turbulence inside him.

When he had finally retreated to the stables for sleep, there were other thoughts that kept him awake. Her answer to his last question.

I thought of getting fucked so thoroughly I would feel it the next day.

His cock twitched, recalling her words from last night. From outside the inn, he could sense that she was in the washroom. But it wasn't until he'd entered the room that he was met with the scent of her recent release.

I thought of getting fucked so thoroughly I would feel it the next day.

The words replayed in his head, and he wanted nothing more than to give his little mate her wish.

Vidorak found a basin outside the stables and splashed cold water on his face. The cool water did nothing to lessen his headache or his desire. At least he'd woken early, even if it meant being in pain and semi-erect. There was one last errand in Ettera to be done before heading out.

He arrived at the little unnamed weapons shop in the alley behind the brothel. A light bell jingled to announce his presence when he opened the door.

"How can I help—" The shopkeeper turned and registered who he was, then dropped the box he was holding and produced a glowing bow and arrow from below the counter. "Stay back! This arrow pierces through all."

From an outside glance, the shopkeeper stood no chance. He was much shorter than Vidorak, about an average human male height. While he had a toned body, it was the slender and wiry physique typical of elven folk.

"Relax, Lucan. I am not here to fight." Vidorak put up his hands, hoping to show he wasn't much of a threat.

After another moment, Lucan set down the bow and ran his hand through his white-blond hair. Unlike his brethren, he kept his short and messy, reminding Vidorak more of a wolf than of the elegant aura of an elf.

"Look, I'm sorry, V. But I told you the shackles weren't a sure thing. Magic-nullifying can get messy. Did a lot of your guys die?"

"Nobody died." *Yet.* "They worked."

Surprise flashed over Lucan's flawless face, then a wide grin broke out. "That's great! Why are you here then?"

"I wanted to know if you had any more of them. Or any other items of similar capabilities."

"Why?" Lucan asked but was met with silence. "Alright, keep it to yourself then. To answer your question, no. Not one I'm confident in. Or at least fifty percent confident in," he added with a rueful smile.

"Are you sure? Because I passed two shops that advertised such items."

"Ever since the royals banned witchcraft, the market has been flooded with items claiming to nullify, harvest, or create magic. Almost all of it is crap."

"Except when it isn't."

"Exactly. Look, I'll keep an ear out and let you know."

Vidorak had known him for almost half his life, but that didn't mean he wasn't familiar with his ways. The elf was tricky and could be someone's best friend while stabbing them in the back. But in this case, Vidorak felt he was telling the truth. The very least for the pure desire for coin.

Vidorak nodded and went to leave the store when the sweet smell of fruit caught his attention. On the counter was a tray of pastries.

"Are those some kind of deadly pastries?" he asked.

"Only to the waistline. Jaison has become quite the baker, and he wanted me to put them out for customers." Lucan was loyal only to two people, himself and his mate.

"I'll take four."

After paying, he left the store and headed back toward the inn to look for Calypso. Jarl Kinar may have the shackles, but Vidorak wouldn't put it past him to purchase more magic-nullifying items. He wanted to do all he could to prevent Jarl Kinar or others from accessing such weapons.

He was licking his fingers after eating two of the pastries when he heard shouts echoing nearby. It was usual for fights to break out in Ettera, but it was rather early for such a ruckus.

The noise radiated down one of the side streets, and he turned to see his flaming-haired witch with her hands on her hips arguing with a merchant. Her red-eyed crow was flittering around her menacingly, acting as her guard.

Without another thought, he changed course.

Calypso didn't notice his approach as she continued her threats toward the unfazed merchant.

"Six silver coins!" she exclaimed. "I could get half a dozen rings for two silver coins in Solar City!"

"Then get them at Solar City." The merchant snatched away his rings and put them back in the basket with the others. "There have been a lot of weddings lately, so supply is low."

"Supply will become nonexistent when I burn down your whole stall." Calypso leaned forward threateningly.

It was time to intervene, because while the merchant didn't look worried, Vidorak knew she was serious. He quickened his steps in their direction.

Before his witch could make good on her promise, he pushed the food into her hands. "Eat this."

Then he turned to the merchant, who clearly possessed a death wish. "How much did you say for the ring?"

"Like I told this madwoman, it's six silver coins for one ring."

Vidorak handed him the coins and took the ring. Then he led a sputtering Calypso away from the market.

"That man completely swindled us!"

"That's how it goes in Ettera. Why do you need the ring?" He frowned at the uneaten food and nudged her hand up toward her mouth.

"Not that it's any of your business, but I want to contact my sisters." She took a bite and lifted her eyebrows. "This isn't bad."

"You need the ring for a spell?"

"I'm just going to write a letter," she answered between bites. "The ring is a bribe for the pigeon that will deliver it. They are a surprisingly covetous sort for shiny things."

The normally silent black bird cawed in agreement.

"Is that why this one helped you?" Vidorak looked at the odd bird.

"No, this one just had the misfortune of meeting his final resting place near where I was tied up." Her eyes looked sad as she said that. "There's a loophole with the shackles. My black magic worked once it left my body, and I could resurrect this one."

That explained the eerie red glow of the crow's eyes. "Some might consider it lucky to be brought back to life."

"They would be wrong." She broke off a chunk of the pastry and held it out for the black bird. "Thank Vidorak for the pastry and you can get another piece." The crow gave another sharp caw, and Calypso broke off a second portion.

Asking why an undead bird needed to eat was on the tip of his tongue, but he thought better of it and remained silent. With an amused shake of his head, he left her to write her letter and bribe the local pigeons while he got the horse and their things together.

When they set off toward the Vestrahorn mountains, she elected to sit behind him on the horse, which he begrudgingly agreed to. He enjoyed wrapping his body around hers for protection, but it was probably better she didn't rub against his aching cock the whole time.

Ettera was the last point of civilization before reaching the mountains. The terrain became more and more desolate as they left the town behind. The tall trees of the forests they'd traveled through for most of their journey were long gone. Here was only brush and prickly plants whose sole purpose was survival.

Even the sun abandoned this place. Endless thick clouds blocked all sunlight the moment they left Ettera, and the atmosphere became colder. There were no noises from the forests here, no birds chirping or wolves howling. There was an occasional blurring at the edge of one's vision of a small snake or creature scurrying along.

"Is this place always this inviting?" Calypso commented.

"This is a good day, actually."

He looked over his shoulder to find her studying the wasteland. "Your clan really should resettle."

Something about the simple way she said that, as if it never occurred to them to do that, brought up a brief chuckle.

"You were likely a child at the time, but there was an orc settlement in the Silver Forest for a short while. The hope was to move the mountain clan down there. Things did not go well, unfortunately."

She hummed in agreement. "Things rarely go well when dealing with humans. Let me guess, they didn't take too kindly to orcs being their new neighbors?"

He nodded. "It was strained at the beginning, but my father felt things were improving as long as we kept a peaceful presence."

"Your father?"

He hadn't meant to mention him. It was too painful for his mother to discuss, and his name had become taboo in the clan. He had faded into the background only to be brought up by his uncle as a cautionary tale.

"My father was chieftain at that time and believed in the settlements. He felt that segregating ourselves in the mountain would hurt us. Not just with resources, but with our place in the realm. Our kind does not have the best reputation."

"You don't say."

"It's become well-deserved now, unfortunately. During that time, things were different, and there was hope for building a relationship. But on a day when most of the clan had returned to the mountain to gather more stock, a violent riot occurred. It killed many at the settlement."

He felt her fingers tap as she processed this. "How did a group of farmers kill off so many orcs? Even if the settlement didn't consist of your top warriors, I know what these village militias look like. An orcling could take them on."

An angry wound burned inside him as he told her of his past. "With the help of the northern guard. It was Johann Von Ahlen who killed my father."

"I'm sorry." Her voice was soft and genuine. "How old were you?"

"I was seven years old." Old enough to have fleeting memories of him. Young enough that it still sometimes felt like a dream.

"I was sixteen." She didn't have to finish the sentence for him to know she was referring to how old she was when her mother was killed.

There was a moment of silence between them before he felt her stiffen behind him.

"What are you thinking?" he asked gruffly, hating the sudden distance after sharing the painful past.

Her voice was unusually cold when she asked, "Who is the chieftain now?"

"Urim Vakgarsson. My uncle."

There was a beat of silence before she huffed, "I do not understand you."

"What do you mean?"

"Not only did you destroy your part of the peace treaty, but now I'm learning it was a treaty your own *uncle* agreed to."

The unfair—in his opinion—accusations from her sparked his own irritation. "You would prefer I had never released you?"

"Of course I'm not saying that!" Her voice became more animated as she spoke, and her body now sat rigid behind him. "I just don't understand why you would keep your people suffering? Didn't you just say getting out of Vestrahorn was something your father believed in? It seems to me you had your chance, and now it's shattered."

Her words dug at the anger that festered in him when it came to the clan. Anger that had built from years under his uncle's rule, anger that his efforts to overthrow him were taking so long, and the cold fear that if everything went wrong, it would be his allies' lives at stake.

He pulled back firmly on the reins, stopping their travel. He got off the horse and walked a few steps away to calm his head before turning back. By this time, she had dismounted as well and was glaring back at him.

"Do not think that I don't know what peace would mean to the clan. You do not know even a fraction of what our life has been like," he countered.

"Then why?!" She put her hands out. "What is your motivation in all of this?"

This was a chance to reveal the truth and tell her she was his mate. However, he didn't want to burden her with this knowledge. While she certainly had affected him from the beginning, she wasn't the sole reason he had set her free.

"Because it would be for nothing. The peace treaty would never last."

She frowned. "What do you mean?"

"My uncle cannot be trusted. The Crown certainly cannot be trusted," he said regretfully. "One would've betrayed the other soon enough, and the clan would be in a worse position."

Vidorak desired peace, but, more importantly, he wanted it to be long-lasting. A peace treaty is only effective if those who were a part of it continue to abide by it. The benefit of peace would be fleeting, because

Vidorak knew his uncle would see this as another sign that he was unstoppable. Eventually, Urim would push the boundaries of the treaty.

"You don't know that," she disagreed, but the steam had left her argument.

"I have spent twenty years watching my uncle degrade all relations with the human towns. I am aware of what he is capable of. The clan is not thriving. A peace treaty based on a woman's sacrifice wouldn't lead to the betterment of the clan."

Several emotions flashed across her face. She was an open book to the fullest extent of the meaning, and he saw the surprise, the disbelief, and finally, the vulnerability.

It lasted just a few silent seconds.

"I hope you are real."

There was no chance of discerning the meaning of her words before she crashed into his chest, hands going to his head and tugging him down toward her lips.

He could not deny her, even if he wanted to. He was helpless to do anything besides embrace her back and be grateful for whatever motivated her to kiss him.

She sighed, body melting into his, and for a moment he believed her to be every bit as desperate as he was. He wanted to devour her, to imprint her scent on every part of him. If he couldn't have forever, he would take this.

Even with his mate wrapped around him, his senses flooded with her, some primal instinct stayed alert. There was a blink of unease, one that even his mind didn't register.

One second, he was embracing her, but the next he pulled her aside as his right arm seized his axe and swung in a wide arc.

The axe sliced through flesh, and a chilling snarl emanated from the shadowy creature that attacked them. The creature tumbled several feet away, then rose to its feet with ease. It resembled a wolf but with legs that were too long, a snout that was too wide, and glowing crimson eyes.

Vidorak pushed Calypso behind him and focused on the creature approaching them. Despite the dark blood gushing from its wound, the creature moved as if unharmed. It took two stalking steps forward before lunging at him. Vidorak slashed quickly, slicing open the creature's belly. Once again, the creature tumbled, unhindered by its falling entrails.

"Stay guarded, it seems I'll need to butcher it," Vidorak called to Calypso as he gripped his axe, bracing for the next attack.

"Behind you!" Calypso yelled out, and a whip of fire struck past him.

He turned to see another of those creatures. Calypso's fire was a flaming collar around its neck.

The first creature took this opportunity to lunge again, this time aiming for his witch. Without hesitation, Vidorak hurled his axe, sending it flying straight into the creature's skull. Then he grabbed the second one and slammed it into the ground. Calypso's flames kept it muzzled as he crushed its head with his fists.

His knuckles became coated in a thick black substance, but both creatures remained unmoving.

"Have you ever seen anything like this?" he asked when she stepped forward to examine them.

She shook her head. "No. But I think I know what they are."

"Enlighten me." He removed his axe with a nauseous squelch from the decaying thing.

"Demon hounds. I've only ever seen them in drawings. They are creations of black magic. Very violent and completely subservient to their master's orders."

The hounds melted into a pool of black liquid, as if disintegrating after having failed their task.

"Last I checked, Captain Von Ahlen doesn't do magic," he said, cleaning off his axe before strapping it back on. "Any idea who sent them?"

"Unfortunately, I do," she responded dryly but didn't explain further. "Come on. This is all the more reason to hurry."

Chapter Eighteen

CALYPSO

C alypso was beginning to question whether the orc clan truly existed as they made their way along the barren crags. The last living things they'd seen for hours had tried to kill them. And those demon hounds barely classified as alive.

She was reaching the end of her patience when he directed the horse into the shadows of the mountainside. Hidden in the darkness was an entrance that was completely unnoticeable unless right next to it.

"We are here." He got off the horse and helped her down, his large hands wrapping around her waist.

"What about the horse?"

"I will send someone to tend to him." His faced her, expression serious. "Remember, you cannot use your magic once inside. If it is discovered you are a witch, there will be repercussions."

She nodded, knowing they needed to maintain the ruse.

Before being swallowed into the mountain, she turned toward her little undead friend on her shoulder. The crow had followed them, unable to act outside of her command.

"This is where our journey ends." She brushed a finger over its inky black head, petting it. "You have served me well. For that, I release you."

For a second, she thought the crow would refuse to leave, but then the prick of its claws disappeared, and the crow flew away with no further response.

She peeled her eyes away, refusing to let them water. Undead creatures rarely lasted so long, and she had grown attached.

At the end of the small cavern was a metal door that Vidorak unlocked before leading her into a stony tunnel.

"Are you sure we won't run into anyone?"

"Everyone should be gathered in the dining hall for the evening meal," he explained as they moved along.

It was dark here with torches lit sporadically. They walked downward on uneven steps, descending deeper into the core of the mountain.

There was a long stretch without torchlight, which Vidorak traversed easily with his Orcish eyesight. Despite holding his hand, Calypso kept bumping into the tunnel sides, as if the space was shrinking around her.

They were completely cut off from the outside light, and even Vidorak's bulky form was lost in the darkness. Her throat started to itch as the sensation of drowning in the darkness overcame her.

Her mind was harshly pulled back to the Sanograd dungeon from years past.

She tugged her hand away. "What is that noise?"

There was a rapid beating that radiated throughout the tunnel. She put her hand to her chest and realized it was her heart.

Everything felt light and disorienting when suddenly large hands enveloped her body.

"Sit down." His voice was soft but commanding, and his steady frame helped her onto the cool stone steps. In a grounding rhythm, his hands petted her shoulders and arms. "Just breathe."

He dared to order her again.

Irritation was a comfortable feeling, and it gave her the strength to take a breath. Then another. Her mind floated back and cleared. She wasn't in the dungeons. She had survived them and would survive this.

"This is your fault," she stated when she finally managed to speak calmly.

He kept gently petting her, waiting for her to continue.

"You bring up things that should stay buried." The small amount she had shared about her mother triggered memories she had suppressed. "If you keep doing this, you will need to accept the consequences."

While she may be losing her mind, it was the kind way he handled her that cut her deeply. She could not afford the changes he was bringing forth, and her words were meant as a threat.

He stroked her hair and tugged on one curl before muttering, "I can manage."

They stood back up, and the orc reached to grab an unlit torch handle. He tilted it toward her, and she lit it with a quick swipe of her hand.

He held the torch with one hand and her with the other. They continued down the stone passage, turning every so often. Calypso could not keep track of the maze-like tunnels and just trusted him to guide her.

They veered off the roughly built stairs onto a flat path that no longer descended. The area was constructed out of the same cold gray stone and reminded her of the corridors of a castle. There were metal torches attached along the wall, illuminating the area, so Vidorak no longer needed to hold theirs.

Narrow paths branched off the main corridor, and she saw the outlines of doors along the smaller passages. This was clearly where the orcs resided. She had assumed their clan lived on the surface of the mountain, and never imagined such an extensive underground system.

It wasn't long before they stopped at a wooden double door.

"These are my family's quarters. Only my mother and I live here." He unlocked the doors and moved aside to allow her to enter. "You'll be safe here."

She stepped into an antechamber and noted two further doors toward the back. A tapestry hung on the far wall, decorated with Orcish writing and motifs. The furniture was sparse—consisting of a table, several stools, and a large chest—but looked sturdy in its build. A couple of plush blankets rested on top of the chest. Overall, the room was small but tidy.

She was about to comment on the area when a voice spoke behind them.

"You're back already?"

They turned to see a muscular older orc walking past the open doors of the antechamber. He had a thick white beard styled into two braids and carried a hefty war hammer at his side.

"Jarl Bruk," Vidorak greeted him. "Yes, I just returned."

"Did Kinar go to meet with the chieftain?"

"Jarl Kinar and the rest are finishing the deal. I had to handle another task." His face gave nothing away.

A friendly smile spread across Jarl Bruk's face. "All the better. I was enjoying the peace without that sly bastard."

"Have things been steady here?"

"As steady as always. I finished at the forge and came to escort Mor to the dining hall."

"She is not here."

"I must've just missed her." Then he gestured toward the tunnels. "Come, you must be starving."

When Vidorak stepped to the side, the older orc finally noticed her presence behind him.

His affable demeanor fell as he looked her over. "More business of Urim's?"

Vidorak stiffened at the mention of his uncle. "Of sorts."

A look passed between them that Calypso couldn't understand, but felt there was no animosity. She sensed they were speaking in code, not quite wishing to be completely direct. Perhaps not all the orcs agreed with the capturing and enslaving of human women?

"Bring your human. She can sit with Mor."

Vidorak looked back at her and gave her a slight reassuring smile. As they walked through the tunnels, the sounds of chatter increased until they reached a great dining hall. The area was an enormous dome with rocky stalactites hanging from the ceiling in quiet threat. Fire ran through a deep indentation that spanned across the walls of the vast room, illuminating a warm glow.

A cold sweat broke out on Calypso's back, and for a moment she considered this might have been a grave mistake.

There were more orcs in this hall than she thought possible. Their physical presence radiated strength and power, most with weapons strapped to them. Like Vidorak, the male orcs didn't wear shirts, their chests bearing their battle scars. There were also female orcs, but in smaller numbers. They were taller than the average human female, and while slimmer than their male counterparts, their bodies were also covered with ropes of muscle.

It was hard not to pity the human men who had gone against these orcs during the years of the war. The orcs were boisterous, shouts radiating around the room. If this was them friendly, the sight of them in attack must be a chilling one.

"My nephew returns!" a booming voice rang through the hall, and most heads turned their way.

Out of instinct, light flames licked her palms, but she immediately extinguished them. Her body sensed the threat around her and was responding without her accord.

Vidorak's knuckles subtly grazed hers. It was enough to calm her for the moment and refocus her attention.

They headed toward the head table, where the chieftain sat with his jarls. She could see why this orc led the clan. He commanded attention, from his aura to the way he towered over the others. His body was huge and muscular; even his hands were so massive she was certain they could easily crush her skull. Like other orcs, his hair was long, and his chest bore both the red markings of his Orcish lineage and the scars from the war.

"Uncle," Vidorak stated, his body language completely changed from what she'd known of him thus far. He was not the most expressive, but now he was completely cold and withdrawn. If it weren't for the slight touch he'd given her earlier, she would've thought him a different person.

"Always so formal," the chieftain said easily, but Calypso noticed wariness in his eyes. "This is an unexpected return."

"Unexpected things have occurred."

"Does that woman have anything to do with that?" The chieftain's gaze narrowed in on her, and Calypso had to actively refrain from summoning flames.

Vidorak tensed at her side. "She is of no concern."

"Of course." The chieftain gestured to a seat nearby. "Come sit. I want to hear what has happened."

"I will join you in a moment." Without waiting for a response, Vidorak led her away toward the back.

She followed stiffly to a table that was mostly occupied by female orcs and several orclings. He stopped next to an orcess who was sitting off to the side, not interacting much with the others.

"Mother," Vidorak said, and the female glanced up, her face relaxed, leaving whatever worries she'd had behind.

"My son, you have returned."

"I have." His voice softened. "Handle this one while I speak with uncle."

Vidorak didn't even glance at Calypso before heading back to the main table. Calypso stood awkwardly, unsure of what the best protocol would be, and hating that she was in this position.

The orcess solved that for her. "Sit and grab some food."

Starving despite her fear moments ago, Calypso filled a plate with meat and root vegetables that were served along the table.

"You can call me Mor. What is your name?" The kindness with which the orcess spoke to her was surprising given their pretext.

"Calypso," she answered, immediately regretting it. It never occurred to her to use an alias during her crimes until just then.

The orcess gave no indication that she recognized who Calypso was and instead looked at her with sympathy. "Everything will be okay. Just be calm and try to eat something."

Calypso took her in, wondering how many times she had repeated those words. Mor was tall and toned, with dark curly hair that fell over her shoulders. Her skin was green like Vidorak's but lighter with shades of gray, and her Orcish red markings peaked from under her clothes at her collarbones.

Mor caught her studying stare, and Calypso was taken aback by how much her eyes resembled Vidorak's. Both were so dark they were almost black, with a thick rim of lashes around them. However, Vidorak's eyes were often guarded and cold, while this woman's eyes held an edge of sadness.

"Am I the only human here?" Calypso asked as she ate.

Mor shook her head, keeping her voice low but steady as she answered. "There are others, but they do not dine here."

"What is expected of them?"

"It varies. Most work in the kitchens or the laundry."

"And how many are taken to the orc's bedchambers at night?" she asked pointedly.

"Focus on your food. The rest of your questions will have to wait until later." Whether Mor didn't want to answer because of discomfort or worry was unclear.

Like an invisible pull, Calypso's eyes periodically drifted to the head table to look at Vidorak. They were too far away to hear their conversation. While the older orcs seemed to laugh and exclaim occasionally, Vidorak remained completely shut off. She didn't even sense anger from him, just a vast emptiness.

Seeing this change was disconcerting, and she forced herself to focus on eating. Despite her silence, she felt the heavy weight of being stared at, and her ears pricked as if she were being discussed.

There was a crash on the other side of the room that broke the tension. Heads turned to gawk as two male orcs exchanged blows. She took that opportunity to glance again at Vidorak, who apparently was thinking the same thing and looked back at her.

Their eyes held, and Calypso felt a current go between them. The abruptness passed, and the connection broke as she turned back to her plate.

Done with eating, Mor stood and gently touched Calypso's hand. "Let's go."

Calypso didn't need to be told twice. She followed Mor out as calmly as she could. Her instincts warned her not to pick up her pace, lest the surrounding predators notice.

Once safely in the tunnels, even Mor relaxed a fraction. "We can speak freely here. To answer your previous question, unfortunately, most of the human women are forced to their beds. But you do not need to worry about that."

"Why do you say that?" Calypso was curious rather than scared.

"Because my son brought you to me. We need to lie low for a few days, but after that, I will arrange your return. Where were you taken from?"

Calypso hesitated, uncertain of how much to say. "Taybe."

They walked in silence for a few moments before Calypso said, "Vidorak said it wasn't always like this."

Mor shook her head. "Ushnar never allowed such things when he was chieftain."

"He was your husband?"

"Not just my husband. He was my mate." Mor smiled at Calypso's surprise. "Didn't know that orcs developed mate bonds?"

"I have heard of mates but not specifically about orcs," she admitted. It was not a phenomenon that occurred with witches. "Is it only between orcs?"

She didn't know what made her ask that last part and didn't want to question why her chest beat eagerly as she awaited Mor's answer.

"I have never heard of an orc forming a mate bond with a human."

Calypso buried the twinge of disappointment that came with those words. It was embarrassing even to admit she felt that. She was not destined for things like love anyway.

Things remained silent between them as they returned to the family quarters, and Mor showed her to a small room with a bed. As Calypso went to move past her, Mor gasped.

The woman's eyes widened in shock. "Your scent. It's mingled with my son's. Have you . . . did he . . ."

Calypso caught on to her unspoken question. "No, he didn't force himself on me. We have spent a lot of time in close quarters, is all."

Mor nodded, her shock melting away. "Of course. Vidorak would never do such a thing. It's only he's become so different these last few years. So cold. I could kill Urim for that alone."

Calypso didn't respond, feeling like the woman was mostly talking to herself now.

When she refocused on Calypso, Mor's empty look from the dining hall returned. "Try to get some sleep. I will make sure you are assigned to the kitchen. It's the most tolerable work and won't chance other males bothering you."

With that, Mor left her alone in the small room. Calypso lay on the mattress, a flickering flame she summoned from her index finger the only light source. It was disorienting being so deep underground.

Her body and mind were weary, but her buzzing thoughts kept her awake. It wasn't until she was in the dining hall that the risk of her decision had truly sunk in. With all her magic, even she couldn't fight off an entire horde if they turned on her. She had put herself completely at the mercy of Vidorak just for a chance to obtain her amulet.

Was her mind already fading into the uncontrollable lust for power that black magic caused? That was the risk with such magic; it made one more powerful but also made them greedy. Caution and logic twisted as the mind slipped toward a singular goal.

Panic closed in on her.

Take a dagger and hurt him while his guard is down.

Since the voice's onset, she had been annoyed and occasionally concerned, but never before had felt as angry toward it as she did now.

Yes, she felt the discomfort of needing to rely on another, but injuring Vidorak was wrong. While Vidorak had initially kidnapped her, everything he'd done since then had been to help her, even when she was undeserving of it.

He planned to hand you over to Davinger.

No, that was the chieftain. Vidorak had let her go, destroying the negotiations in the process. Something that was bound to have its repercussions.

Who would give up peace for a single witch?

That gave her pause. It bothered her that she didn't understand why he'd made such a sacrifice.

Perhaps carrying a dagger may not be a bad idea. Vidorak wouldn't be able to be with her constantly in the mountain, and having a weapon that wasn't magic could have its uses.

The quarters were filled with weapons. All she had to do was slip out and grab one to keep on her.

Before she could act on those thoughts, Calypso heard the clanking sound of the doors to the family quarters open.

Chapter Nineteen

VIDORAK

I t was a mistake to bring her here. He was rarely at ease in the mountains, but having his recently discovered mate nearby tested his control. When his uncle had turned his attention toward her, Vidorak had felt his vision turn red. If Urim had made any comments indicating he might hurt her, there was no doubt Vidorak would've attacked him.

Thankfully, his uncle was more interested in questioning him regarding his early return to the mountain. Urim easily accepted Vidorak's explanation because afterward he shared his new endeavor. He was planning not only a large raid but also a takeover. Of none other than the witch's stronghold in Taybe.

Turmoil swirled within him when he entered the family quarters. It would be difficult to find sleep knowing he'd need to tell Calypso what his uncle planned to do. Witnessing her rage firsthand worried him about what her reaction would be. He shuddered at the idea of her fighting his uncle, formidable as she may be.

The second he entered the antechamber, he felt her eyes on him. Even in the dark, he spotted her speckled golden eyes studying him from the opening of her room.

Even though they'd just spent days together traveling to the mountain, he didn't realize how much calmer he felt with just the two of them. They'd been apart for simply one evening meal, but it wasn't until this moment that he felt like he could truly breathe.

He advanced toward her, unable to stop himself, and offered his hand. She put her soft hand in his, and the mate bond hummed with contentment.

He pulled her into the antechamber to talk, but she tugged her hand away. When he looked back, her eyes were blazing with an undercurrent of anger and suspicion.

"I'm sorry for the treatment in the dining hall." Acting as if she didn't matter felt wrong, but he couldn't risk Urim's curiosity growing.

"I don't care about that." Her words were clipped, and he saw her eyes flitter to the wall of weapons.

The idea of her being frightened of him made him sick. He couldn't blame her for her suspicion. It was necessary to treat her coldly to avoid drawing attention.

"Take what you want. Though if you want to incapacitate me, burning my eyes would be more efficient than stabbing."

After a moment of hesitation, she reached for one of his daggers and took it. Her fingers ran over the sharp, forged metal. "I think I am having a hard time being enclosed underground."

The urge to walk over and embrace her was tough to tamp down. "It is difficult spending most of the day out of natural light."

Her fingers danced over the dagger once more before she returned it to its original spot. "It's not just that. It brings back memories."

"From your time in the Sanograd dungeon?"

She nodded. "It was hard to tell time there too. Everything was just so dark." Suddenly, she crumbled and covered her face with her hands.

"Goddess, I feel so foolish complaining about it when I was only there for a few days."

This time he didn't hold back in comforting her. He gathered her small body in his arms and, luckily, she didn't push him away. "You were just a child."

"It wasn't a secret the Purist sect of the nobility loathed my mother. But I was too busy enjoying the freedom of being the daughter of a royal advisor. Right until they detained us."

"These things cannot be predicted. No good comes from torturing yourself." He knew that well. Even though he was just an orcling, he often wondered if his father's end could've been avoided.

"She freed me, you know."

He knew that; she'd told him days earlier, but he let her speak through her tumultuous thoughts.

"My mother used the last of her strength to melt the lock on my chains before distracting the guards. She promised she'd meet me at the sanctuary in Solar City, but by the time I got there, they had already killed her."

There weren't any words he could say to soften the traumatic past she'd lived through, so he stroked her hair until she stopped trembling. "I cannot take you to the surface. But I can bring you to a place that I find peaceful."

The tension in her face relaxed, and he felt a glimmer of longing. She stepped away from his embrace, then took his hand. "Show me."

He led her to a part of the mountain unknown to others. The path there was undeveloped and difficult to traverse. There were no torches hanging, and he moved solely by memory.

"You can use your fire if the darkness bothers you," he told her, recalling how strongly she'd responded to the dark earlier.

When the tunnels remained unlit, he felt the warmth of her trust spread in his chest. Even if she didn't admit it, his witch was starting to let her guard down around him. He wanted nothing more than to make sure she never regretted that decision.

They arrived, and he temporarily let go of her hand to push a large boulder aside. Once shifted, they walked in, and he moved the boulder back, shutting them off from the rest of the mountain.

"It's beautiful."

The cavern was warm from the hot springs, and the plants that grew around the thermal waters emitted a greenish-blue light.

He walked up behind her but left a small amount of space between them so they weren't touching. "I used to come here with my father when I was an orcling. I don't think he even told my mother about it."

"Your mother mentioned they were mates."

He nodded. "They were. There hasn't been another mate pair in years."

"Why?"

There were many opinions regarding this. The occasional periods of low food, the lack of sunlight. But those things had persisted for years when mate bonds were common. What many in the clan didn't dare say too loudly was that it was likely a result of Urim's war.

"It's unknown. There is a lot of discontent within the clan. Not enough babes are born, and the war takes our young male warriors."

"I thought the females fought as well."

"They used to." Some were as formidable as the other males in the horde. "My uncle forbade it several years back once the numbers fell."

"Sounds like things aren't going too well with Urim as chieftain."

He grunted in agreement. "Unless he is challenged, his command remains."

"Tell me what will happen when Urim finds out."

He knew she referred to what would happen when Jarl Kinar returned and told of her assisted escape.

"Nothing that I can't handle."

She gave him an unhappy look but didn't push him further. Instead, she stepped to the edge of the hot springs and kneeled to dip her hand in the water.

"It's warm," she commented happily. "Perfect for a swim."

She glanced over her shoulder at him for a moment before reaching up and undoing the ties of her dress. The untied dress pooled at her feet, leaving her only in undergarments, which she slipped off next.

His breath caught in his lungs as his eyes roamed over her naked back. She was so beautiful that it didn't seem real. He wanted to touch her and assure himself that she was truly there. The thought of her soft skin under his hands caused him to instantly become hard.

She was his mate. She was naked and wanted him. He took a step toward her before he even realized what he was doing. The mate bond was demanding he go to her and show her that she was his.

He dug his claws into his palms to clear the need that gripped him and stopped in his tracks. As much as his hands ached to touch her, he fought to regain control.

Without turning back, she walked over to the hot springs and slowly stepped in. Between the glow, her bare tattooed form, and her curly crimson hair, she looked every bit a mystical being come to life.

The water was up to her shoulders, and she swam a few feet away before turning around and looking back at him with an amused tilt to her lips. "Did you bring me all this way just to stare?"

He put his weapons on the ground, realizing he hadn't even taken the time to store them before leaving for here. "I don't trust myself to enter."

The depths of his desire for her scared him. He longed to caress her body, to bury his face in her cunt, to rut her like an animal and watch as release washed over her. Being so close to her with these thoughts running through his mind was dangerous. He would never force himself on her, but his desire for her engulfed his mind, and the beastly part of him threatened to take over.

Suddenly, he felt that coming here might not have been the best idea. He would let her swim, then take her back and put distance between them until his head cleared.

Her golden eyes focused on him with a heated look. "Use your question of truth to ask me what I've decided."

He hadn't asked a question yet this day, but he hadn't been able to decide between the several he had. Part of him wanted those answers to come naturally and not as payment for a deal. A secret part of him felt he wanted too much. An orc like him knew only a life of war, loss, and deceit. The dream of being together without the troubles that surrounded them both seemed a fantasy that even a mate bond could never overcome.

He paused for a minute before asking his question, as if he was pondering it, despite knowing he'd inevitably do what she asked. "What have you decided?"

"I've decided to let you taste my pussy. If you want." She said it so simply as if they were discussing the weather, but the words went straight to his cock.

It was on the tip of his tongue to ask what made her decide that, but he wasn't stupid enough to question whatever blessing this was.

He took off his boots and entered the water with his trousers still on. She had said he could taste her, not put his cock in her, so while his hard length was not subtle, it would stay away.

The spring was shallow and reached just above his hips when standing. He grabbed his mate by her waist and hauled her to him, crushing her bare breasts to his chest. A small inhale of surprise escaped her at his quick movement. Her lips curved into a satisfied smile, and her legs went around his waist, bringing her naked cunt against his hardness.

His lips skimmed over the curve of her neck, inhaling her scent. "Are you sure about what you said, little witch?"

He loved that she leaned into his touch, exposing more of her neck for him. He couldn't resist leaving a trail of kisses from her shoulder to her ear. Her little sigh at that was so addicting, he did it again.

She gave an impatient squirm, her warm core rubbing into him. His lips went to her ear, and he gave her a chastising nip. "Answer my question."

She blinked a couple of times before responding. "Yes, Vidorak, I'm very sure."

With that, he captured her mouth, his tongue dipping inside. He tasted her, moving like he wanted to do with his cock. She followed his lead and allowed him to leave her breathless. His headstrong witch melted into him, letting him do what he wanted, and that was such a heady feeling.

As delicious as her mouth was, he was eager to taste her everywhere. With her round bottom in his hands, he walked to the edge of the springs and sat her on the flat warm stones. The greenery was soft so she wouldn't be uncomfortable.

Sitting on the stones, her full breasts were level with his face. Her rosy nipples pebbled, calling out to him. He leaned forward and took one into his mouth while palming the other. She sighed with pleasure, and her hands went to his hair to hold him in place. As if anything could pry him away at the moment. He felt like he could spend hours exploring every inch of her body, watching her reaction to his touches.

After his thumb had rubbed over her nipple to a hard point, he switched sides, not wanting to neglect the other of his mouth.

While he could stay there much longer, his mouth watered for another part of her. He kissed her chest and moved down her belly. He pulled up her knees and opened her wide for his eyes. His lovely witch wasn't shy and let him see her glistening pussy unabashedly.

"You're perfect," he whispered, gently caressing her thighs as he moved toward her core.

"And you're taking too long." She tilted her hips when his fingers skimmed over her folds, trying to increase the pressure.

"So eager." He caressed her cunt leisurely, studying every reaction to learn what triggered each moan and sharp inhale.

Her wetness coated his entire hand, and he brought it to his mouth to lick each finger clean. Her taste was divine; however, the sharpness of his claws posed a problem. Savagely biting his claw, he tore the end off and then repeated the process on a second finger.

Claws now taken care of, he pushed one finger into her tight warm channel. His hips inadvertently thrust forward in the water. She would feel so good wrapped around his cock. "Tell me, what did you think about the night you touched yourself in the tub?"

Her eyes were closed, and she rocked herself upon his finger as he rubbed her clit with his thumb. "You already asked about that."

He stilled her movements with an iron hand on her hip and moved his thumb away from the circles he was doing.

A frustrated sound left her lips, and her eyes flew open. Her hair was wild, a red flush forming on her cheeks and chest, and she glared at him. Gods, he'd never been as aroused as he was at this moment. "Fine! Yes, I thought of you!"

His satisfaction was intense.

He rewarded his witch for her honesty and brought his mouth down on her cunt. He removed his hand and cupped her bottom, holding her firmly against him. Then he ate her like the starving orc he was. His large tongue reaching deep inside. Her hands flew to his hair, holding on tight as he fucked her with his tongue.

Her wetness was the sweetest nectar to him. Hers was a unique and perfect taste, and he wanted to rub it all over his face. He wanted to lick her like this every day to have her scent on him always.

Her breath was heavy, and he wanted her to get her release.

She reached down to rub her clit, but he pushed her hand aside, growling, "*Mine*," before closing his mouth over her clit.

He licked her eagerly, and when he sucked over her clit, she arched off the stones with a half scream. Focusing on the area that had her tensing, he pushed one of his fingers back inside her. He stroked her like that before pushing in a second finger.

"Oh, fuck, right there!" she cried out.

Her hands clenched at him desperately as her breath became more rapid. Then he felt her come as she pulsated and tightened around his fingers, and her thighs clamped his head in what was his new favorite place in the world.

When her body went slack, he removed his fingers but kept his hold on her, caressing her thighs.

She looked down at him with half-lidded eyes.

"Hopefully, I lived up to the fantasy, little witch." He gently kissed the inner part of her knee and then tugged her forward so that she was back in the water. He held her with one arm under her knees and the other at her back.

Her satisfied smile turned wicked. "I don't remember. I think we may need to do that a few more times to be sure."

With a laugh, he embraced her closer. They soaked a bit more, but when she yawned, he pulled her out of the water. He regathered his weapons, and they redressed without hurry, both wanting to prolong the inevitable.

They left the springs holding hands and returned to his family quarters. Once inside, they retreated into their separate rooms, one thin wall standing between them. As wrong as it felt to be without her, it was too risky to have her that close all night. He didn't think he'd sleep without her next to him, but exhaustion overtook him.

It wasn't until the very end that he realized he hadn't told her about Urim's plans to attack the witch stronghold.

Chapter Twenty

CALYPSO

Calypso woke up contented and relaxed from the afterglow of last night's earth-shattering orgasm. If she had known orc tongues had such capabilities, they could've had more interesting nights during her initial capture.

Her brightness instantly dimmed when she saw the seriousness on Vidorak's face. To be fair, it was always like that, but now it looked acutely grave.

"What is it?"

"I need to talk to you about my uncle's plans."

"I have a feeling I won't like them." She crossed her arms over her chest to keep from fidgeting.

His expression was grim. "You won't. He plans to attack your stronghold in Taybe. He sees your coven as weak."

This time she didn't even correct him in referring to it as a stronghold. She had not anticipated this possibility. Coils of disgust swirled within her. She had been relishing his kisses and pleasure while her sisters, the rescued witches, and all she strived for were at risk.

If her mind could be so easily swayed, then she was too weak to carry out her plans. She steeled her heart as she looked at Vidorak. He may desire her, but that didn't mean his loyalties automatically lay with her. While he clearly had his disagreements with the chieftain, Urim was still his blood relation.

"I see," she said through gritted teeth.

His dark eyes hardened in response, and he stalked toward her. She stiffened, flames licking at her fingertips. If this were a trap, she was completely at his mercy. Could she trust him and risk ruining all the plans she'd set into motion?

"Stay back!" she warned, her eyes turning golden around the edges as she warred with her mind.

He didn't slow in his progress, taking her by the shoulders and wrapping her in his embrace. The small tendrils of fire born of her restless emotions swiped at his skin. She wanted to control them, but she felt too much.

She struggled to get out of his grasp, but his hold only tightened.

His hand went to her chin. "Look at me, Calypso."

He rarely used her name, and hearing it did something to her. Her golden eyes went to his dark ones, and she felt anchored once more.

"I will not let that happen," he promised. "I will protect you. It doesn't matter if that is against my uncle or against the king."

Her heart beat fast at these words. "Why?"

It was too much. The gentle way he touched her, the loving words he spoke—it messed with her already fragile mind. It made the hurt and lonely part of her wish for more. She loved her sisters fiercely, but she knew the ugly parts of her got in the way. With Vidorak, she'd not held back, but he persisted in showing her compassion that mended the cracks in her heart.

"Because you have bewitched me," he started, but then hesitated. The tumultuousness she felt inside her was reflected in his eyes. "Because it is what's right, and it's something I should have done long ago."

He does his duty against a tyrant chieftain.

Unlike the previous evening, she didn't feel confident enough to refute the voice's claims. Her rapidly softening heart wanted to hope his proclamation of protecting her was more, but she didn't trust the judgement of her maddening mind.

She pulled out of his hold, having regained some control. As intoxicating as things between them were, she reminded herself that love was not for her. In a way, it might not be for him either. She had her revenge, and he had his clan.

"He is your uncle and chieftain. I do not see how you have a choice but to follow his plan," she stated.

"There is always a choice. I've been preparing to challenge my uncle."

"Challenge him?" she repeated.

Grabbing power for himself was a motivation she could understand, but she felt it was more given all that she'd seen from Vidorak. He cared for the clan and wasn't happy about the hardships they were suffering. From his mother's words last night, clearly not all supported Urim's leadership.

"You were correct last night. Things have worsened since my uncle became chieftain. I am not sure if it was his grief after my father died or if he was always this way, but the clan will be destroyed if we continue like this."

"What do you plan to do?" she asked.

"The clan will only support a chieftain who wins through challenge. I have spent months ensuring everything is in place for this, but we need to worry about his plans first."

She wanted to push him more about it, but could tell by the hardness in his eyes he didn't want to discuss it further. For all his evil deeds, Urim was still his blood relation. She couldn't imagine Vidorak making this choice easily and wondered how deep Urim's violence went.

As much as she wanted to know more, she let it go. "Tell me why he has set his sights on Taybe."

"He wants to attack because there have been more sightings of the demon hounds by patrols in the wastelands. He thinks the witches sent them as revenge for kidnapping you. I won't let that happen." He gave her hand a reassuring squeeze. "But there is more to this you haven't told me."

Denial was on the tip of her tongue, but he had earned her trust, and she chose to answer him. "Hugh Davinger is sending the demon hounds. He must have realized I'd escaped capture somehow."

Vidorak frowned at the mention of the king regent. "He's a man."

"That's debatable," she muttered, but understood what he meant. "It's rare for men to perform magic, but some can perform simple spells with the help of runes."

"This does not seem like a simple spell."

She shook her head. "It's not. Davinger has become quite powerful."

"How?"

"I am not sure." She grimaced, hating that she still lacked so much information. "I think that's why he had my mother killed. She must've found out what he was doing."

"And now he's the most powerful man in the realm," Vidorak finished for her. "I see your motivation in wanting to stop him."

She gave a bitter laugh. "Don't make it out to be more noble than it is. I am not doing this for the betterment of a realm that abandoned us. There is no hope for witchkind. I am doing this for revenge."

He stared at her for a moment before speaking. "You are not without hope."

That healed another crack in her heart even though she knew it was a lie. "The amulet would certainly help. I will need all the magical aid I can get."

He nodded. "I will meet with my uncle and the jarls today. But tomorrow, I plan on getting the amulet you seek. Then Nazghor will escort you to Taybe."

She should've been happy getting what she had been searching for after all these years, but the idea of parting from him caused an ache in her chest.

"I could help you here with your challenge against Urim," she offered. "You have seen what my fire can do."

"I know. But you need to get back to your coven."

Unfortunately, he was right. She had been absent for too long.

He kissed her forehead, which made her scowl, and then took a step back. "I need to go now. My mother will help you during the day."

With that, he left the quarters and disappeared down the stone corridor. It wasn't long after that Mor left her bedroom and came up to her. Calypso wondered whether she'd overheard them, given her Orcish hearing.

"How are you feeling?" Mor asked.

That was a question she wasn't ready to analyze too closely. "As well as I can be a hundred feet underground."

"If Vidorak says he'll get you back home, he will." She put a reassuring hand on Calypso's arm. "He's a lot like his father. He has a strong sense of responsibility but is very stubborn in accepting help. I always imagined Vidorak mated to someone strong-willed."

Calypso's mood darkened with the sudden rush of jealousy at the thought of Vidorak mated. The question had been on the tip of her tongue to ask at the springs last night, but she couldn't muster the courage. The thought of him forming a deep bond with another female made her unreasonably furious and bloodthirsty. Even knowing he'd likely had prior orcess lovers pricked at her.

She kept these thoughts to herself because there was no way she was going to talk to Vidorak's mother about her son's past lovers.

"Can you show me the kitchen? I am eager to distract my mind for the moment."

Mor took her to the kitchens through a winding tunnel branching off the main corridor. The path was still difficult to memorize despite her going through it for the third time.

They reached a crossing point, but instead of going straight into the dining hall, they turned to the left. The kitchen came into view shortly after that.

For the first time since entering the mountain, Calypso saw non-orcs. A dozen human females of varying ages were completing tasks while an orcess stood guard at the entrance of the kitchens, her half-shaved head highlighting the red Orcish markings on her scalp. Mor filled a bowl of porridge and handed it to Calypso before going to talk to the orcess guard.

While they chatted, Calypso scarfed down her food and observed the other women. From what she could see, they didn't seem to have any bruising, and their clothes, while plain, were clean. That was a small mercy, given they were captives here and forced to do labor.

After she finished eating, the orcess guard came over to her, carrying a hefty bucket filled with root vegetables. She set it on the ground and handed her a small dull knife.

"Peel."

Calypso raised her eyebrows at the short, gruff command, but wordlessly started her task. No one talked to her, and the women worked stiffly.

That was fine with Calypso, and she took out her frustrations on the potatoes. She was not one to sit still when there was something she wanted. The amulet was within her reach, and she wanted to slam this dull dagger in Urim's eye and grab the Eye of Azara herself. It spoke to how much she trusted Vidorak that she reined in her natural urges and continued to prep the food.

From time to time, male orcs would come by with excuses of wanting something to eat while stealing glances at them until the orcess guard chased them off.

"You'll last longer if you choose one and go to their bed."

Calypso looked over her shoulder to find a young woman about her age with round, stormy blue eyes and short-cropped brown hair. "I have no interest in taking any of them to bed."

She only had interest in one orc.

"The others stay away for a bit when they sense the smell on you. It's not too bad if you get one that's more careful. Sometimes they even give you gifts." She started mixing dough next to Calypso, giving her a soft, friendly smile. "I'm Dalia."

Those words burned Calypso like hot coals inside of her. To be glad of such a pittance for the use of her body.

"Calypso." After a beat, she asked, "Where are you from?"

"Rava."

Calypso paused her chopping. The cliffs of Rava spanned the southeastern border of Shalimar. "I did not know the orcs raided so far south."

"They don't. I was visiting my aunt up north when I got captured. What about you?"

"Taybe." Which was more or less the truth. Then Calypso recalled what Dalia had first said. "What do you mean, last longer?"

The orcess guard towered over them, killing their conversation. "Less talk, more work. Evening meal is soon." Her speech was guttural, as if she weren't quite comfortable with the feel of the common tongue.

With a silent nod, Dalia moved away and went to finish her task. They rushed to complete the cooking as hungry orcs appeared in the dining room. There was no time to say more than a few words of direction as they fed the mountain.

Calypso observed the different orcs that arrived to eat. Because of the war, many of the clans across the realm had migrated north seeking refuge at the mountain. It wasn't easy, but she spotted patterns in their appearances.

She thought of one type as the "bead orcs." They were tall and their bodies slim, but toned, reminding her of the elven kind. Their faces appeared softer with their shorter tusks, and their hair had strands interwoven with colorful beads. While most orcs wore their hair long, a few preferred it short to the scalp. That group had dark green skin and short and stout bodies. She saw many with hoops up their pointed ears, like Vidorak, and others that wore necklaces of bones.

That's as far as her analysis went, as half of them spoke Orcish to her and she couldn't understand a word of it. Perhaps she should ask Vidorak to teach her some phrases. It would only help her here.

It wasn't until they were washing the dishes that she had another moment to chat with Dalia.

"Explain to me what you meant earlier."

Dalia looked around before lowering her voice and speaking quickly. "I don't want to frighten you, but it's important you know. Once a lunar cycle, one or two of the human women go missing."

"Where do they go?" Calypso growled out.

Dalia's blue eyes filled with sadness. "No one knows. I've been here three years and have yet to see any of them return."

"What about the others?" Calypso glanced over the other women.

"They haven't been here as long. The ones that take a warrior to bed are less likely to disappear."

The noise outside the kitchen told them their time for conversation would be coming to an end.

"We will speak more later," Calypso promised.

Dalia nodded and walked away, but not before Calypso caught a glimpse of a black mark of magic at her ankle.

It seemed she wasn't the only witch currently at the mountain.

CHAPTER TWENTY-ONE

VIDORAK

It was probably not the best idea to run back to the family quarters with how tightly wound he felt. After spending the whole day under the analyzing eye of his uncle and the jarls, Vidorak felt his control buckling.

Nazghor jogged up from behind him. "You are a hard orc to track down. Can we speak for a moment?"

Speaking with Nazghor was not high on his priority list at the moment, and he scrambled for excuses to give him.

Nazghor sensed this, and a wide grin split his face. "Come, let's go to the training grounds. The way you look now, I'm not sure you could open a door without tearing it off its hinges."

Unfortunately, he was right. While every part of him demanded to return to his mate, he wasn't sure how he'd react upon seeing her. Once her addicting smell hit him, he was likely to lose all control and either tie her to him or fuck her senseless or possibly both.

Such a move might not be received very well. Getting rid of some pent-up energy was the smarter choice.

"Make it quick." Vidorak changed directions and followed Nazghor down the familiar tunnels.

They exited onto the flat basin that sat between several mountain peaks. Their bulky orc bodies made it difficult to train within the mountain, so they kept the training to the outside grounds.

The clan was busy enjoying their evening meal, so Nazghor and Vidorak were outside alone. They warmed up, stretching out the stiffness that had built throughout the day. It was nighttime, and for once, the moon glowed unimpeded by clouds.

"Something tells me things did not go as planned with your trip," Nazghor began, testing the waters of how much Vidorak was willing to share without coming out directly and asking. Normally, Vidorak appreciated this, but currently, he was finding it bothersome. There was something refreshing about the way Calypso just demanded exactly what she wanted to know. Without coyness or hesitation.

"If you keep thinking about your mate every other minute, we will get nowhere," Nazghor interrupted his thoughts.

That quickly got Vidorak's attention. "How did you know?"

"Your scents are starting to mix. Your clan might've forgotten what a mated pair smells like over the years, but it is recent in my mind."

Despite all the loss he had suffered, Nazghor still maintained such an even-tempered demeanor, always so skilled at making others feel at ease. The plague that had ravaged Rava ten years back had decimated the orc clan that resided there—Nazghor's mate included. Having now experienced a mate bond, Vidorak couldn't imagine surviving the grief.

"I did not think it was possible since she is not an orcess," he admitted.

"Why not? It's a connection of the souls after all, not the physical body." Nazghor shrugged. "Now if you're disappointed with your beautiful mate, I can certainly relieve you of the burden."

Vidorak's fist connected with Nazghor's face before he even processed what was happening. His possessiveness clawed at him to punish the threat regardless of it being his friend.

The only thing that stopped him from pummeling his face again was the bloody grin that Nazghor held and the complete lack of interest Vidorak sensed from him.

"Good to see you are no exception to how territorial mated orcs are." Nazghor wiped the blood from the small gash at the corner of his lip. "Why do you seem sullen? More than the regular amount anyhow."

Vidorak wouldn't apologize for punching him; it was clear Nazghor knew what he was doing by goading him.

"Because it does not matter if she is my mate when we have no future!" he bellowed. The ache in his chest felt suffocating. "I hate being reminded of that every time I see her."

"Why would there be no future? I think—"

"By the end of the fortnight, I will challenge my uncle for control of the clan." Vidorak silenced him.

For once, Nazghor's relaxed manner turned into concern.

"It's too soon. Most of the jarls still support Urim. And we still haven't heard from the Bear Lake clan."

The colony lay far to the northeast of the realm. It was under the king's control on maps alone. In reality, the frozen tundra ruled itself in segregation. It was the only orc clan untouched by disease or war.

Vidorak shook his head. "There is no more time. Urim has forced my hand in this. I won't discuss it further. What I want to know is whether you will lead Calypso out of the mountain tomorrow and take her back to Taybe."

"Vidorak…" Nazghor began, set to argue, but then paused and nodded. "You can trust me. What about Mor?"

"I'll speak with Grushag about that. Once the challenge begins, she'll need to be taken away." He hesitated, knowing the depth of heartbreak his mother already carried. "I do not want her to see."

It wasn't simply about the fight with his uncle, but also about what would happen next. If he won, leading with dissenting jarls risked breaking apart the entire clan. If he lost, he did not want his mother to witness his death.

Nazghor nodded, his jaw clenched. Unhappy but also not opposing what would come to be.

After that, they trained silently, Nazghor pushing him harder than he ever had in the past. It wasn't until Vidorak completely exhausted himself that he returned to the family quarters.

Upon entering, he heard Calypso before seeing her. She sounded as if she were having a conversation with someone.

"Go away!" The hiss in her command caused him to burst into her room.

He found her alone, lying on her side in bed with her eyes closed. She didn't glance his way as he stood in the doorway.

"Are you in pain?" he asked, searching for a threat that wasn't there.

She opened her eyes, expression unreadable. "I am fine. You weren't in the dining hall when we served the food."

"Nazghor and I were training," he answered, but he could tell her mind was elsewhere. "You looked lost in thought."

"I want to ask you something. You can come in." She sat up and crossed her legs on the small mattress.

Vidorak entered, careful to keep distance between them. "Ask away."

"How much do you know about the human captives disappearing from the mountain?"

"There have been rumors about a male taking them, but I could never discover who was behind it. With Nazghor and Grushag's help, I send as many as I can back to their villages, but we've had to act covertly."

"Urim never ordered you to handle the captives?"

"My uncle used me when he had more violent orders."

Her expression was contemplative. "It's the secrecy that I find odd. Your uncle doesn't strike me as someone who hides his violence."

No, he wasn't, which made Vidorak think he wasn't killing these women. "Urim is more greedy than violent."

Silence fell between them as she considered what he'd said.

"Who were you talking to when I came into the room?" he asked.

Her eyes darted away at that question. "My mother."

He frowned, not quite catching her meaning.

With a breath, she looked back at him and explained, "Occupational hazard of the black magic. Sometimes I see people who have died or hear voices that aren't mine."

Another cost to her black magic. Her words unnerved him, not because he was horrified by her, but because he was scared *for* her.

"That must be frightening." As much as he loved his father, the idea of seeing him at random, following him like a ghost, would be horrifying.

She shrugged. "It is what it is. I cannot change it."

"Even if you stop your black magic?"

Her eyes sharpened. "There's no stopping what is already part of me. But I have not added anymore blood tattoos in months."

He was glad of that for the simple fact that it was clearly harming her. She may believe in her need for revenge at all costs, but it was not worth destroying her mind.

"What helps when you have these visions?"

"Being around others. It reminds me who's actually alive."

"I can stay with you tonight, if you'd like," he offered, barely holding back from crossing the room.

She did not reach for him. Instead, she shook her head and laid back in bed. "I would prefer to be alone."

For a moment, he considered ignoring that and going over to comfort her. To embrace and distract her from the thoughts that plagued her. He wanted to show her how he desired her, all of her, even the dark parts she wanted to hide.

"Goodnight, Calypso," he grunted before retreating to his room.

He'd given in to his desires last night, and it only temporarily satiated the ache. In fact, he craved her even more. He wanted to get lost in the pleasure between them, shut out the rest of the world.

But to do that would be selfish. As much as every part of him rebelled at the thought, the truth was there was no forever for them.

Chapter Twenty-Two

CALYPSO

Calypso cursed under her breath as the smell of burned porridge suddenly hit her. This was the third batch she had ruined, and she had half a mind to serve it as is rather than start again. The complete disbelief at how difficult this task was proving to be even had her genuinely considering apologizing to Paola when she returned to the estate. And she never apologized to anyone. Ever.

"Switch with me," Dalia said as she pushed a bowl of onions that needed chopping into Calypso's hands.

More than willing to part ways with the porridge, Calypso took the onions to the counter and started chopping.

"Are you the only one in your family?" Calypso asked, making use of the small moment they had to speak.

"The only what?"

"Witch."

Dalia stiffened, keeping her eyes focused on her own task. "I don't know what you are talking about."

"I saw your mark."

The silence stretched between them, and Calypso felt a twinge of guilt about making a woman who showed her kindness uncomfortable.

"Does it matter if I am?" Dalia finally spoke again. "It is a death sentence in this realm. I am better off living as a slave for the orcs."

The urge to protest burned within her, but she realized Dalia was right in her assessment. Some loving families chose to protect their witch relatives. Without family or friends, surviving in the realm was near impossible.

We can create a place for witches to go.

The thought rang through her mind in Nyx's voice, and Calypso scowled.

Before they could speak any further, the half-shaven orcess guard approached them. "Female, bring food and tea. The chieftain demons it."

"It's not female, it's Calypso," she snapped. "It's also not *demons* but *demands.*"

Surprisingly, the orcess did not look angry at being corrected but intrigued.

"Demands it," she repeated quietly.

As Calypso gathered ingredients, the thought of slipping a laxative in the drink crossed her mind, but the guard kept a constant watch.

Meal prepared, they headed into the tunnels. Calypso tried to memorize the directions they took, but after three turns, it all started to blend together. She was never good at walking through the shadows patiently like Nyx, instead preferring to charge forward like a bull.

They approached a wide set of doors, and the guard warned over her shoulder, "Do this with silence. Your eyes down."

The guard knocked and waited for permission before allowing Calypso to enter the council chamber. At the head of the wooden circular table was the chieftain, sitting on an intricate metal throne with sharp spikes that ran up its sides and back. Should she stumble and fall on it, she would get impaled.

Around him were half a dozen other orcs, some she recognized as the older jarls she met on the first day, others she didn't recognize at all. Most notably, Vidorak was not present.

There was actual sunlight streaming in from the heavy glass windows in the room. It seems they were close enough to the surface to allow natural light in. It took a moment for her eyes to adjust, having spent over a day only in torchlight and dark tunnels.

"You can place it here," Jarl Bruk instructed her, gesturing toward an empty section on the table.

Her steps were quiet as she walked over to the table, her eyes low but keeping the orcs in her periphery. They paid her no mind and continued talking, in half-Orcish with common language words sprinkled through-out.

As she set the plates off the tray one by one, her ears pricked up at what was being spoken. Even in the gruff orc tongue, it was unmistakable when they spoke the words "witch" and "Taybe."

She slowed her movements, letting her eyes travel to the parchment that was scattered at the center of the table. Most were maps of the realm with markings on top of them.

The valley surrounding the northern district caught her eye, as did the gleam of fresh ink that marked it. She hadn't doubted Vidorak, but it confirmed his claims about Urim's intentions with the stronghold.

Even with the unexpected return of his nephew, he was very confident the deal would go through. So much so that he was moving forward with his plans for Taybe.

Little did he know, the witch who took the stronghold was right under his nose. While she was here for the amulet, these maps would also come with her. There was no way she would let a vicious orc impede her plans for revenge.

The parchment partially obstructed a word in the corner of the Taybe map. It looked to be written in the common language, and she could just make out the beginning of it. It was recognizable, but she just needed a better look.

She leaned forward a fraction too much, and her elbow hit one of the teacups, sending it rocking precariously. Some liquid sloshed out, but the cup settled without toppling.

She let out a sigh of relief and reached for a handkerchief to clean up the droplets.

The room became tense. The hairs on the back of her neck stood as the chieftain towered over her. She could have stopped him, but instead had to endure him backhanding her so roughly she fell.

"Be careful, you stupid wench!" Urim growled loudly enough that she could hear it over the ringing in her ear.

Humiliation ignited deep in her chest. There was nothing she wanted more than to reach for her magic and strike back. She could release her fire and leave a blistering mark on his cheek matching the one she now had.

Swallowing her immediate urges was not easy or natural for her. Calypso didn't like burying her hurt. She preferred to unleash it on those who wronged her.

But for once, she accepted the foolishness of doing such a thing. There was a bigger picture at play.

Keeping her head down, she crawled forward and apologized through gritted teeth. "Forgive me, Chieftain." It wasn't the best performance, but it was all she could bear to do.

"Clean up your mess and go." His boots disappeared from her sight. However, something remained that caught her eye. A long black strand of orc hair.

Calypso palmed it and stuffed it in her apron before standing up and quickly finishing her task. She left the chamber with no more disturbances and found the orcess guard shaking her head at her silently.

They returned to the kitchen, and Calypso couldn't focus on anything else besides the hair that was burning a hole in her pocket. The hours droned on as she eagerly awaited the evening.

Once the evening meal concluded, she rushed to the quarters and found them empty. She was hoping to find Vidorak and tell him of her intentions. He had informed her he was getting the amulet, and she attributed his absence to that. Though not having an easy way to reach him was frustrating.

She gathered the hair and a pair of candles that were illuminating the room. Then she searched through the quarters for crystals to borrow. Jewels were plentiful in the mountain, and she removed a few décor pieces from the walls. She would return them after her spell.

Based on prior attempts at dreamwalking, she knew rest was beneficial, but her body was buzzing impatiently. The last time she had entered someone's mind had been several years back when she was gathering evidence for her mother's trial. She had entered the mind of Joseph Collier, the royal treasurer, and learned of his insecurities, which proved helpful during his interrogation.

It was an entire year after that when Gemma had been able to procure a hairbrush of Davinger's and sent it to Calypso. That was when she attempted to dreamwalk Hugh Davinger's mind and ended up comatose for days. His mind was re-enforced by corrupted black magic, and it attacked her immediately. Only through Nyx and Astra's care had she survived.

It'd be a lie to say there wasn't a current of anxiety with attempting such a spell again. However, she didn't sense any black magic from Urim. Just bloodthirst and orc magic.

Calypso held out until she couldn't wait any longer and began her spell. There was no need for the spellbook. Calling upon a power of this magnitude was scorched into her mind. She put the crystals at the five points of the pentagram and then lit the candles in front of her.

In a smooth motion, she walked to the center of the formation and sat. A shiver of anticipation ran through her body. Once she spoke the words, there would be no backing out. Not only was there a risk of the other mind lashing out, but there was the risk that she could get stuck in the dreamland.

A scoff left her lips. If she were weak enough to get trapped in the mind of someone like Urim, then she deserved that fate.

Decision made, she recited, *"Goddess, I call upon you. Grant me the power to walk through the mind of another. Grant me guidance to traverse the paths of the dreamlands. Grant me protection to return to the body that is my own."*

"I give you the essence of one asleep." She kneeled in the center of the pentagram before a small wooden bowl and placed Urim's hair.

"I give you the blood of my veins." She sliced her hand with her nails, letting the blood drip into the bowl.

"I give you access to my mind."

The transition was instantaneous. One moment she was in the room, surrounded by candles. The next, she was enveloped by thick, dark mists that obscured her vision.

It was both disorienting and thrilling. Every time she entered the dreamlands was different. It was impossible to prepare for, so she could only react in the moment.

Silk fabric touched her skin, and she looked down to see that she was dressed in a white chemise. Barefoot, she ventured forward into the mist.

She walked on and on until a sweat of worry broke out at the back of her neck. Just before she could convince herself to turn around, crisp grass fell underfoot, and the mist cleared.

A narrow path was now visible, demarcated by snowy ridges on the sides. The feeling that she should remain on the grass and that stepping onto the snow would be fatal was strong. There was no moon present, but the snow radiated a dim light of its own.

The guided path led to a solitary wooden cabin. She was confident she would find Urim's mind in there. The door was unlocked, so she entered easily. The second the door shut behind her, the scene changed.

Gone was the dusty dark cabin, replaced by a boisterous tavern filled with music and dance. Orcs and humans drank and sang while servers passed around food and mead. Was this a memory or perhaps just a dream? There was an ease here that she had yet to see amongst the clan.

What there wasn't was any sign of Urim.

Perhaps all the best, since she had to test something first. She walked up to a server at the bar and waved in front of his face. No reaction.

"Can I have some mead, please?" she said, but the response was the same.

"Hey, I am speaking to you." This time she reached out and touched his shoulder. His eyes lit up as if seeing her for the first time.

This was good. She was invisible until she directly interacted with the scene.

"Of course, miss."

He quickly filled her mug, which she took but didn't drink. "Where can I find Chieftain Urim?"

The server frowned. "You mean Chieftain Ushnar? He's in the room at the back of the hallway."

Interesting. This must be an old memory from Urim's youth.

She left the drink and made her way toward the back. Even though it was only a few paces away, the lively energy of the other room quickly died down as she entered the hallway. There were no orcs walking around here, and the only light was radiating from below a closed door at the end of the corridor.

She paused in front of the door, listening for a moment. When no sound came, she carefully turned the doorknob and opened it just enough to slip in.

Engrossed in tense conversation stood Urim and his brother. Calypso's breath caught in her throat at how similar Vidorak looked to his father. Ushnar's red markings also ran across his cheeks. Even frowning in frustration, Ushnar radiated a warm and strong demeanor.

Urim, on the other hand, looked the same as he had earlier today in the war council chamber. A man stuck between the present and the past.

"We have to attack before they do!" Urim insisted, slamming his clawed hand on the table between them.

"Why? Everything is going smoothly."

"Barely. I see how the humans look at us. Orcs will never be equal to them."

Vidorak's father's look of exasperation was that of someone who's had the same argument many times. "They look with fear, but only until they get to know us. If we stay locked in the mountains, that will never happen."

"I should never have allowed you to do this."

Gone was the calm exterior as Ushnar's patience waned. "You are not someone to allow me to do anything. I am the chieftain of the clan, lest you forget."

At Ushnar's hard stare, Urim relented, his shoulders sagging slightly. "Forgive me, brother. I want only the best for our clan."

This was good enough for Ushnar, and the tension left his body.

"As do I. Each year, we are blessed with orclings and outside orcs that join our clan. Even more so after the plague in Rava. We can't sustain them all at Vestrahorn. We need to expand, and the Silver Forest is where we will do this."

Urim nodded.

"Come. Let's enjoy the festivities and then get some rest. I plan to wake early and ride back to my Mor."

With those words, Ushnar turned toward the door, facing Calypso. Behind him, she watched Urim's mask drop as he drew a dagger from his side.

A yell of warning was on the tip of her tongue, but she bit it down, knowing the scene before her would play out, regardless. It was just a dream of a memory. She couldn't get too involved and risk getting stuck.

All she could do was watch as Urim thrust the dagger into his brother's back.

"Sorry, brother, but I will not stay and watch you lead the clan to ruin. We need strength. And that strength will be me."

Red blood ran down Ushnar's back, pooling at his feet. His eyes never left Calypso's as he slid toward the ground. When his lips silently said the name of his mate, Calypso felt an ache deep in her chest that took her breath.

"Now it is time for you to see the chieftain."

She was so focused on the fallen orc, it took her a moment to realize that statement was directed toward her. Her eyes flickered up to see Urim staring back at her. Her eyebrows furrowed, not understanding what was happening. She hadn't talked or interacted with anyone in the room, so he shouldn't be sensing her right now.

Before she could do anything further, something wrenched her mind away, and everything went black. She gasped and coughed as if emerging from a lake she'd almost drowned in.

Vision slowly crept back as she blinked a few times. A blurry form of an orc stood above her, and for a second her heart picked up, thinking it was Vidorak. But as he came into view, dread settled in.

"I said, we are going to the chieftain." Mabanok roughly hauled her up. "Where he'll cut off your head and ship it to the capital."

Chapter Twenty-Three

VIDORAK

In a single day, Vidorak had committed half a dozen offenses that could get him executed, all to help that demanding witch.

He scowled even as his heart softened with thoughts of her. The frustration stemmed from how long this was taking. He thought locating the amulet would be simple, allowing him to return and share a final meal with his mate before sending her to Taybe.

The evening meal had come and gone, and his witch was probably asleep or awake and furious with him. She'd be even more furious if he returned without the amulet.

He had been overly confident that he would find it in his uncle's treasure room. That's where other prized relics were stored when not worn or in use.

Anyone entering the chamber without permission committed a punishable violation, even if related to the chieftain. His treason was ultimately for nothing as he left empty-handed.

Thinking his uncle's ego might've led him to store the amulet in his own bedchambers, Vidorak checked there next. The search there was also unsuccessful. The rest of the day was filled with speaking to orcs he trusted and gathering more information about the amulet without inciting suspicion.

That led him here. Deep in the heart of the mountain lay the forgotten orc forge. It had taken over an hour just to get here as most of the tunnels had broken down.

The mountain of Vestrahorn contained a vast amount of buried gems and metals. The clan crafted their weapons from the metals and used the gems for décor and jewelry. While coveted deeply by humans, for the orcs, their value had dimmed. Gemstones were not edible, and they couldn't make soil fertile or keep a body warm. No one would trade for them because of the war, so in essence they were worthless.

Once, the forge had been an area of pride, but over the years, the knowledge of working these materials waned as the young orcs joined the war efforts and raiding parties. Now, only the elders would visit the deepest part of the mountain.

Vidorak felt the heat of the fire before seeing it. He stepped off the last stair and entered the forge. A cart full of metal ingots waiting to be processed stood to the side. Scattered shards of gems decorated the ground.

There was the rhythmic clanking of metal against metal as the old blacksmith flattened a sword on his anvil. The elder orc didn't falter in his work as Vidorak came into his view.

"It's been a long time since I've seen you, Vidorak Ushnarsson."

It had been many years since he'd set foot in the forge. Once, this had been a place of refuge from his uncle's brutal training. A place he could mention his father safe from his mother's pain and uncle's anger. With time, coming here felt more like a weakness, and he stopped.

"Just Vidorak now, Kallsson," Vidorak responded, and the elderly orc grunted his disapproval, having always preferred the old ways of naming. "Still prefer to work through the night, I see."

"Old habits are hard to change. But you aren't here to discuss my work hours." Placing down the flattened metal, Kallsson looked up with his one good eye. "What can I help you with, just Vidorak?"

It was a shock to see him and notice the changes of age. While the muscles he'd earned from his trade were still strong, the once looming orc now appeared shorter, and his hair was completely white. His hands still bore the red Orcish markings, but his knuckles had swollen and fingers twisted with age.

"I'm searching for the dragon's eye amulet. I heard it was sent here to be fixed."

The old orc made a tsking sound. "You heard wrong. The amulet sent down by the chieftain was a reproduction I made a long time ago. The true one has been safely stored for the past seventeen years."

Since the raid on the sanctuary.

"Urim never wore the true amulet?" Vidorak asked, surprised at the admission.

Kallsson was an honest orc who valued tradition above all else. It was not like him to do these kinds of tricks.

"Such a powerful thing would've been dangerous in his hands." Kallsson's statement was blatantly treasonous.

"My uncle doesn't need the amulet to be dangerous." Then Vidorak asked, "Where is it?"

The older orc seemed undisturbed by the truth he had just shared. "A better question is not where it is but why you need it?"

Vidorak hesitated before answering, "I am searching for it for my mate."

Whether he was surprised, Kallsson didn't show it. "Strong motivation indeed." He too had been a mated orc, but his mate had died before Vidorak had been born.

The orc continued to talk casually as he wrapped leather around the knife handle. "Do you know the amulet's origin?"

Impatience sparked at Kallsson's avoidant questions, but Vidorak stamped it down. "Everyone on the mountain has heard of its legacy."

Worn by conquerors of Shalimar past, the dragon's eye amulet was rumored to magically aid whoever possessed it. Urim often reiterated that and wore the amulet as if it were an approval from the gods.

Kallsson grunted in displeasure. "I did not ask about the legacy, but about its origins. Luckily for you, I have time to educate the youth."

Vidorak bristled at being referred to as a youth, but took a seat on the stool next to him, knowing better than to rush the old orc.

"In the days of dragons, magic was different. It flowed throughout the entire realm and was often unpredictable and fickle. At that time, humans lived very harsh lives as they couldn't harvest magic the way other beings could. Because of this, their numbers lessened quickly. Until that fickle and unpredictable flow of magic decided to give the humans a fighting chance. A chance in the form of a sword."

"The sword of King Duran," Vidorak recalled, remembering the tales his mother told when he was an orcling.

Kallsson nodded. "King Duran's sword was laced with magic that allowed him to slay the dragons and steal their treasure. The problem is once such power and wealth were tasted, it was hard to stop. He killed dragons young and old, driving him deeper into his madness and bloodlust, until the proclaimed last dragon, Azara."

"I'm aware of orcling stories, Kallsson. The king slew the last dragon and then fully gave in to his madness, killing himself."

"You never did like to wait." Kallsson chuckled. "That ending isn't what happened. He didn't kill Azara. The king killed her remaining young, and in turn, she killed him. Having lost her young, the dragon wailed from the heartbreak. The earth flooded and shook with her sorrow until an old witch took pity on her. She offered the dragon a deal. To bring back her young in exchange for Azara's life. The last dragon accepted, and the spell was cast.

The witch placed the spirit into an unassuming amulet, to await the day when the dragon could be safely reborn."

Both versions were tales of warning about the destructive nature of possessing magic. His mother had often ended the tale with a warning against greed and trusting in your own strength. In an unexpected moment of nostalgia, he recalled a memory of his father overhearing the story one night near the evening fire. His father had jokingly commented on how fortunate he was to have a mate so concerned with the risk of greed that she took preventative measures of relinquishing him of his treasures.

There was something worrisome about the version Kallsson shared. It was a story left unfinished. It was clear his mate believed some power truly sat within the amulet, and she meant to use it. What would the price of that be?

Kallsson stepped away and reached into a chest of malformed and broken weapons. He rummaged for a moment before pulling out the object he was looking for. The sacrifice of a mother for a death that shouldn't have happened.

He held up his fist and let the ruby amulet dangle from the silver chain like a drop of blood. Without hesitation, he walked to Vidorak with a slight limp in his gait and dropped the amulet in his palm.

It sat small and light in his hand, nothing that seemed worth traversing all of Shalimar for. "It does not feel magical."

"That's because it requires a sacrifice of magic to unlock it. Whoever unlocks it would tap into powers that have been long gone in this world."

"Thank you, Kallsson. I appreciate it."

The orc patted him on the shoulder. "Tell your witch to be careful. The amulet demands a price for its use."

He didn't like the sound of that, or the story Kallsson had shared. The old orc had been right to hide the amulet, and Vidorak wondered if it wasn't better to keep it that way.

However, he had made a promise to his mate. She was the one who dealt in magic and could tell him more about her intentions with it.

Pocketing the amulet, he left the depths of the mountain and ascended. He hoped to kiss her at least one more time before she left. To feel her soft lips and breathe in her scent. That way, the taste of his mate would be the last thing he remembered before facing probable death.

The ache in his heart was a blessing. Some orcs went their whole lives without finding a mate. Not to have known the warmth and love of such a bond would've felt like a life not lived. While he yearned for more than just these few days, he knew even years would not be enough. He would always desire more, desire eternity.

"In another life perhaps," he muttered to himself.

He arrived at his quarters to see Nazghor approaching him. Vidorak was relieved he wouldn't need to go searching throughout for him. Finding the amulet took so much time that they would need to delay the journey until the following evening.

The look on Nazghor's face made him forget that and instead he asked, "What has happened?"

"He has her."

Ice-cold rage slashed through his veins. "Who?"

"Your uncle. They are at the fighting grounds." Nazghor hesitated before adding, "Vidorak, he means to execute her."

CHAPTER TWENTY-FOUR

VIDORAK

The arena echoed with incomprehensible shouting from the gathered crowd. It seemed the entire orc clan was currently here, and Vidorak had to force his way toward the chieftain's throne.

His uncle sat on the throne surrounded by his jarls, but Vidorak didn't spare them more than a glance. When he spotted Calypso's small body, he felt fury overtake him. The magic-nullifying shackles were back on her wrists, holding them above her head, chained against the stone wall. He vowed to destroy those shackles once he got her free.

She remained still, and only when he cleared the crowd did he notice her chest gently rising and falling. It was the only thing that stopped him from descending into a mindless rage.

He hated himself for failing to protect his mate. The mountain was dangerous, and he should never have brought her here.

He advanced toward her when somebody stepped in front to block his way. Without pause, he swung his heavy fist straight into Mabanok's face. The orc went down, and Vidorak continued toward his mate.

She was indeed unconscious, with a light red swelling on her cheek showing someone had hit her. He cupped her face, and she let out a small groan at his touch.

"My little witch. I am sorry I didn't protect you." He spoke softly as he caressed her face. "Open your eyes. Please."

The seconds it took before he heard her voice were torture.

"Vidorak," she muttered, and her eyes fluttered open. "Why do I always end up bound around you?"

In the distance, voices called him, but his focus was completely on her.

Leaning in, he stared desperately into her eyes. "Listen to me. Do you see the tunnel at the far corner behind the throne? That will take you out of the mountains. There should be horses there as well."

"Why are you telling me this?"

The guards were approaching him. He had seconds left.

He slipped the amulet into her dress pocket. "I will find a way to free you. Then you must escape. Tell me you understand, Calypso."

She nodded.

He made to turn from her, but she called out, "Wait! Vidorak, it was your uncle. He killed your father."

Truthfully, that statement didn't come as a surprise to Vidorak. With all of Urim's brutality and thirst for power, it made perfect sense. Vidorak had always wondered how Captain Von Ahlen could best a strong warrior like his father. He would naturally be less cautious with his own brother, and Urim took advantage of that.

Calypso seemed to take his hesitance as disbelief and added hurriedly, "I dreamwalked in his mind last night and saw."

Someone dragged him away before they could speak more. Her words were still ringing in his head as he was forced in front of the chieftain. Hearing the truth in her voice, which confirmed suspicions he'd carried for years, made reality sink in.

It was all so disgustingly pathetic. The countless years of war, the suffering of their people, the degradation of their culture—all done so Urim could grab power. In an alternate reality, his father would be leading the clan toward prosperity within the realm, and Vidorak would be bringing his mate home with the respect she deserved, not under the guise of a slave.

Vidorak had closed off all emotions for years, and now, seeing his uncle sitting on the throne and his mate shackled at his side, he felt the wall break. His body shook with a chuckle at the horror that he'd spent most of his life unknowingly in servitude to his father's killer.

Suddenly, his head snapped back, but he barely registered the pain, even as Mabanok pummeled him again.

"Stop, Mabanok," Urim commanded, and the orc stepped back, roughly pulling Vidorak onto his knees. "I want to hear why my own nephew destroyed the clan's chance for peace."

Vidorak spat out the blood that welled in his mouth. "A peace you wouldn't have honored. All you have done is led our clan to ruin."

Urim stood up and stalked toward him. He crouched so that his face was inches from Vidorak's and snarled, "Be careful what you say, nephew. Your relation to me will only protect you so far."

Vidorak went to his feet and, without hesitation, bellowed his challenge before the clan. "I, Vidorak Ushnarsson challenge you for the throne." Then he lowered his voice. "Something I should've done years ago."

All chatter and commotion completely died. There was a hushed shock that spread through the arena.

"No!"

He recognized his mother's scream that broke the silence but didn't turn to look at her. When no further protest came, he knew either Nazghor or Grushag had taken her away. His mother played a part in delaying his challenge for the clan. She had broken after losing her mate, and he feared what would become of her if he died as well.

The sound of metal unsheathed rang through the air as Kinar took out his short sword and approached. Urim put out a hand, stopping the jarl. "Does anyone second him?"

A challenge to lead the clan must be backed by one of the jarls or it wouldn't be valid. If no one backed him, there would be no fight, but an execution instead.

"I do." All eyes went to the older, well-respected orc. Throughout the years, Jarl Bruk had attempted to steer Urim away from his more savage decisions. He did it wisely, never overstepping enough to be ousted.

Jarl Bruk was putting his life on the line with this statement. Vidorak's loss would mean his death as well.

Even Urim turned, the fury in his stare making it clear he hadn't expected that. But the statement had been clear, and there was no refuting it.

"You heard my nephew. He has challenged me in the way of orcs, seconded by Jarl Bruk. I will respect his challenge as custom dictates. Bring the shaman!"

Mabanok and the other orc guards drew back, giving them space. Urim undid the fur cloak that rested around his shoulders, threw it to the side, and stepped forward bare-chested.

Wearing the ritualistic bone mask, Rhunga entered the arena. His hair was piled on top of his head, held up by two needle-like daggers. For once, there wasn't a glint of humor in the young shaman's eyes.

Dipping his fingers into a pot of red dye, Rhunga painted both of their chests and faces. "The blessings of the gods are among us. May they favor the strongest and wisest to lead the clan."

As was the custom, they brought out a choice of weapons. Vidorak declined the choices, opting to use his father's dagger, the one kept on him at all times. His uncle took hold of his axe.

They moved to the flattened ground where just the other day he'd fought with Nazghor. Above them, black crows circled as if expecting the death that was to come. The tension felt thick in the cool air, and small droplets of rain hit Vidorak's chest.

No one had dared to challenge Urim for over a decade. Even at his advanced age, he was incredibly strong and utterly vicious.

A benefit of his uncle's merciless training was that he'd raised Vidorak to be as fierce as him.

"I had high hopes for you, Vidorak," Urim broke the silence in the arena as he circled Vidorak carefully. "I saw you as a son."

In a way, Vidorak believed him, and was glad that Urim never had children of his own. There were years he spent training until he lost consciousness, years he was forced to kill, to be brutal at too young an age.

"Raise your weapon and start the challenge," Vidorak roared, eager to get his uncle's blood on his hands.

Urim gripped the axe tightly, his body tensing. "Your father would be so disappointed."

Without further warning, Urim lunged, axe slashing swiftly at him. Vidorak dove away, but not before the tip of the axe grazed his arm. If he had been a second slower, the axe would have separated his shoulder from his body.

Urim's comment was meant to distract him and make him sloppy. It angered Vidorak that it had worked. He allowed himself to stagger more than he needed to, letting Urim think he was thrown off.

When Urim's following attack came, Vidorak was ready and blocked him at the forearm. It gave him an opening, and he took it, coming at Urim with everything he had. All the rage and anger that had boiled inside him for years spilled out.

He swiped a leg, and Urim's colossal frame tumbled back. Vidorak was on him, slamming his fist into his uncle's face. In this position, his axe did nothing to help him, and Urim was at his mercy.

"Do not mention my father!" Vidorak snarled between blows. "You didn't have the courage to challenge him."

Urim remained unfazed at the revelation that Vidorak had discovered the truth. The rain had become a downpour, and rivulets of blood flowed from Urim's wounds.

"Why?!" Vidorak demanded, slamming his uncle's head against the ground. "Why did you kill him? Was it all for greed?"

His uncle lashed out and grabbed Vidorak's neck, pulling him down until they were inches apart. "Because he was weak."

The words were audible only to him and dripped with malice despite Urim's swollen face. Shaking with rage, Vidorak recoiled and gripped his dagger tighter, poised to kill his uncle.

A sharp inhale of pain stole Vidorak's attention in a sudden and primal way. His eyes flew up to see Mabanok with a knife pressed against his mate. While Mabanok wouldn't interfere directly with the challenge, his threat was apparent.

The distraction was enough for Urim to take advantage and hurl Vidorak off. He crashed onto his back, the wind knocked out of him, and his dagger tumbled away, having slipped from his grasp.

Something deep and evil within Vidorak unleashed. Nothing else mattered but getting his mate to safety.

He sprang up just as his uncle attacked him with a swing of his axe. He couldn't maneuver away quickly, and a deep slice cut into his chest. Without pause, his uncle aimed for another strike, but Vidorak grabbed onto his uncle's wrist, stopping the descent of the axe. The deadly blow was blocked, but it came at the price of Vidorak leaving himself open, and Urim took advantage. His uncle struck his face, battering him relentlessly. Vidorak's vision dotted, but he continued to hold, not letting the axe get any closer.

With his sight obscured by blood, Vidorak slammed his head forward, hearing a satisfying crunch as he shattered his uncle's nose. The blow was hard enough to temporarily lose hearing, but the pressure of the oncoming axe lessened.

"This is for threatening my mate." Vidorak slammed his fist into Urim's jaw.

"This is for breaking my mother's heart." He kicked Urim's chest, sending him flying backward onto the ground.

Vidorak stalked forward, bending down to pick up the fallen dagger. Urim made to sit up, but Vidorak was there in one smooth motion and slammed the dagger down to the hilt into his uncle's heart.

"That is for the clan," he nearly whispered. For the sorrow, the suffering, and the hardships he had brought them, his uncle deserved this death.

Chapter Twenty-Five

CALYPSO

Her head throbbed mercilessly as the rain plastered her crimson hair to her scalp. She had been naïve to hope she wouldn't see the orcs who had captured her a week ago again. In fact, the one whose name she hadn't bothered to remember had taken particular joy in rendering her unconscious and shackling her once more.

The second she was free, she would bury those shackles in the deepest grave possible. As appealing as it was to possess a magical artifact like that, she would be happy never to lay eyes on them again.

There was only the question of getting free.

Vidorak had told her how to escape the arena, but getting down from the elevated way she was chained would be difficult. Her shoulders throbbed from the extreme angle, and she had to point her toes to keep touching the ground. There were few options without anyone's help.

The jeering of the crowd brought her attention back to the fighting arena, and the sight of Vidorak's bloodied chest stopped her breath. Even though his uncle was also battered, Urim moved with an eager calm that made her feel sick.

Vidorak was going to die.

Like trapped prey, frantic desperation overtook her, and she did the only thing she could think to do. She stopped trying to hold up her weight, and let her body hang, applying a jolting pressure at her wrists.

She bit the inside of her cheek to keep from screaming as the sharp pain dug deep into her joints. Her suffering wasn't without effort, and her right wrist began to slip through the metal cuff, shearing skin along with it.

Tears flooded her eyes, and her mind lost all thought beyond the brutal pain she was inflicting on herself. With a final tug, her right wrist slipped free of the shackles. The comforting tingling of magic weakly reawakened. She continued to hold her wrist high above her head as she caught her breath.

Her mind was so numb from pain she didn't notice the fluttering near her ear until the crow tugged on her hair.

Despite being released, the undead, red-eyed crow had returned. Calypso could've cried from relief.

She cleared her throat and whispered, "Get me the key."

The crow flew toward the orc standing several feet away, completely focused on the fight. With light movements, the bird grasped the key with its claws and tugged.

The orc jostled his body, and terror spiked through Calypso. She imagined him turning and killing the bird in one motion.

Thankfully, he continued to watch. With quiet precision, the undead crow seized the key and returned to Calypso once more.

She clutched it, but before she could use it, the leering orc turned away from the fight. Unhappiness was evident on his face as he stalked back toward her. He was confident in the shackles and didn't bother to even glance at her wrists.

Without speaking a word, he took out a knife and dug its sharp tip into her side. Calypso couldn't help the soft cry that left her.

"Cry out again, witch. I want Vidorak to hear how he failed you before he dies." The orc switched his attention back to the fight, eager to see the result of his threat.

Calypso had had enough.

"I'd much rather hear you cry." She closed her free hand over his wrist, forcing every ounce of fire within her to sear his skin.

Being half-shackled was limiting, but she held nothing back. The orc dropped the knife, hissing at the sudden burn that blistered up his green skin.

The orc rushed to grab his knife as she unlocked her other wrist and dropped to the ground, freed from her restraints.

Now would've been the perfect time to run. To blind the orc with her fire and run toward the tunnels that Vidorak told her about. She was free. She had her amulet.

Instead, like the fool she was, she started siphoning her magic toward her undamaged hand, intending to hurl a ball of fire at the chieftain. Interfering with the challenge was likely against the rules, but screw it. If they could play dirty, so could she.

Her plans were cut short when the orc recovered and slammed her back toward the stone wall, hand around her neck. The way he did it was significantly less appealing than the way Vidorak did it.

Pressure increased at her neck, and her air was cut off. Her fingers clawed and burned at his wrists, but the orc was decidedly pushing through the pain with his anger.

"Let her go, Mabanok." The low, raspy command sounded so quietly that she almost missed it.

The pressure released after a second, and air rushed into her lungs. From the corner of her eye, she noticed a tall, brawny orc who had half of his face covered in burn marks. He was bald on the left side of his head, where the scars extended into his scalp, and his ears were covered with heavy rings. His red orc marks ran from neck to his collarbones, untouched by his extensive burn scars. He had to be the most frightening orc she'd seen thus far, and she'd seen plenty.

"Leave, Grushag, or you'll be next," the apparent Mabanok growled.

Despite Mabanok's threat, his grip around her neck disappeared. She pushed away, not bothering to figure out what was going on between the two orcs.

Her heart stopped when she saw Vidorak hold back the sharp axe that was descending slowly as he absorbed hit after hit.

Between the rainstorm and the shackles, her magic wasn't recovering fast enough, and she moved forward, ready to run into the arena. She would not let Urim kill Vidorak. Not when they still had so much between them left unsaid.

Before she could take a second step, the scarred orc, who had just helped her seconds ago, yanked her back. His hold was firm and not painful, but that wouldn't save him from her ire.

She snapped his way, ready to lash out at him when Vidorak's voice cracked through the arena.

"This is for threatening my mate."

For a moment, Calypso's mind went blank.

Then a wave of cold rage hit her. That fucking bastard. How dare he do all those things to her, make her want all those things, all the while having a mate!

He had kissed and caressed her like something to be cherished, and asked all those probing, and at times flirtatious, questions that healed her heart. Except not only did he have a mate, but one that he would kill for!

The painful throb in her heart was too much to bear, and she poured the acid of her anger over it. She would help him kill Urim and then fight Vidorak herself!

Before she could implement any of her plans, everything suddenly came to an end.

Vidorak crouched over his uncle, family dagger buried deep in Urim's chest. Urim lay unmoving, even the red blood that bubbled from his chest came to a stop. The whole arena was frozen in time as the death of the chieftain sank in.

Vidorak slowly stood, his dark eyes immediately going to hers before facing the others.

His voice was raw but steady as he spoke. "I stand before you as the new chieftain. Things are going to change. My uncle failed the clan, and his way of doing things has only brought more hardships. Some of you may not agree." Calypso noticed he looked in the eyes of several of the stiffer warriors. "You can challenge me, as is our way. But make no mistake. You will lose."

With those words spoken, he turned and stalked toward Calypso. The intensity of his gaze caused her heart to beat with anticipation and fear. Little sparks of fire remained at her palms as he closed the distance between them.

He grasped her firmly by the shoulders and tugged her to his chest. Then he leaned down until their foreheads touched, and she thought he would kiss her.

He didn't. Instead, he put one of his hands on her cheek, simply keeping her close.

The fire at her palms extinguished into nothing. She blinked away raindrops, not daring to take her eyes off him.

She didn't know how long they'd stood like that, but it felt too soon when he withdrew. Without letting her go, he led her toward the throne that rose above the arena.

He sat down, and Calypso took a moment to look at him, eyes skimming over his harsh face, sharp tusks, and pointed ears. Gone was the restraining braid, and instead, his long black hair was loose and wild around him. He sat with calm strength, even with the deep wounds on his bare chest still bleeding. He looked every bit the orc chieftain that he now was.

"Come sit," he commanded her.

Her eyes went down to his muscular thigh. She raised an eyebrow. "Shouldn't that be for your mate?"

He dared to give her an annoyed look. "Are you serious, Calypso?"

Oh, she was very serious. New chieftain or not, he would answer for his behavior.

She opened her mouth to argue when a slow realization set in. Her voice shook when she said, "I am not an orcess."

"I know."

She swallowed hard, not quite believing what he was insinuating. Of everything that had passed in these last days, this filled her with more fear than anything.

"I can't be your mate."

A quick flash of irritation went across his face. "Says who?"

"Says me! We have not even known each other for a lunar cycle."

"The bond can happen instantaneously." Patience had run its course, and he leaned forward. "Come sit. Or do you prefer I pick you up and place you on my lap myself?"

Still brimming with questions she didn't know how to put into words, Calypso stepped forward and sat on his thigh. As confused as she might feel, leaning into him felt right, and sometimes all one could do was what felt right in the moment and sort through the rest later.

Violence still radiated from him, yet all she wanted was to rub against his broad chest. The exhilaration of the fight and their near death intertwined with a sudden longing for him. Was it the mate bond that made her want to kneel before him at the throne and take his cock in her mouth, onlookers be damned.

Her mind was brimming with mixed emotions when the shaman approached Vidorak's throne. He gave a brief bow before placing a bloody bone necklace over Vidorak's head.

"The gods have chosen a new chieftain," the shaman said loudly before the others. "I know you will lead us well, Vidorak Ushnarsson."

Chapter Twenty-Six

CALYPSO

The stunned silence across the clan broke, and everyone lined up to pledge their allegiance to the new chieftain.

The first to step forward were the broad-shouldered forms of Urim's prior jarls, led by Bruk. Pride shone in the old orc's eyes as he pledged his loyalty.

"I saw our clan suffer for many years and am ashamed that I did not stop it. You have protected the clan, and your father would be proud." He inclined his head. "For my failures, I relinquish my post as jarl."

"I do not accept that," Vidorak answered. "I wish you to remain as jarl. The past holds many regrets, but the clan's welfare comes first."

Jarl Bruk nodded his acceptance and moved on. The rest followed suit until Kinar stepped forward, tension rising between them. The jarl's eyes burned, but he held his tongue as he lowered his head in acquiescence.

"I should kill you where you stand," Vidorak stated before Kinar could leave. "However, too much orc blood has been spilled already. Don't mistake my mercy for weakness. I strongly suggest you are gone by the morning."

Kinar responded with a huff before fleeing the arena. It would be cleaner to kill him now. A man like Kinar didn't just fade into the distance. He would be a problem in the future.

After the jarls recognized him, Mor stepped forward accompanied by a male orc that Calypso had seen around Vidorak. Mor's eyes were red and puffy from tears, but her face remained calm. The male orc looked worse for wear, with his nose still bleeding and a nice bruise blossoming at his ribs. It seems Vidorak's mother didn't appreciate being dragged away during the fight.

"My son. Our new chieftain." She kneeled before him as the jarls had done.

"You do not need to kneel before me, Mother," Vidorak said softly.

She stood and walked up the steps to the throne. She took his free hand, squeezing it once, before leaning down to say something in his ear. Calypso couldn't make it out as it was in Orcish.

Before Mor stepped away, she turned toward Calypso and surprised her by also touching her hand as well. "My son's mate. It is a blessing that he found you. This marks a favorable future for the clan."

If Rhunga felt annoyed that his role as prophesier was overshadowed, he didn't show it. Instead, the young shaman nodded respectfully at Mor as she passed him.

The rest of the clan stepped forward to kneel before the new chieftain. Eyes skittered in Calypso's direction as the orcs approached, their expressions ranging from curiosity to excitement. The stares felt odd, but even if Calypso wanted to leave his lap, Vidorak's iron grip held her in place.

Even though Vidorak sat calmly as the clan stepped forward, she suspected he was concealing inner turmoil. While she held no grief for Urim, she wondered if Vidorak felt the same. Despite all his evil, Urim had still been his uncle.

With the pledging of loyalty concluded, Vidorak stood and pulled her away unceremoniously.

"There are a few things to discuss, Chieftain." The shaman stopped them.

"Later, Rhunga."

"Of course." The shaman's eyes glittered with amusement as he glanced at Calypso. "It has been a long day. I will send a medicinal salve to the chieftain's quarters, along with water for a bath."

Vidorak paused, and she hoped he was thinking the same thing as she was. Being in the space that Urim had occupied for decades didn't seem appealing at the moment. "Bring them to the chamber on the north summit. Also, clear the chieftain's quarters of all possessions."

Rhunga nodded and left to follow through on the instructions.

Avoiding further interruptions, Vidorak tugged Calypso through an entryway across the grounds, and they ascended a curving staircase. He was rushing her along, but she dug her heels in, forcing him to stop and face her.

"How long have you known?" She didn't need to specify for him to realize what she was referring to.

"I sensed something from the beginning, but the bond did not form until the first time we kissed."

"The kiss was a test to see if we were mates?"

His hand reached up to cup her cheek. "I simply wanted to kiss you. Having a mate wasn't something I thought would be possible for me."

Her chest tightened at those words. How many times had she said a similar thing to herself? Love and happiness felt unattainable for her. For so long, pain and revenge had completely consumed her thoughts.

"That doesn't excuse not telling me."

Regret briefly crossed his face, and he glanced downward. "Our start was not a very trusting one, little witch, most of which was my doing. I barely understood what was happening to me, let alone understood how to tell you."

"We are still far from understanding one another," she stated grimly.

"I know. The bond may have happened without our input, but we will continue how we see fit." When she said nothing, he added, "Or not at all, if you so choose."

There was sadness in those words but no anger or ill-will.

"You would let me go if I refused . . ." it was hard to say the words, "whatever this is?"

"I won't deny the thought of letting you go is difficult." His hands when to her shoulders, gently tugging her toward him as if his body didn't want to entertain that idea even verbally. "But I do not want you to feel like a hostage. The bond is not complete until we are physically joined. After that, I do not think I'd be able to."

That made her snort in amusement. "Did you not learn by now that no one can keep me hostage? Bond or not, I will always do what I want."

His mouth twitched. "Did you forget I practically handed the keys to your crow that night?"

"That was not my only plan! Next, I would've laced your drink with a powerful laxative, so consider yourself lucky."

They smiled at each other for a moment before she spoke again. "A lot has happened recently. I need time to think about this."

"Take all the time you need." His thumb rubbed over her hand before heading back up the stairs.

A short walk further, and they approached a door off the winding staircase. He opened it to reveal a modest but pleasant room. It looked comfortable and had natural light pouring in from a window.

"Is this where we will stay?" The bed seemed small, but she supposed it would do.

"It is your room. Mine is further up." He showed the direction to go. "Someone will bring you a meal soon. Now I need to wash off the fight, but tonight we will speak regarding the return to Taybe."

With a parting nod of his head, he closed the door behind him. Calypso was alone in a room all for herself. This arrangement made the most sense if she was seeking space. Yet, she'd assumed they'd be in the same quarters as if it was the most natural thing in the world.

Sitting on the edge of the bed, she examined her injuries. Now that the intensity of the fight had dissipated, pain was setting in. The worst of it was her wrist, with the skin sheared away, but even that had stopped bleeding. Fortunately, the stab wound Mabanok gave her appeared superficial. The orc had been more concerned with disturbing the fight than actually delivering an efficient wound.

Rest felt impossible. She took out the dragon's eye amulet from her pocket. The ruby hung like a drop of blood and was cool to the touch. Even in its dormant state, she could sense the magic within the small ruby necklace.

The voice in her mind stayed silent, but she felt a hum of satisfaction that she knew wasn't her own. *It* was happy to be in possession of the amulet. She should be happy to have received what she came for, should be eager to leave this dark mountain and return to her sisters.

Yet all she could think about was that leaving here meant leaving Vidorak. Leaving someone who not only challenged her but also cared for her so gently that her hardened heart was softening.

Restless energy taking over, she stood and paced in front of the bed.

Her need to avenge her mother hadn't changed, but for the first time since her death, Calypso wondered if it was possible to lead another life. Such a thought, even uttered in her mind, felt like a betrayal of her mother and her sisters.

But now that she had thought it, it was impossible to silence. She imagined herself by Vidorak's side seriously, helping him with the orc clan while he, in turn, helped her with the new coven in Taybe. For a moment she ached for that reality, so much it hurt her deep in her chest.

Her hand touched the doorknob, but she paused. Reality was never so easy or pretty. She hadn't lied to Vidorak when she'd stated she'd do what she wanted. For better or worse, she was an emotional and chaotic being. Over time, would she end up hurting him with her relentless nature?

Logically, completing the mate bond was not a wise choice. It was safe to stay in the comfort of their roles, she the mad witch out for revenge, and he the war-torn orc set to lead his clan.

She repeated this to herself even as she left her room and hurried up the stairs. Just as he'd said, there was a room further up, and she burst in without knocking.

Vidorak had finished bathing, and his long hair was damp, but neatly combed and loose at his back. He paused, rubbing healing salve over the wounds on his chest, and looked up at her.

"How can I be certain this isn't a lie?" Subconsciously, she rubbed over her heart as if expecting to sense something there. "I do not feel anything binding me to you."

He put away the salve but stayed on the far side of the room.

"I imagine the bond feels different to non-orcs. To me, it feels like a string connecting us, like my body is attuned to yours. Like nothing else matters except for you and your safety."

There was a twinge of jealousy at his certainty. She wanted the confidence he had, wanted to fall into the attraction between them, but the risk still felt too great.

"I am too much." The words slipped out before she even realized what she was saying. "You will regret it."

"Not possible."

She shook her head, seeing how foolish her spontaneous decision to come here was. It would make leaving him all the more painful. "I cannot be what you want me to be! My revenge against the Crown will not be cast aside, and I will see it through."

"You do not know what I want," he answered, voice laced with tension.

"No, perhaps not. But it certainly wouldn't be a witch plagued by madness and the need for vengeance," she yelled, angry at the world and herself. "You need someone steady by your side, not someone unpredictable."

Someone unlovable.

"Do not presume to know what I am thinking." This time, his composure vanished, and she noticed his hands clench in frustration. "I need my fierce mate beside me."

Another crack in her heart healed at his words, no matter how much she tried to fight him. How did he take these ugly, angry parts of her and make them beautiful? It was easier to drown in her pain than to let herself be loved.

Despite her words, Calypso couldn't bear the distance between them any longer and threw herself at him. Desperately, she clutched his shoulders, pressing into the hard planes of his chest.

Control snapped, he buried his hand in her hair and boldly kissed her, his tongue probing his mouth as if she were all his to explore as he wished. His other hand was at her back, not allowing her to step away now that she had closed the distance. Her breath caught at the feel of his hardness, and she couldn't help but rub up against his length.

He groaned before speaking through gritted teeth. "Not consummating the mating bond is affecting my control, especially after the fight." He inhaled deeply at her neck but then pulled himself back. "If you don't want me, then you need to leave now."

Lust dilated his pupils, and he gripped her hips despite what he'd said about letting her leave. Seeing him on the edge of control spurred her own desire, clenching deep in her lower belly. The need to touch his body drowned all hesitations and questions. She had ached for him, and here he was, wanting her just as fiercely.

She pushed his chest slightly, and his hands fell immediately. He was telling the truth that he would let her go if she chose that.

But she didn't want to let him go.

Calypso dropped to her knees before him, her hands sliding up his trousers, nimbly untying the material. His enormous cock sprang free, and she almost moaned at the sight of it. Since that day in the forest, the memory of his gorgeous cock plagued her thoughts. She ran her fingernails over the prominent veins leading up to his bulbous head. There was a drop of pre-cum at the tip, and she leaned forward to lick it, eager for the taste of him.

He sharply inhaled at the contact. Having had a taste, she became hungry for more, longing to fully break his control. She licked his entire length then took him into her mouth as far as she could. With the size of his head, she could barely get much in before gagging.

There was so much of him, she could wrap both of her hands around his length and glide up and down as she sucked at his head. Seeing him up close just made her ache with need and anticipation. He would stretch her so much she wondered if he would fit all the way.

"You are so perfect, my witch." His breathing was ragged, and his hips inadvertently thrust forward.

She melted under the devoted way he looked at her. He loomed so large and powerful, his muscular strength rippling with barely contained restraint, and all of it was focused solely on her.

Her lips popped off his head, and she continued to stroke him as she teasingly said, "That's not my name, dear mate."

Then she took him into her mouth again, bringing him as deep as she could until her eyes filled with tears.

"Fuck, Calypso," he groaned, hand tightening in her hair and his claws lightly scratching at her scalp.

She loved it when he said her name in that deep and rumbling way. She steadied her rhythm as her orc became undone.

"Move if you don't want my seed," he growled, and she felt his balls tighten with his impending release.

She stayed where she was, mouth wrapped around his thick cock as he groaned, and warm liquid hit the back of her throat. She swallowed what she could but had to move back when it became too much.

The rest of his seed fell onto the front of her dress. It seemed wrong that it wasn't on her bare skin instead. In the forest he'd marked her with his scent out of necessity, but now the idea of the clan knowing she was his thrilled her.

He pulled her up and slammed his mouth onto hers. She wrapped her arms around his neck and her legs around his waist when he picked her up. He walked while easily carrying her, but she paid no mind to it as he devoured her mouth.

Her legs tightened with the overwhelming urge to feel him closer. Her core was desperate to be touched and filled. She kissed his jaw, his tusks, his neck, and then bit his shoulder. "I need you now."

"My impatient mate." One of his hands then moved under her dress and slid up her bare skin until he reached her throbbing clit. She moaned into his chest and moved her hips, wanting more of that pressure.

She felt a nudge near her bottom and realized he was hard again. That made her want to push him down and just take over herself.

He placed her down on a pile of furs, but that is all she registered with the raw need coursing through her veins. This orc had taken over all her senses and all her mind, and at the moment all she wanted was to be claimed.

A second later he lowered himself on top of her, but he came at her infuriatingly slow, his touches too soft and his kisses too gentle. She felt so close to the edge, but every time she tried to increase the pressure, he slowed it down. He regained some control after his release, but lust was propelling her into madness.

She groaned in frustration as his kisses made lazy movements down her neck, leisurely lowering her dress. That damned orc smiled in amusement at her desperation.

"Tell me what you need, sweet mate."

Sweet mate. The way he said those words made her pussy clench, and she couldn't imagine her need becoming greater. Her dress was now pulled down to her waist, and his hand was over her breast, slowly rolling over the nipple.

"I need to come." Goddess, help her if he continued his teasing touches and slow kisses.

Her orc seemed to have taken pity on her torture because one minute she was on her back and the next he'd flipped her over onto her knees, her hips pulled up. She put her hands out to steady herself and felt the fabric of her undergarments rip, exposing her aching core.

He pushed in a finger and then another, finally giving her something to satiate her need to be filled. She arched her hips back and moved with him, fucking herself on his fingers.

"You're so wet and so tight. I don't want to hurt you," he said as his thumb rubbed over her clit with steady pressure.

"I can take it," she moaned, basing that confidence on nothing but mindless desire. The pleasure that had already built didn't take long to peak, and she tightened over his hand, flooding it with her release.

He held her hips up as her body became languid and she fell onto her elbows. As she worked to steady her breathing, she felt him run his length over the folds of her pussy, coating himself in her wetness. Despite having just come, she tilted her hips back, ready to accept more.

She felt him nudge at her opening, and she moaned as he pushed in. Even dripping from her release, he still stretched her more than she'd ever been. He moved in and out slowly, letting her adjust to his large size, and her desire built again.

His rough hands caressed her body, setting her aflame until she was moving her hips back herself onto his length. She felt so full, so stretched, so completely encompassed by him.

"Vidorak, please," she moaned, unable to fully form words of what she needed from him.

With that desperate plea, he slammed his hips, seating fully inside her. She screamed out, her hands fisting in the furs. She didn't know if it was the bond or simply Vidorak, but she felt as though he had imprinted on her soul.

"Faster," she breathlessly commanded. She didn't want to walk without feeling him between her, torturing her long after their mating was done.

Holding her securely by the hips, he thrust hard into her, his large sac swinging forward. There was no strength left in her, and she completely yielded to him, letting the waves of pleasure wash over.

His thrusts became more erratic, and his breaths ragged. Then his hand moved around to rub her clit, and she became completely incoherent.

"I want to hear you come again, Calypso," he demanded in her ear.

With that, she became utterly undone, her orgasm dismantling her perfectly. Behind her, she felt him thrust hard one last time before hot liquid spilled inside her, and he followed her over the edge.

He gently helped her onto her back, and she closed her eyes as her breath slowed to a normal pace. Exhaustion set in as her orc cleaned her off before laying down beside her. She rested her head on her mate's chest, quickly falling asleep. While she may not understand the bond, she could not deny they were linked eternally.

Chapter Twenty-Seven

VIDORAK

She was still asleep when Vidorak returned to the bedchamber. He set down a tray of tea and food on the table and got back into the fur-covered bed. The way she curled around him in sleep satisfied something within him.

Having consummated their mate bond, he thought the savage possessiveness would simmer down. Instead, it had intensified, and he craved to know everything about her. He wanted her mind, her passions, her sweet smiles and her wicked ones. Thinking back to what she'd told him about her hallucinations, he realized he even wanted the dark parts of her, if only to help her fight them.

A selfish part of him desired to hide her away for only himself, but he knew that wasn't who he had mated. They were not just Calypso and just Vidorak, able to steal away and fully explore the nuances of what was happening between them in peace. No, he was Vidorak, chieftain of the mountain orcs, and she was Calypso, the mad witch.

His fingers moved over her arm, tracing the dark tattoos of her black magic. Having seen her unclothed a few times, he realized the markings were changing. The black band with dots that was once on her upper arm now spiraled up toward her collarbone.

What began as light, curious touches roused more lustful thoughts, and his cock stiffened. Especially since Calypso stirred awake and conducted her own lazy exploration.

"We have more to discuss." She pressed kisses along the side of his chest.

"If you continue doing that, we won't be talking," he grunted. "You should eat."

She made an unhappy noise but peered at the tray where bread, cheese, meat, and tea were waiting for her.

"The tea is to control fertility," he explained. "We never discussed pregnancy."

She looked at him curiously. "Vidorak, I am a witch. I began controlling my fertility long ago." Then she reached for a piece of cheese and asked, "Are children something you desire?"

Having a mate and children was not an idea he'd entertained while Urim was chieftain. A family meant having someone who could be taken at any moment, leaving their loved ones husks of their former selves.

He watched her eat and pictured her round and heavy with his orcling. It stirred a longing in his chest so great that it scared him.

"I enjoy picturing you as a mother." He spoke the thought out loud before being able to stop it. "For years, my focus was on ending my uncle's tyranny. Having a mate and orclings wasn't a consideration."

She stared at him with silent understanding before speaking. "I am not known for being maternal. I think you just like the idea of breeding me."

Then, she took a piece of meat from her plate and brought it to his lips. He ate the bite, capturing her wrist before she could pull away, and kissed her palm.

"Perhaps you are correct."

A heated look passed between them before she sobered up and returned to eating. "Do you want to discuss what I saw in the dreamlands?"

Truthfully, he did not.

He wanted to bask in the naked beauty of his mate, not bring up tragedies of the past. But this would continue to sit between him and there was no avoiding it.

"Tell me."

She recounted everything she saw in the dreamlands in a calm and observant way, repeating the conversation between his uncle and father word for word.

"Dreams are not pure memories. That might not be exactly how things occurred, although I think it's likely close."

Vidorak would agree with that assessment. It was painful to discuss, but everything fell into place. It had always puzzled him how Von Ahlen could've bested his father.

But it was never about being bested. It was about betrayal. Brother killing brother just for more power.

"He killed my father to lead the clan," Vidorak summed up. "And with all that power, he brought nothing good."

She put the plate of food aside and then crawled into his lap. She kissed the corner of his lips and then pushed his chest until his back hit the furs. "It is not his clan anymore. It is yours."

That reality felt unbelievable. His uncle loomed so large in his mind that beating him had felt improbable. He hadn't truly considered what he would do if he won. How was he going to untangle the mess Urim had created?

Rather than dwell on those questions, he chose to concentrate on the mate in his arms. He pulled her down for another kiss, nipping at her to open her mouth. She obliged for a minute, melting into him, before pushing away.

"No more kissing until you tell me if there is anything else to know about the mate bond."

He thought about it. "Over time, some mates can sense each other's emotions even across great distances."

"I don't need the bond to tell me what you are feeling." To prove her point, she moved her pussy along his hard length. "Since I'm not an orc, perhaps it won't have the same effect on me."

"I wouldn't be so sure about that," he mumbled, fingers tracing over a red marking on the left side of her chest that resembled the kind orcs were born with. All her skin markings were black, and this one was definitely new.

She looked down at where he was touching. "Well, that is interesting. It seems the mate bond does affect me."

His hand left the new red tattoo and traveled down her belly to her cunt, sliding a finger between her wet folds.

"I don't need the bond to tell me that," he repeated her prior statement.

She inhaled softly and then gave him a smirk while leaning down to lick his tusk. "That has nothing to do with the bond. I craved you even before." She stopped right before her lips touched his, suddenly realizing something. "Could my ability to see in the dark become as good as an orc's? That would be useful."

"Time will tell." He tugged her down, crashing her mouth to his.

Her hands moved greedily over his chest, and her hips ground against him. He felt male satisfaction at her hurried desire for him.

He gripped her hips and pulled her up his chest until her dripping cunt was over his face and sat her down on her new seat. His need to lick and taste her was driven even stronger by the mate bond. Bringing his mate to orgasm helped increase chances of fertility, and even though they were not trying to get pregnant, the urge was irresistible. And the mewling noises she made were just as irresistible.

He devoured her, leisurely enjoying every second, until her noises became more desperate. Then he gave her consistent stimulation that caused her body to go taut before reaching her peak. Seeing such a powerful woman come undone was a heady experience.

As she caught her breath, he continued to lick through every tremor. With a dreamy look, she kissed down his body until she settled at his hips. She took his cock in hand and stroked him.

There was a knock at the door.

"You're the chieftain. Tell him to go away," Calypso said.

Nazghor's voice sounded from the other side of the door. "There are things that even the chieftain can't make go away. If you don't come out, I will be forced to enter."

Calypso didn't seem bothered by this and continued to stroke him. "Onlookers don't bother me."

While orcs were not prudish, the thought of someone seeing Calypso's naked body filled him with jealousy.

Regretfully, he moved her off of him. "Nazghor is not joking when he says he will enter. If he sees you naked, I'll be forced to remove his eyes from his head. That'll put a strain on our friendship."

She chuckled and got up to dress. Vidorak also rose, handing her a new clean dress to wear, but it was made for an orcess, so it pooled at her feet slightly. He watched her put the amulet around her neck and hide it under the dress.

"Since you know I won't betray you, what does the amulet do?"

"Make me a great conqueror, haven't you heard the legends?" She evaded his question.

He took her by the shoulders, forcing her to look at him. "Do not tell me nonsense after last night. The legend is nothing more than a fool's dream."

While his witch may be rash and bold and passionate, she was not a fool. Not for a second did he believe she risked so much just for greed, like his uncle, and he disliked that she still wanted to hide from him.

Irritation colored her pale skin. "Just because we are apparently new mates doesn't mean I need to divulge everything with you."

"We have a deal of truth."

The pained surprise that flashed across her face tore at him. "Are we still doing that?"

"Answer my question, Calypso," he demanded.

Her body burned with anger, but she didn't renege on their deal. "The amulet is nothing more than a rock until I activate it. Once I do, it will grant me the strength of a dragon. Then not even the royal army could stop me from storming Sanograd."

"And you will use this power to kill Hugh Davinger?" he concluded, the realization of her goals sinking in. He understood her need for vengeance, but what would become of her at the end of it? Suddenly, he felt unable to breathe at the thought of her putting herself at risk.

"Yes, I will kill Hugh Davinger," she snapped. "What else would I do?"

"You could protect your coven."

Her entire body tensed at his sharp criticism, and for a second he wondered if she would attack him. These thoughts had been on his mind throughout their travels. He already considered her powerful even without the dragon's magic and felt she could accomplish so much more than single-minded revenge. Regardless of her claims, what she'd done at Taybe and in rescuing the other witches signaled that deep down she also desired more.

"There will be no more covens, Vidorak. This realm has condemned us. All I need is for Davinger to die," she snarled, her eyes staring daggers at him. "I've answered your questions. Now let me go."

His hand went to her throat, ignoring the lick of flames as he leaned down. "For you, there's a lot I would tolerate. But I will not allow you to believe you are damned."

He turned on his heel and stalked out of the room. Thankfully, she didn't come after him or fight him. He was brimming with so much anger that the idea of finding those magic-blocking shackles and chaining her up again sounded appealing.

"What did you do?" Nazghor asked with a hint of amusement. "You don't look as relaxed as I'd expect after you disappeared with your mate."

Vidorak's jaw clenched, in no mood for Nazghor's teasing. "Go back to my witch. I don't want her to leave your sight."

"Anyplace off limits?"

Vidorak thought about this but shook his head. "No. Just keep her safe."

There was a lot of fallout that would need to be sorted with his taking over as chieftain. While he knew his mate was strong, he wouldn't let her go around undefended. And the mountain tunnels would be difficult to traverse without a guide.

Regret replaced his anger by the time he finished the trek to the gathering hall. He knew his mate was driven by the pain in her past and didn't take well to being controlled. But his mind had gone numb at the thought of her being hurt, which made him speak too forcefully.

The past didn't have to dictate the future, and she didn't need to bear her burdens alone. He would tell her that when they spoke again. While she may not see it now, they were stronger together.

Chapter Twenty-Eight

CALYPSO

C alypso let Vidorak walk away because if she went after him, she risked either setting him aflame or having sex with him. Her body still felt the delightful soreness from their fucking even as she boiled with anger.

Instead, she finished getting ready as calmly as she could before stomping out of the bedchamber. Leaning against the wall of the stone staircase was the orc she'd seen around Vidorak and Mor.

"Good morning, my queen. We haven't officially met. I'm Nazghor." He gave her as charming a smile as one can have with two tusks at the ends. His face was clear of scars and classically handsome, reminding her of the refined beauty of the elven kind. There were beads interwoven through his long black hair, which was currently pulled back in a low ponytail. If one overlooked the green skin, pointed ears, and red Orcish marks that spanned from his fingertips to shoulders, he had the air of a nobleman.

"I am not your queen," Calypso responded.

"You are the chieftain's mate, which makes you our queen. Or it will once the mate ceremony is completed."

Her head started pounding. Her *mate* had left out some details, it seems.

Through gritted teeth she asked, "Where is Vidorak?"

Ignoring her irritable mood, Nazghor easily responded, "The chieftain is in the gathering hall. Kinar departed overnight, joined by several warriors. As a result, Vidorak will need to speak with the horde."

That took the edge off her fury. While she knew Vidorak had planned to challenge Urim, the situation had forced his hand. It wouldn't be a small task to lead jarls who had followed his ruthless uncle for decades.

Deciding to leave him to his work, Calypso turned her attention to other questions on her mind. "I'm assuming you have been assigned to monitor me."

"Think of me more as a guide."

"Take me to the kitchens, Nazghor," she directed. "And on the way, tell me exactly what an orc mating ceremony entails."

He casually led her through the tunnels as if they were old friends. "It's slightly different with each clan, but the general customs are the same. Here, I've heard it's done at a sacred lake in the central dip of the mountains. The mates enter from opposite sides under moonlight and approach one another."

"What happens when they get to one another?"

"Traditionally, the shaman says a prayer as the mating pair exchange vows. Once that is done, there is a public mating followed by a feast."

Calypso paused and looked at Nazghor, but he was completely serious. From everything she'd seen, it wasn't entirely shocking to find out orcs were such exhibitionists.

"Do you have a mate?"

"Not anymore." A fleeting grimace of pain crossed his face.

He led her to the kitchen, where the human women were working as they had the other day. They probably heard about the change, but to them it was just another orc that owned them.

The work in the kitchen came to a halt as the captive women looked at them with guarded expressions.

Dalia was the first one to step forward and speak. "Is it true? Is the chieftain dead?"

Nazghor nodded. "Vidorak Ushnarsson is our new chieftain."

There was no change in her neutral expression as she accepted the development. Calypso waited to see if the witch would ask the burning question, but Dalia remained silent. Was it fear or hopelessness that kept her from asking what would come of them with the new chieftain?

Calypso indicated she wanted to speak privately, and the three of them stepped aside. "I want to know more about the women going missing. Do you know why they were chosen?"

Dalia's gaze flittered to Nazghor. "I don't know what you are talking about."

"It's okay, please share," Nazghor reassured her.

She hesitated, but answered. "No one ever asks. It's too risky to draw attention."

Calypso didn't judge the woman, who was simply acting in self-preservation. Speaking out when there was nothing she could do would only get her killed. Calypso could do something about this, but she needed direction.

She looked over toward Nazghor, but he just shrugged his shoulders regretfully. "I was not privy to this. Whatever Urim did, he kept it between someone he trusted."

They went to leave when Dalia spoke up again. "Is he dead too?"

"Who?"

"The orc who would take the women."

They paused, and Nazghor asked, "You saw him?"

"Yes, I caught a glimpse of him once leading a woman out of the mountain. He is the one with the short hair and bone piercings in his ears."

Knowing exactly who Dalia referred to, Calypso faced Nazghor and asked, "The orc that Grushag took away, is he still alive?"

"Mabanok? He's alive, but not for much longer." Nazghor hesitated. "I don't like the look in your eyes."

Calypso stopped herself from smiling too quickly.

"Let's go pay our soon-to-be-departed orc a visit, Nazghor." Then she turned toward Dalia. "You can tell the others that the new chieftain plans to change things around here. They will be returned to their homes."

There wasn't the wash of relief that Calypso expected to see. Dalia went to leave, face still somber, when Calypso stopped her once more. "A coven in Taybe has been established. You are welcome to go there once you leave the mountain."

Without responding, Dalia nodded briskly before resuming her work.

The disapproval on Nazghor's face was clear. "The chieftain won't be happy about this."

"About what exactly?" Calypso stilled. She had no position of power in the orc clan and likely shouldn't have spoken for him. However, if Vidorak didn't release the captive women, she would see him as an enemy, mate bond or not.

"He would not want you to visit Mabanok in the dungeons," Nazghor clarified. "I need to tell him."

Calypso waved a hand in dismissal. "Is that all? Show me the way, then tell him."

He led her through the tunnels descending deeper into the mountain. The air became stale and thick. Calypso smelled the sharp tang of blood before she saw it. They reached a large metal door with a heavy lock that Nazghor pointedly didn't reach to unlock for her.

"Stay here. The chieftain is nearby, so I will go speak to him first," Nazghor instructed before disappearing into the darkness.

Calypso examined the lock, tilting it up.

Vidorak was a busy orc, and there was no need to wait on things she could handle.

With a blast of her fire, the lock cracked and separated enough to be slipped off, and the door opened. A whiff of rotted flesh and urine hit her nostrils.

Grimacing, she entered, the sound of her steps echoing throughout the stone-covered dungeon. It was pitch black here, but she spotted a torch handle near the entrance and lit it.

Picking it up carefully, she let her vision adjust. Unlike the dungeon in Sanograd where she had been imprisoned, there were no cell doors here. There was no need for them. Shackles and chains hung on the walls, designed to restrain prisoners.

This was a room of death. No windows, no light, no noise. Just air that suffocated you and a maddening silence.

Calypso observed the area, noting a couple of orc bodies that had likely died months ago. It seemed Urim wasn't one for keeping a clean torture chamber.

She moved forward slowly, letting the flames illuminate the room further until a shadowy form at the very end caught her eye. Hanging by metal chains wrapped around his wrists was the barely recognizable body of Mabanok. Swelling had disfigured his face, and dried blood and grime coated his torso.

For a moment, she thought he was already dead. His chest barely rose in the fire's glow.

"Can you open your eyes?" Her voice sounded too harsh in the morbid silence.

The large orc's face twitched in response, but his eyes remained shut, likely too swollen to open.

"That's probably for the better in here," Calypso said as she approached. "I just need you to hear me anyway."

The orc gave a bloody cough in response, mumbling something in Orcish.

"Oh, come on now. We aren't in the forest anymore, so let's not play games." Calypso grabbed his balls with a flaming hand. "I know you speak the common tongue."

Mabanok screamed, voice hoarse and raw.

She let go after a couple of seconds. Seems she still held a grudge about the little game he set up in the forest to decide which orc would force himself on her. "Let's try things again."

He gave a pained groan but spoke this time. "What do you want, witch?"

"Answers. What did you do with the female captives who are disappearing from the mountain?"

His lips twitched. "I have no idea what you are talking about."

She cocked her head. "Is that so? Would you like me to refresh your memory?"

He flinched when she reached for him. Instead of striking, she ran a long fingernail over the numerous wounds on his chest. "I am feeling generous, so I'll make you a deal instead."

"You cannot tempt me with lies of being released."

She shook her head even though he couldn't see her. "We both know that's not possible at this point. Your death approaches. How quickly is up to you. If you keep your secret, I will cauterize these wounds and let your clansmen hurt you again only to heal you afterward. It would not be a pleasant way to go." She leaned forward and whispered in his ear, "Tell me what I want to know, and I will set you free. You will not feel it. I promise."

A heartbeat passed. Mabanok hung so still that she wondered if he'd lost consciousness.

"Urim had me sell them for gold."

"To whom?"

"Some woman. We meet once a month in the ruins outside of Ettera."

"Why is she buying them?"

"I don't know." His voice became weaker. "I bring her the girls, and she gives me gold."

"When is the next meeting?"

"Tomorrow."

She may not know what the buyer's motives were, but Calypso doubted she'd deal with orcs if she had good intentions. These women were being treated like cattle, passed from one owner to the next.

Calypso put a finger under his chin and tilted up his drooping head. "You do not deserve mercy. But I do not break promises."

With that, her nails sharpened to deadly points. She plunged her hand into his chest, gripped his heart, and squeezed it to silence. As promised, it was over in less than a second. He had not even emitted a sound before his life faded.

Calypso stepped back and spared him one last glance before turning around. Near the entrance of the dungeon stood her orc, watching her silently in the shadows.

When she approached, he reached for her bloodied hand and took out his waterskin. Cool water poured over her hand, cleaning off the blood.

"Do you disapprove?" she asked with a guarded expression.

He shook his head. "I am unburdened from having to deal with him. Though, I'd rather you waited for me to join you."

"I was not in danger."

Skin clean from traces of her killing, he pulled her to his chest. His arms wrapped around her, chin resting on top of her head. "I know. Did it bother you? Having to take his life."

Only honesty should be between them. "No. Does it bother you that it doesn't bother me?"

"There's not much you can do that would bother me." He buried his head in her hair and sniffed. Calypso smiled, loving how he enjoyed doing that.

"I think that's an answer from your cock." To prove her point, she rubbed against his hardness. "Tell me the truth."

"It doesn't bother me," he repeated. "Though I think you consider yourself crueler than you are."

She made a noncommittal noise, not wanting to analyze herself any further today.

"I'm assuming you heard it all. The next exchange is tomorrow."

She felt Vidorak stiffen under her embrace. "You mean to leave the mountain and meet with the buyer?"

She pulled away in order to look at his face when she responded. "If no one shows, it will be suspicious, and by the next meeting the news of the new chieftain will have spread. This woman shouldn't be allowed to get away with this."

There were warring emotions in his eyes, and she braced herself. Vidorak was not a male who was prone to being defied. But she was not a woman who would tolerate being controlled.

"Grushag and Nazghor will join," he finally said. "Unfortunately, there is more I need to do here."

Even as he said it, she could see he was considering coming. She put a hand to his cheek. "We will be fine. Who we are makes it impossible to always be with one another."

He scowled. "Don't say such things. Even if it is true. It makes my monstrous side want to lock you up again."

If he meant to be scary, it didn't work because she laughed. "Don't worry. We won't be gone long. I plan to be back in time for my mating ceremony after all."

To her delight, her scary orc actually blushed at her words and mumbled, "I meant to say something."

She laughed again. "Don't worry, Nazghor filled me in on your voyeuristic ways."

"Nazghor talks too much. We don't need to do all that. Just entering the lake and exchanging vows is enough."

"And miss my chance to show off how good you fuck me? I don't think so."

When he said nothing back right away, she worried she had scandalized her dear orc, but then he pulled her to a stop. "Consider our deal of truth over."

She drew back, unsure of how to feel about that. Even with the argument this morning, she had grown to enjoy his questions, enjoyed how he pushed her to open up. She wanted to share these things, but the first step was too difficult.

"I still want to know all of you." He caressed her hair. "But I want you to share these things willingly."

"It will take time." What surprised her most was that she actually wanted to try, sought to put her trust in him, and that scared her beyond belief.

"One more thing," he said as they left the dungeon behind. "Promise me we will discuss the amulet more before you use it."

Her fingers went to the cool stone around her neck. "I promise."

Chapter Twenty-Nine

CALYPSO

The ruins outside of Ettera held the last remnants of old Shalimar. Most of the ancient cities had turned to dust or had been built upon throughout the years. No one had wanted to live in the barren wasteland between the Vestrahorn mountains and Ettera, so the old city had been left to ruin.

Half-collapsed towers and buildings remained, desperately resisting the ravages of time with their last breath. Most structures had one or two walls that had crumbled, and inside she could see indiscernible household objects covered in sand and dirt.

The real unsettling sight was the old castle that loomed above this city of death. Unlike the rest of the ruins, the castle looked preserved, whether by chance or some ancient magic, she didn't know.

What made her skin crawl was the way the city looked destroyed but frozen in time. It was as if one day there was life and the next it had become completely abandoned.

"Why didn't Urim ever loot the castle?" Calypso observed the dark windows along the structure.

Vidorak had known of the ruins, but only in passing. Neither he nor the orcs she traveled with had actually set foot in these deserted remains.

"Fear." The hoarse answer came from Grushag. It was the first word he'd spoken in their entire journey together.

"Urim was greedy, but he was also superstitious," Nazghor explained. "It is warned that whoever comes to steal from Old Shalimar never leaves it. The taverns of Ettera are always full of stories about grave robbers attempting their luck and never returning."

"Do you believe the stories?"

"I believe the wasteland is dangerous, and drunkards are prone to getting lost. Though I don't want to linger any longer than necessary."

They were in agreement there. While Calypso didn't sense any living presence here, her instincts were screaming at her to leave this place.

They stopped their horses and dismounted outside the castle courtyard. There were three arched entrances to the courtyard with connecting pillars surrounding the periphery of the area. A vast maze began at the far side of the courtyard, extending toward the castle. She could imagine the gardens that once flourished here must've been a striking sight.

Calypso made to step forward when Grushag blocked her path. His unusual green eyes glared down at her. "You stay here."

She looked at him incredulously. "You can't be serious."

To his credit, he didn't back down.

Nazghor came over to explain. "This could be a trap. Mabanok isn't exactly trustworthy. We will clear the area first and then come to get you if it is safe."

It was annoying, but she could see the reasoning behind that. "Fine, I will stay back for now, but I will not wait long."

It was the best she could promise.

Nazghor accepted her response and glanced over toward Grushag. "Let's go."

She watched from the arched entryway as the orcs disappeared into the courtyard. Eyeing the precarious lean of one arch, she scoffed. There was a higher risk of the ruins collapsing on her than the buyer harming her.

The buyer was expecting a weak human woman after all. When she got her hands on this person, she'd burn them from the inside out. Though not before she found out what they had done with the other captives.

She acknowledged this was a lot of effort for someone who vehemently avoided helping her own kind. Vidorak's words from their argument still rang in her mind. He had touched on something she had buried. Something that her own sisters were trying to get her to face.

Of course, she'd love to see the covens reform across the realm. She hated the persecution that still existed and burned with fury at the death that had spread. Which made her even more scared at the prospect of things getting better only for it to happen again.

She'd rather face Hugh Davinger or Ker Beck a thousand times than attempt to resurrect the covens only to have them get destroyed. It was one thing to fail herself, but the idea of failing thousands of witches made her sick.

Impatience overtaking her, Calypso abandoned her post and entered the courtyard. The orcs would just have to accept they had taken too long.

Just as she entered, she saw a cloud of dust in the distance. Staying hidden from sight, she peered around the corner and watched as a hooded figure rode in their direction. The rider dismounted at the side entrance and confidently walked into the courtyard.

"Damn it!" Calypso cursed under her breath and stepped behind a stone pillar to block herself from view.

In the center of the courtyard stood Grushag and Nazghor, their postures tense as the hooded figure approached. From her position, she wasn't able to see clearly, but could hear their conversation.

"You are not the orc I usually deal with. Where is Mabanok?" the woman asked.

"He had other matters to attend to. You will deal with us," Nazghor said in a colder tone than she'd ever heard from him.

"More important than this? I want proof Chieftain Urim sent you."

Nazghor scoffed. "You don't make demands of us."

Things didn't appear to be going as they had hoped, and Calypso braced to intervene.

"You do if you don't want the entire northern guard coming to the mountains," the woman threatened them, but Calypso detected a falter in her voice.

"We are leaving," Grushag's low raspy voice stated.

There were brief sounds of footsteps shuffling before the woman called out again.

"Fine! But this better not happen again. If Mabanok isn't here next month, then I am done here."

The steps halted, and the orcs walked back. "Where is the gold?"

"Product first."

"You are as greedy as Mabanok said you were. I will get the woman, but you aren't getting near her without the payment," Nazghor commented, then he turned to leave the courtyard.

The plan was for him to grab her and drag her forth, loosely bound to give the appearance of capture. From her position behind the pillar, he would be able to spot her without problem. The only issue was that she left the rope they would bind her with back with the horses.

Nazghor didn't make it to the pillar before the woman's tone changed. "Funny. Mabanok always said I overpaid. That these women weren't worth half the gold I gave Urim."

Dread blossomed through Calypso's chest as she felt their rouse fall apart. Not waiting any longer, she sprung from around the pillar in time to see the cloaked figure throw a glass vial at the feet of the orcs. The explosion released a gas, and the orcs roared from the scalding pain.

Grushag plowed through the gas even as his skin blistered from the substance, but the woman had already turned on her heel, running out into the maze beyond the courtyard.

Without missing a beat, Calypso dashed after the woman, circumventing her poison. The woman had the advantage of starting ahead, and Calypso kept an eye on the billowing cloak.

The maze was complex, with multiple turns, but the walls had degraded over time, and it helped her see far enough ahead to follow the buyer.

Calypso was closing the distance when the cloaked woman turned and slammed another vial into the ground behind her. The liquid quickly rose, creating a massive block of ice, walling off that path of the maze.

This area of the maze was still intact, and she'd have to backtrack quite a bit to find a broken-down opening. Motivated to get through the ice, she channeled her flames into one spot, but the ice was melting too slowly.

A whooshing sound came from behind her, and by a hair an axe passed her ear, slamming into the ice. There was a loud crack as it splintered through to the other side. Over her shoulder, she saw Grushag's burned form barreling forth.

The damage was enough to sink her flames into the cracks and speed up melting the ice. The orcs caught up and slammed at the weakened section, opening it enough for Calypso to go through.

"Go!" Nazghor yelled in between assaults. "We will follow when we can."

She squeezed through, leaving them to work on widening the wall for their larger frames. Not wasting a second, she continued running, but no longer saw traces of the buyer. She kept her speed until she reached a point where the maze split in two directions.

Anger and anxiety and frustration built upon themselves as the seconds ticked by. The idea of just releasing her fire in one tremendous explosion became more and more appealing as her indecision grew. She closed her eyes and breathed deeply, trying to clear the fog of her impending failure.

The scent of sulfur entered her nostrils, and her eyes flew open. That gas was sulfur-based and likely had stuck to the cloak. She stepped forward, and the potent smell unquestionably followed the path to the left.

Back on the trail, Calypso ran as fast as she could, desperate not to let the opportunity slip by. If the buyer got away, they would lose all chance of figuring out what was happening to the women in the mountain.

In the distance, she saw the end of the maze as it opened onto the steps of the castle. The buyer was desperately trying to reach her horse, hurrying her steps once she spotted Calypso emerging from the maze's exit.

Uninhibited by structures, Calypso sent a ball of fire toward the woman, but she easily dodged it without slowing down.

Calypso prepared to send her fire once before, but a small blur sped past her. Her undead crow flipped the woman's cloak over her eyes, pecking at her mercilessly.

The seconds that slowed her down were priceless, and Calypso caught up easily after that. The buyer tumbled to the ground but quickly got back on her feet. There was a flash of metal from a knife before the woman lunged toward Calypso.

The knife sliced at her arm, but Calypso moved to the side and kicked the woman in the chest, sending her flying backward.

The woman recovered quickly and braced to lunge again, but Calypso struck without hesitation and slammed her into the maze's stone outer wall. She scalded her wrist until the woman dropped the knife, which Calypso quickly grabbed before ripping off her cloak.

Light blue eyes that had once held a sad loneliness, now radiated contempt.

"Priestess Levorn," Calypso bit out. "I did not realize the sanctuary was in the business of trafficking women."

The priestess spat at her. "The sanctuary's affairs do not concern you."

Calypso pressed the knife into the priestess's neck, causing a tiny bead of blood to appear. "Why are you purchasing women from the orcs?"

"Don't make it so ugly. I'm merely taking those who are lost and giving them a greater purpose."

A chill went down Calypso's spine at the priestess's words.

"What does that mean? Does the head sanctuary know about this?" Calypso asked her questions but saw the look in the Priestess Levorn's eyes.

There was a brief moment of struggle before the priestess answered, "I will not speak those words."

It wasn't a question of whether she would tell her, but rather, *could* she tell her. Their silence bound them in ways that were unknown. The fact that whatever the women were being used for was blocked by their vow of silence told Calypso that the Sanctuary in Solar City was behind all this.

Calypso groaned out of frustration, then leaned in menacingly. "Figure out which words you can say then. Believe me, you don't want me to motivate you."

Even binding rituals had loopholes. While the priestess could not be direct regarding the fates of the women, there were things they could share.

"I will *not* speak those words!" the priestess ground out.

"The sanctuary protects all. Isn't that what's carved into every one of your sacred houses? You are harming these women, and I will find out why," Calypso swore, suddenly being pulled back into the past. For all her criticism of the sanctuaries, if it weren't for the refuge there ten years ago, she would've met her death long ago. To think that throughout the years so much has changed that they now preyed on the most vulnerable without hesitation shook her to her core.

"You judge me, but I do what I must for our place in the realm. What will happen to the witches who followed you during the takeover of Taybe? While you indulge in selfish whims, your coven meets its end by the royal army."

Calypso reared back. "What?"

The priestess gave her a dark smile. "I suppose news doesn't travel fast to the mountains. The regent king brings the royal army to Taybe. The days are numbered for you and your kind."

Calypso didn't notice that the priestess had pulled out a small vial until she'd already drunk all the contents.

"What have you done?" Calypso said in horror, knowing there was nothing to stop what would come next.

"I go to Mother Selene knowing I have served her. And soon, she will return."

With those words, the woman sagged forward, life leaving her body behind. Calypso placed the body on the ground, staring into her face, which had been alive and brimming with indignation only seconds ago.

Was she any different from the priestess? Her only focus had been her own desires, which until this point had been her revenge and now her orc. In truth, she wasn't the only who suffered during the genocide of the witches. The fury and pain that had festered in her for years had made her selfish. Made her blind.

Her mother wouldn't be thankful that she had spent her life on murder and revenge, with plans to go out in a literal blaze of glory. The hard truth sat bitterly as Calypso examined the dead priestess's body, searching for anything important.

If she continued isolating herself, she would end up exactly like the priestess. Poisoned by her own delusions and sense of self-righteousness. If she truly wanted to avenge her mother, she needed to help witchkind, not just self-destruct on a murderous spree.

Nazghor showed up shortly after. "Are you hurt?"

"I am fine."

Calypso stood, not finding anything else of importance on the body. "I'm going to burn the priestess."

He looked down at the dead body but didn't stop her. "I will bring our horses around so we can leave when you are finished."

She released her flames, letting her anger and disgust fuel their strength until they turned almost white. It was so hot that the air seemed to dance and her clothes blackened, but Calypso stood unblinking at her task. Sanctuary magic was a guarded secret, so Calypso decided she would burn the priestess's bones to ash so there was no chance she could return.

She should have left for Taybe as soon as she'd gotten the amulet. She had let herself become influenced by her heart, let herself indulge in a moment of pleasure. All the while her sisters suffered.

Task done, she stepped away from the gray ash, letting the wind take it. She headed to the horses, where Nazghor and Grushag were waiting for her.

"I need to return to my people," she told them. "The royal army is headed to Taybe."

Nazghor looked torn but then nodded sharply. "Anything I should pass along to the chieftain?"

Calypso hesitated, unsure of what to say. There was a mess of emotions she couldn't put into words. None of it felt right to pass through someone else either.

"Just tell him thank you."

Chapter Thirty

CALYPSO

There was a familiar caress of magic when she passed through the wards surrounding the estate. No one was out in the fields, but Calypso knew her crossing informed Astra of her arrival.

Seconds later, the tall woman appeared in the distance, barreling toward her, blonde braid whipping behind her. Calypso jumped off her horse and ran to her friend, meeting her halfway.

They embraced tightly. It had been only a couple of weeks, but Calypso had dearly missed her sister.

"Do not do that again," Astra whispered, and when she pulled back, Calypso saw her green eyes were wet with unshed tears.

"Wouldn't dream of it." Calypso kept her tone light. "Where is Nyx? I would've expected her to be patrolling the fields."

"She's in the infirmary. Recovering."

Calypso's face fell, and she felt a sick pang in her stomach. "What has happened?"

"Too much. And I imagine the same goes for you." Astra put her arm through hers and held her close as they walked back toward the manor. "Come, she will be eager to see you."

Calypso stayed silent on their walk, her mind reeling with the news that her sister had been injured. She should have returned as soon as possible and not wasted that time at the mountain.

On their way to the infirmary, she spotted witches she hadn't met before, and the manor felt busier. When they passed the women who'd followed them the past year, they stopped to embrace Calypso in greeting. The affection made her uncomfortable, but she couldn't bring herself to reject them.

They arrived at the infirmary to hear a crash and see Marianna storm out. She came to a screeching halt when she spotted them and, instead of greeting them, threw up her hands. "She's impossible! I've done what I can. The rest is out of my hands."

Gone was the frightened woman dragged to a public trial, and instead Marianna now carried herself with confidence. Her skin had a healthy glow, and her brown eyes sparked with emotion, the current one being exasperation.

Aileen followed calmly behind, pausing to lightly touch Calypso's hand. "You are back."

"Of course I am," Calypso replied at the preposterous statement, sensing the quick assessment of her feelings from Aileen's sway in that brief contact.

Aileen shook her head with a smile. "Nyx will be happy to see you. I will go after our irritated healer."

With no further interruptions, Astra and Calypso entered the infirmary. There were four beds lined up, all empty except the one next to the window, which currently occupied a sullen black-haired witch.

"If you expect me to apologize, Marianna, you are in for disappointment," Nyx clipped out, not bothering to turn her face toward them.

"I'm gone for a couple of weeks and the entire realm has turned upside down," Calypso answered.

Nyx whipped around and went to stand when she saw her but quickly crumpled to the floor. Calypso rushed over and helped her back onto the edge of the bed.

Despite her injury, Nyx embraced her tightly. It took a second for Calypso to return the hug, feeling touched by the show of affection from her typically aloof friend.

"Stop leaving the bed," Astra chided. "Marianna has the patience of a saint. I told her to render you unconscious days ago."

Nyx ignored the scolding but pulled back and settled into the bed once more.

Calypso grinned. "Missed my charming personality?"

"I'm glad you are back, because now I can kill you myself."

Well, so much for the warm welcome.

Astra jumped in to speak, "The pigeon delivered your letter stating your travels to the mountain. We were glad to hear you were free, but the details were sparse."

"What in the world were you thinking?" Apparently, the injury was making Nyx impatient. "How many times do I need to tell you that you are strong, but your power isn't limitless? With those magic-nullifying shackles, they could've held you captive again. We would never have been able to get you out of that mountain!"

"I would never expect you to do that." Calypso was bewildered at the thought, but the tension on Nyx's face told her it was the wrong thing to say.

"Of course you don't. Because the only thing that matters is what you think is best. I'm beginning to think you made that pact with only yourself."

"That is unfair to say, Nyx." Astra gave her a pointed look at her injured side.

The two women shared a tense bout of eye contact as Calypso looked between them. Her eyes skimmed Nyx's side, seeing the outline of bandages under her gown that were wrapped around her chest.

"How did you get hurt?"

Nyx looked away, and Calypso thought she'd refuse to speak, but then she answered, "After Gemma arrived with a medicinal witch, I went after the merchant who was planning on purchasing them."

"Gemma returned? Is she well?" Calypso asked, hands tightening in the sheets of the bed. She still carried the guilt of almost getting her killed at the trials.

Nyx nodded. "She has healed well physically. But I am not sending her to Sanograd anytime soon, despite her protests."

"The merchant?"

"Dead." Nyx fell silent for a moment before continuing. "Though not before stabbing me with the sharp edge of a broken wineglass."

"I'm surprised he got close enough to do that." It wasn't criticism. While Calypso liked her fights up close and personal, liked to feel the skin blister and blood gush out, Nyx preferred to kill from the shadows.

"I was rushing and didn't confirm he was truly unconscious after I struck him. He recovered while I was busy unlocking a cage containing two elven women." Nyx scowled while recounting the event.

"Odessa said something interesting. The medicinal witch who arrived with Gemma." Astra added, seeing Calypso's confused expression. "She said an orc helped them to safety and gave them coin to travel back here."

Vidorak had told her what he'd done, but hearing how he'd helped the women made her immensely grateful once more. He had been under no obligation to do that, and her heart warmed at the knowledge he'd done it regardless.

"That was one of the orcs who had captured me, though he later helped free me as well. The orc clan was going through its own power struggles, but the chieftain who made the deal for my capture has since been deposed." Calypso took a breath before the next part. "I know I often let my ambitions cloud my judgement, but I needed to go to the mountain, and I'm glad I did. Because I realized you were right."

The statement was so uncharacteristic that it silenced the other women. Calypso continued, "The pact we made has been my focus for so long. It was what gave me life and purpose in a world that rejected us. In the mountains, I saw the true hopelessness of abandonment. I met a witch who preferred to stay with her captors than return to the realm because there was nothing to return to. She is not wrong to feel that way because there is no place of safety for our kind. I also discovered that the prior orc chieftain was trafficking some of the human women to the priestesses of Mother Selene's sanctuary."

Astra gasped at the revelation, "How could that be?"

While they shared their distaste for the private sanctuary rituals, housing the needy was part of their mother's tenets.

"The priestess facilitating these exchanges was the same one I visited here recently. I could not get much information out of her before she ended her life, but I am certain the main sanctuary is leading this. Davinger must be stopped at all costs, but that revenge would be hollow when many others hold such sentiments. Our strength could mean so much more, not just for us but for all of our kind."

Astra reached out and touched her shoulder. "I am happy to hear you say that."

Nyx remained silent, and Calypso turned toward her. "This should not be an estate to loot on the way toward the next part of our plan. This could be a stronghold for our new coven. One that will protect any witch who needs refuge."

Nyx shook her head in bewilderment. "Who would've thought that being taken by orcs would finally make you see reason."

"It wasn't just that. There were a few things that opened my eyes. Willingly or not." Calypso smiled, thinking about her recently discovered mate.

"I am glad we are finally in agreement."

Calypso nodded before turning serious once more. "We need to discuss Hugh Davinger. I hear the royal army approaches."

Astra spoke up. "We are aware. We have been tracking his movements since he left Sanograd."

"I suppose it's flattering he considers us enough of a threat to bring such a force. Do you know how many soldiers he brings with him?" Calypso asked.

"Reports aren't exact, but likely four to five hundred."

"This complicates things." That was the kindest way Calypso could think of to phrase things. Their small coven of witches was no match against hundreds of royal army soldiers.

She wanted to delve into preparations, but she noticed the exhaustion around Nyx's silver eyes. "Luckily, complicated is what I do best. But let's plan after some rest."

Nyx straightened. "Don't stop on my account. This is too important to put off."

"It's not you. I need some rest. I rode here straight from Ettera." Two days of no sleep was taking its toll.

Worry swirled in Nyx's eyes, but exhaustion won and she relented, embracing Calypso one last time before closing her eyes to sleep.

Calypso stepped out of the infirmary, guilt burning inside her. Her motivation had changed, but unfortunately, her plans did not. Fighting against the royal army was a death sentence unless she used the Eye of Azara. She may not be able to save herself, but she was going to do all she could to avoid dragging the others down with her.

Hopefully, her friends would find it in them to forgive her after some time. The question of her mate's forgiveness was another matter.

Glass in hand, she walked onto the balcony from her bedroom. Calypso tipped back the glass of wine, finishing the red liquid before setting it aside. The moon was full and unobstructed by clouds tonight.

That was good. It would help the binding take better. The first part of this spell was something she'd done many times once she opened the door to black magic. Most black magic started with a binding. A sacrifice of blood. At its core, black magic wasn't evil; it was just magic that drew its power from the essence of life.

She took a knife and sliced down the middle of her forearm. The pain was sharp and immediate, but she focused on the flow of the blood. She moved her forearm over the amulet, allowing the crimson rivulets to pour over the gemstone. The ruby absorbed it, emitting a soft glow as if awakening from a slumber before returning to its prior form. It didn't look different, but Calypso could sense the change within.

"And so, it is done," she mumbled to herself and slipped the amulet back on. It would take a night for the binding to hold, but come dawn, she could complete the spell.

The cool stone sat nestled between her breasts, and she bandaged her forearm on the balcony, not wanting to return inside just yet. The choice was cowardly and she knew it, but she would take every minute she could before facing the inevitable of telling her sisters about the amulet. Especially now that she had bloodied it, there was no hiding the truth anymore.

Her thoughts were so full of dread that she almost missed the blur in the distance.

It was brief, simply a movement of shadows in the corner of her eye. She snapped her focus in that direction, studying the darkness of the trees and field. Everything remained completely still.

Yet, her heart rate picked up.

There was something there. Something that had bypassed the wards Astra set up.

Closing her eyes, she internally traced the boundary of the estate wards, feeling for any breaks. It was intact, which meant no one should be able to breach it.

Again, her instincts screamed that something was out there watching her.

Fists clenched, she descended the balcony stairs, craving a fight. She wanted the pain, wanted to let out all the turmoil in her heart.

Still clad in her thin slip, she reached the grounds. Her mouth curved in a wicked smile. Whatever creature Davinger had summoned to spy on them was going to meet a very brutal end.

The grass was cool under her bare feet, and she walked soundlessly in the dark until the noises of the manor died down. She stopped and took a breath. Then another.

She sensed the presence coming from her left. With an eager chuckle, she took off into the darkness, leading whatever chased her further away from the estate. She didn't want anyone to get accidentally caught up in the fight.

Goosebumps broke out on her skin as she felt her pursuer get closer. She didn't bother looking back and pivoted to the right.

Weaving between trees, the distance grew between them. She quickly scurried in front of a large oak tree, back pressed against the rough bark. Her skin itched with anticipation for the upcoming fight.

Several silent seconds passed, and she worried that the creature might have circled back toward the manor. She peered around the tree, searching in the darkness.

A snap of a branch came from in front, and Calypso jumped, starting the chase again. The creature was smarter than she realized. It seemed capable of hiding itself whenever it wanted. Which meant that it wanted her running, wanted the chase.

That was good because she wanted the chase as well.

Her path broke away from the trees, and she found herself in the fields north of the manor. It herded her to a place that contained no protection for her, no obstacles to weave between or hide behind.

However, she knew up ahead was a patch of rough brush before leading back into the woods. If she could just make it there, then she could catch the creature at a disadvantage as it entered.

She sprinted across the field, her arms swinging and eyes fixed ahead.

Without warning, she was suddenly tackled toward the ground. The creature hit the ground first and they rolled around a few times, ending with its heavy weight pressing her into the grass.

Then a familiar voice rumbled in her ear. "You think you can run away from me, little witch? You are mine."

Chapter Thirty-One

VIDORAK

He hadn't meant to chase her. He simply got caught up watching her before he planned to make himself known. His witch still had too many secrets, and he wanted to know what they were.

When she had cut herself, he'd almost emerged from the tree line then and there, but had held back when he noted no distress on her face. In fact, she looked quite somber during the act. Her blood dripped onto the amulet, and he swore it emitted a glow before dulling once more. From what she'd mentioned prior, he suspected this had to do with her black magic, but exactly what was unclear. The cost of her prior use of black magic was the voices and images that haunted her. Would the amulet demand more?

He pondered this, planning on waiting until the morning before confronting her. But then she'd run. All intentions disappeared, and what remained was a primal urge to chase her. All he could focus on was his need to capture his mate, to fuck her, and to mark her so she never thought about leaving him again.

"This is the second time you've tackled me in the woods, orc." Her words came out breathlessly while writhing against him. "Though I must say, this time it's much more enjoyable."

He trapped her underneath him, not letting her turn over. His face buried in her neck, breathing in her scent that he'd craved since the moment she left.

"I told you once before not to run from me." He nipped at her shoulder.

"In all fairness, I didn't know it was you."

He growled and flipped her over, still pinning her to the ground. "You left the estate unguarded wearing nothing?"

Worry and irritation at her careless behavior pierced through his haze of lust.

"Don't exaggerate. I am dressed." She wrapped her legs around him, tugging him closer to her core. "Besides, I was in the mood for a fight."

It seemed to him his mate was in the mood for something else. One hand trapped her wrists above her head, while the other gripped the collar of her flimsy slip, tearing it easily down the center.

Vidorak ignored the quick flash of outrage on her face, instead focusing on her perfect breasts that were illuminated in the moonlight. Her nipples pebbled in the midnight breeze, beckoning to him.

He closed his mouth over one breast while pinching the nipple of the other. He had never wanted someone so deeply and this mindlessly before. Never felt as if all his senses became alive by the mere sight of her.

"There is no time." She breathed the statement so quietly that he almost missed it from the desire pounding in his veins.

He would find a way to stop time. He would learn to control the moon and sun if only to spend a minute more by her side.

"You are mine, witch. I have caught you, and I will take as long as I want with you."

With that promise, he kissed her lips and plunged his tongue into her mouth. Their tongues danced together, intertwining and tasting. The kisses became breathless until he couldn't stand it anymore.

Letting go of her wrists, he kissed down her chest and belly, savoring each inch. His hands roamed her skin, unwilling to spend even a second not touching her.

He gazed at his beautiful mate with her wild mane of red hair and flushed cheeks, whose eyes filled with lust. He thought how she was so beautiful it hurt, right before pushing her knees further apart and ravishing her cunt with desperation.

The taste of her was intoxicating, and he craved it more than anything. He plunged his tongue deep in her cunt with his tusks pushing into her upper thighs. Her moans echoed in the darkness as she gripped his hair, tugging him closer to her writhing body.

With a hard suck at her clit, he earned a view of her back arching and breasts glistening from the wetness of his mouth earlier. She was an absolute goddess, and he wanted to spend the rest of his days worshiping her.

She was giving him needy sounds signifying she was close but not quite there. Keeping his mouth on her clit, he pushed into her with one finger before adding another in her tight cunt. The pressure caused her to moan.

He removed his mouth and used his thumb to rub at her clit instead. While pumping his fingers, he turned his head toward her thigh and bit the soft inner part. He did it hard enough to leave a mark but not too hard to really hurt her.

She sharply inhaled. "Marking your territory?" The question was laced with breathless amusement.

Yes.

As savage as it was, he wanted to mark himself all over her with bites and rough kisses. He wanted to paint her with his seed so the world would know she was his and his alone.

He didn't say any of that, too taken aback by the intensity of his possessiveness. Instead, he returned to licking her apex.

Between his mouth and fingers, it didn't take long before she clamped her thighs around his head and tensed with her release. Vidorak was determined to suck every drop of her and draw it out.

Her body went slack, and Vidorak resisted the urge to bring her knees up and slam into her immediately. Instead, he kissed back up her body and captured her mouth. She kissed him back fervently, fighting him for control.

She suddenly pulled back and asked, "Are you mad?"

His nose grazed up her neck. "It feels like madness. But no, I'm not angry. I understand why you had to go."

"Good. Because I'm not sorry."

He chuckled, loving his headstrong and arrogant witch. He loved how brazenly she expressed herself. She was unapologetic, while he had spent years hiding behind a wall, fighting to remember who he wanted to be. "Good."

He was kissing the smooth skin of her shoulder when she pushed him onto his back. Her hands grabbed his trousers, freeing him. He groaned as she moved expertly over his cock.

"I'm the one who captured you. You should be yielding to my desires."

"You are taking too long," she said with a wicked grin before stopping her caresses and straddling him. She sank down onto his entire length in one merciless movement. When she rode him, Vidorak experienced pleasure like never before.

She was a sight to behold, her hair tangled around her face, her breaths deep, her eyes flooded with power. She was a creation of magic and wildness. Untamed perfection. Yet, she was his.

His hands went to her hips, unable to hold back any longer. He pumped into her, needing her ingrained into his soul. When that wasn't enough, he flipped them both over again, bringing her leg over his shoulder so he could sink deeper into her.

The rest of the world stopped existing. There was nothing else except their desperation for one another. He fucked her so hard her back moved up the grass with each thrust.

Her head arched back as her own wave of ecstasy hit her, and he felt her clench around him, milking him cruelly. He snarled, mind void of reason, and bit down on the curve of her perfect neck. His hand fisted her red curls to keep her immobile. His sack tightened, and his movements became erratic as he spilled his seed into her depths.

He let go of her neck, leaving kisses while he caught his breath. Her fingers gingerly touched where he had bitten. "Is the biting something I get to look forward to every time we get together?"

Shame for puncturing her perfect skin sunk in. He turned his body, taking her with him, so he wouldn't be crushing her. "Are you in much pain?"

"Barely." Her fingers absentmindedly moved over his chest. "I get the urge. I want to mark you as well, lest any orcesses get ideas."

The thought of her biting him was appealing, and his cock hardened again despite their recent activities.

"Again?" she asked, noticing the effects. "You will have to do all the work though. I don't have any strength left."

He shook his head in amusement. "Ignore it. I don't think I will ever stop getting hard for you."

Embracing her closely, his fingers drifted near the laceration on her forearm. "What happens now?"

The amulet had remained on throughout their lovemaking, and he sensed no difference in the teardrop-shaped ruby.

"Infusing the amulet with my blood is the first part. Once it takes, I can complete the second part of the spell."

"You don't sound pleased."

The unsettled feeling in his gut returned as he recalled Kallsson's warning about the amulet. Suddenly, he felt awash with the urge to take her again to assure himself she was here and safe. The dark rims of her eyes and sleepy blinking held him back.

She hesitated before responding, "I am thinking about my sisters. We had a conversation that had needed to happen for some time. It was good, though initially tense."

He waited, but she didn't expound. Irritation sparked within Vidorak at her continued insistence on closing off her heart.

Then a thought came to him. "Was it about me? Are they unhappy that I formed a mate bond with you?"

She gave him a look of bewilderment before bursting out laughing. Clearly, that wasn't the right answer.

"Sorry," she apologized between chuckles. "Honestly, you didn't come up at all."

He'd be lying if that didn't sting a bit. The first thing he did as chieftain was present her as his mate to the clan. Clearly, she didn't feel the need to share the news right away with her people.

"Come now, don't sulk." She pressed a kiss on his chin.

"I'm not sulking."

"Okay, my misinterpretation." Her fingers gently petted him. "I would rather have talked about you."

They stayed silent for several minutes, neither wanting to break contact. When she yawned, the urge to put her to bed so she could sleep was too great, and he stood to dress himself.

"You should be back with your clan," she mumbled sleepily.

"My clan is my responsibility." He picked up her still-naked body in his arms. "We will talk more tomorrow."

She didn't protest being carried. Instead, she leaned into him and traced his skin as they walked. "In a different life, I think we would've traveled the realm instead of fighting wars. We would spend our days eating sweets and fucking everywhere."

He smiled at the thought. "I would take you in any life I can."

It wasn't long after that he felt his witch drift off to sleep, her body becoming limp in his arms.

CHAPTER THIRTY-TWO

CALYPSO

C alypso awoke to shouting. She sprang out of bed, braced for the threat. Her room was empty, and instead, the voices were radiating from outside the manor.

The events of last night came flooding back.

She threw on the first dress she saw and hurried out onto the balcony attached to the bedchamber. Barreling down the balcony stairs toward the grounds, she saw Astra with a knife to Vidorak's throat. Flames sparked at her hands before she realized what was happening.

"Stay back, Calypso. It seems Davinger has sent more orcs to finish their contract," Astra shouted, oblivious to the target of Calypso's sudden draw of power.

"Let him go, Astra." Her command was sharp and direct.

Astra leaned her knife in, drawing a bead of blood. "No need to waste your energy. I can take care of a single orc."

Vidorak held her back defensively, trying not to hurt her sister. While Astra was a strong fighter, Vidorak could easily overtake her.

"I don't understand," Nyx said from behind Astra, her eyebrows furrowed. "The wards are still intact. It's impossible for him to have passed the barrier without even an alert."

There were other witches outside watching them but keeping their distance. As far as Calypso could see, there was no destruction, and no one looked injured. Yet.

"The mate bond let him." Calypso pushed herself between them. "Now step back."

Astra retreated, eyes widening in astonishment. "This orc is bonded to you?"

"Actually, it seems they bonded with each other." Nyx muttered as her silver eyes focused on the red tattoos on Calypso's chest.

The thin slip Calypso wore didn't hide the red, Orcish-like mark on her left chest that had appeared after their mate bond.

"You are right, he is my mate," Calypso confirmed, then stepped aside so they could meet more calmly. "This is Vidorak Ushnarsson. He is also the new chieftain of the Vestrahorn mountain clan."

There was a moment of stunned silence as the women didn't know how to respond. Slowly, Astra sheathed her dagger.

"This is . . ." Astra began, clearly not knowing how to phrase things next, "unexpected."

"I'm assuming this was the orc who let you go?" Nyx asked, her face unreadable.

"She did that on her own," Vidorak said before she could respond.

She had enough self-awareness to realize that her plan with the crow likely wouldn't have worked without Vidorak's help, but she didn't correct him. Instead, Calypso added, "He is the one who helped Gemma."

That softened Nyx's face. "Thank you for helping her."

The tension had lessened, but Calypso could tell her sisters were still shocked by this news. "I know a lot has changed these past couple of weeks. The bond was unexpected, but I'm grateful for the truths it has helped me see. And I want you to know I am happy."

That seemed to be the right thing to say because the tension dissipated and she saw her sisters relax.

"That is good." Nyx actually smiled at that before returning to her neutral expression.

Astra embraced her wordlessly, but when she pulled back, Calypso saw she had tears in her eyes. "You have a mate!"

Calypso felt completely undeserving of their affection. She put them through so much with her moods and unyielding nature, yet even with the war that approached, they still cared for her happiness.

Nyx stepped closer, and Calypso could feel her studying her closely.

"Is that the only thing you are hiding?" Nyx asked quietly.

Before Calypso could respond, Nyx grabbed the amulet hanging around her neck and pulled it toward her, causing her to stumble forward. She could've pushed back, but she didn't want to hurt her sister. Vidorak stiffened at the treatment, but thankfully didn't intervene.

"It actually exists." Nyx's voice was full of wonder as she turned over the stone before releasing it abruptly. "Seems you've bloodied it already."

"What's going on? What do you mean?" Astra clamored, looking between them.

"This is why I went to the Vestrahorn Mountain," Calypso explained, hiding the amulet under her dress. "This is the Eye of Azara. Once I complete the spell, we will be a genuine threat to the royal army."

An excited smile broke out across Astra's face. "This is great! They won't stand a chance with a dragon on our side."

"It is," Calypso responded half-heartedly.

"I actually believed the things you said about working together for the greater good of witchkind," Nyx spat out. "As always, it is half-truths as you make unilateral decisions."

Astra looked back, confusion furrowing her brow. "What do you mean?"

Calypso just stared at her furious sister, half willing her to hold her tongue and half eager to reveal all the secrets.

"Are you going to tell her?" Nyx challenged with an arched black brow. "Because I am eager to know what your *mate* will think of your impending sacrifice."

Suddenly, it all became just too much.

Like a coward, Calypso muttered she needed to go and turned on her heel to run back to the manor. She didn't look back as she dashed up the stairs and entered the bedchamber only to be met with the still form of Thomas Haworth in the corner of the room. His chest was a bloody red hole, and his eyes were two black pits.

"Not now." Her voice shook, and she tore her eyes from the hallucination.

Her trembling hands were searching a pile of clothes for a proper dress when she heard Vidorak enter the room, and the tension rose around them.

"Explain."

She didn't dare look at him. "There's nothing more to say. You already know there is a price for all magic."

Hands gripped her upper arms, whirling her around, and pressing her into the wall. "You test my patience too much, mate."

Another evasion sat at the tip of her tongue, but it seemed too exhausting all the sudden. Perhaps his anger would be better than his pain.

"The spell brings forth a life, and for that, it requires a life. The one who casts the spell is sacrificed to provide the magic needed to summon a dragon."

There was a gasp, and for a moment Calypso thought the Howarth's ghost had spoken. Instead, she turned to see that Nyx and Astra had followed them into the bedchamber.

"Is that true?" Astra asked, looking at her and then looking back at Nyx.

Nyx's eyes stared back at her with a cold anger. "Answer her, Calypso."

She could not speak, could not find the words. As the daughter of the royal advisor, Calypso had access to the vast royal library. Even before her powers had awakened, she would spend hours reading through various texts about magic and spells and the history of witchkind.

The story of Azara was always one she found interesting, perhaps because there was something sad and unfinished within it. When she'd discovered the spell to unlock the amulet, it had become a bit of an intriguing fantasy. After Davinger's decree and their escape from Sanograd, it turned into an obsession.

From the beginning, she knew the price. The final part of the spell required sacrificing her life for the summoning of the last dragon. She didn't care. Once her mother was murdered, there was no thought of a future for her. She just wanted revenge. Giving her life to an unstoppable otherworldly force felt apt for the moment.

Everyone stared at her, and Calypso protected herself in the only way she knew how. She retreated deep within herself and hardened her heart. "I have always known. When did you find out about this?"

"Do you value my skills so little?" Even Nyx's cool composure broke, and her hand shook with anger. "I've been gathering any information I could over the past year as you became more erratic with your black magic. I recently received a letter from Sanograd detailing the specifics of the spell."

"Yesterday you said that you wanted to focus on rebuilding the covens. Was that all a lie?" Astra asked.

"No!" Calypso exclaimed. "I want the covens to be rebuilt."

"You just don't plan on being a part of it," Nyx concluded bitterly.

Next to Haworth's ghost, a bruised Mabanok appeared. Neither man spoke, but they looked just as real as everybody else in the room. Calypso swallowed her shock and peeled her eyes away from the hallucinations. "When does the royal army arrive?"

Astra hesitated but then answered. "Less than a week. We received notice that he had crossed the Ihoi River two nights back."

Five hundred royal soldiers would appear on their doorstep in less than a week, led by none other than the king regent. Even with the newcomers, she doubted there were two dozen witches on the premises. "Perfect. We can end this once and for all."

"Don't you dare," a deep growl came from Vidorak, who'd remained silent since the other women had come into the room. "Don't you dare refer to your death as perfect."

The look in his eyes almost made her falter. She stepped forward, unsure of whether she was going to comfort him or plead her case. "It's the only way to end this. We are not powerful enough to take on the royal army otherwise."

Vidorak's jaw tensed in anger. "What is to stop the dragon from attacking the town instead of the army?"

Calypso shook her head and repeated, "There's no other way. It's an army of five hundred, Vidorak."

Her mate growled his response, but Calypso didn't process his words as the image of Joseph Collier appeared beside him.

She spun around the room, seeing figure after figure appear. Soon the room filled with past victims, even some whose names she didn't remember. They were all silent, staring, expecting something.

Suddenly, Astra stepped right up to her, taking her hands and staring into her with pleading eyes until all Calypso could see was forest green. "The pact was supposed to make us partners. It was a binding between us and for us. Let us all come up with a plan."

The pact was originally Astra's idea. Nyx had arrived at the sanctuary a shell of a person, spending more days in solitude than speaking to others. Calypso had been too angry to think beyond her rage. It was Astra who had gathered them and given them purpose. Given them a reason to wake in the morning.

"I love you." Calypso felt like her heart was breaking as she stepped out of Astra's hold. "But there is no other way."

Too much emotion battered at her unstable defenses, and Calypso felt suffocated by the sudden slip into insanity. She needed to leave, and she needed to leave now. Otherwise, the flames that were bursting within her would erupt so ferociously that she could burn down the manor.

Chapter Thirty-Three

VIDORAK

The clenching in Vidorak's chest worsened with each passing minute. He felt his mate's distress pulse along their bond, which only made him even more desperate in his search. The grounds were extensive, and Calypso was good at hiding when she didn't want to be found.

Vidorak had been searching for her for nearly an hour with no success. He left the stables, scanning the area carefully as he crossed the estate. He'd already searched the small building nearby, which turned out to be staff quarters.

Located past that building were the gardens. The plants were growing peacefully in the sun, oblivious to the impending danger. Seeing the calm around him did nothing to soothe the pang in his chest.

"Damn it," Vidorak muttered and marched toward the forests beyond. He wasn't sure if she'd run that far, but he didn't have any other ideas.

Abnormal warmth radiated from his right and drew his attention toward the garden shed in the far corner. Frowning, he changed directions and stalked toward the lone structure. The warmth increased as he got closer, giving a shimmer to the air.

A sheen of sweat broke out on his forehead, and his eyes burned as he got closer. His body braced for what he might find there.

He rounded the corner and spotted his fearless mate sitting on the ground, hugging her knees to her chest, face hidden from view. While her body was completely still, flames danced upon her skin, moving around her arms and down her back. The fire had blackened the surrounding grass.

How she could look so small and fragile and yet be completely dangerous, he couldn't understand.

"Calypso," he called, but she didn't answer. He ignored the slight blurring of his vision as he approached her and kneeled at her level.

"Are you real?" The question was quiet, but he heard her clearly.

"I am." He reached out, but before he could make contact, she stiffened.

"Don't. Just leave."

"I'm not going anywhere."

Her head tilted up, and he saw her eyes were completely flooded with gold, pupils lost in the flames that swirled. "If you do not leave, I will hurt you. Do you understand?"

It dawned on him that she wasn't holding herself together. She was holding herself back.

He understood too well the feeling of one's mind betraying them. The fight for control, when the thing being fought was oneself, felt like a loss either way. That was even more evident in his mate, who liked to teeter on the edge of madness.

First, he would help her regain control. Then they would talk.

In a smooth motion, without thinking of anything else, he picked Calypso up. The flames scalded his flesh as he carried her away.

"Stop! I'm burning you!"

He held her tighter. "It's only skin. It'll be over soon."

She stopped her struggles, seeing it only burned him more, then said through clenched teeth, "I just need time. I will control it."

She didn't look like she could control her own breathing right now, let alone her consuming flames, but he would not say that.

"Don't control it," he said, finally reaching the edge of the pond he'd seen earlier. "Let it out."

With that, he tossed her into the water. With a splash, she went under and disappeared.

There was a moment of stillness, as if nothing had happened. Then, the water started to simmer. He counted the seconds in his mind and stared as the water absorbed all that she threw at it.

His body twitched with worry when he reached a minute, but the water still boiled from her assault.

When she didn't break the surface at the two-minute mark, he couldn't take it anymore. He dived into the hot water and pushed toward the source.

Her eyes were closed as he wrapped his arms around her and swam up with her swaying limply in his hold.

This was a stupid idea, he thought as panic rammed in.

They broke the surface, and he placed her onto the grass. He examined her body for breathing that wasn't there. He pressed down on her chest, willing it to move, when her eyes flickered open. She turned to her side, hurling up water that was deep in her lungs.

He patted her back as she coughed out the water. After gathering her breath, she turned to glare at him, but her eyes were back to normal. "You almost drowned me!"

"I'm so sorry." He crushed her to his chest. "I didn't know you couldn't swim."

He moved back when her hands pushed at him. He braced for her anger, but she just muttered. "Well, now you know."

They sat near one another, catching their breath, not quite touching. After a few minutes, he spoke. "We need to talk."

"There's nothing to say except you should return to the Vestrahorn mountains."

He growled. "Enough of that. I will stay here with you. Besides, my horde will be here in a day or two."

Calypso's head whipped toward him, eyes wide. This might've been the first time he truly shocked her.

"Are you out of your mind?!" she yelled. "You just got control of your clan and you are bringing them to fight in another war?"

Without waiting for an answer, she jumped up and began pacing, hands tightened into fists. Little flames flickered in annoyance from her feet.

"Take a breath or I'll dunk you in the water again." The comment earned him another glare, but she stopped her pacing. "The responsibility of my clan falls on no one but me. I don't do this just because you are my mate. If you hadn't taken over Taybe, Davinger would be marching to the mountains right now. He doesn't want peace with orcs. He wants to keep us as brutes for his armies. The reality is we are better together."

She still wasn't happy but seemed to simmer down and sat down once more, keeping space between them. He could accept her unhappiness as long as she was safe.

"Tell them to turn around."

"No." His eyes flashed. "You can keep the horde from coming onto the estate, but you can't stop us from going against Davinger."

"You are just risking their lives when it is not needed."

"Not needed because you plan to sacrifice yourself like a martyr?"

"This was always the plan," she snapped back at him. "For years, I planned on ending things like this."

"Is that what you truly want to do?"

"I don't know." A moment passed. "No."

For all her talk of revenge being her only goal, Vidorak suspected she cared deeply for her sisters and would do anything for them, including sacrificing herself. Her plan was fraught with flaws, but she was too stubborn and panicked to see it.

"The royal army is sizeable, but an uncontrollable beast doesn't guarantee a win. Certainly not at the cost of your life." He wasn't sure if his words were getting through to her, but persisted. "We will figure this out together. You cannot fix everything yourself, and you need to let others in."

Much to his surprise, she crawled onto his lap, hands clenching at his wet shirt as if she didn't know whether she wanted him close or to push him away. He felt silent tremors go across her back, and his heart clenched at the feel of her tears. With everything they'd been through, he had never seen her cry. He wished he could shed the tears for her, to take away her pain. While he couldn't do that, he would be here to help heal the wounds that were left.

"My mother was the smartest witch I knew, and even she couldn't stop it."

She sobbed into his chest, and he knew it was more than just the situation at present. It was as if she were mourning things she hadn't allowed herself to do prior. Throughout it all, he petted her back and whispered words of comfort into her hair.

When she finally quieted, her body sagged against him in pure exhaustion. He picked her up and returned to the manor. He gently settled her in bed and wanted nothing more than to join her in her rest so she would know he was nearby. But that wasn't possible at the moment.

He changed his clothes and went downstairs in search of the other witches. They needed to discuss a plan for dealing with the royal army that kept his mate alive.

CHAPTER THIRTY-FOUR

VIDORAK

Thus far only one stabbing had occurred, and it had been by one of his warriors with a carrot in the kitchen. Otherwise, the first few days between the horde and the coven had been a relative success.

"What are the current numbers?" Vidorak asked Nyx, who was presently organizing a set of maps upon the long dining table. They were making do with what they had, so the dining hall was turned into a makeshift war council area.

"Let's see." Nyx flipped through one of her parchments before answering. "We are up to thirty-one witches and sixty-eight orc warriors. Two of yours are in the infirmary after getting in a drunken fight."

Vidorak grunted, "If they can stand, they can fight."

Sentiment among his warriors was mixed. A lot of changes had happened in a short amount of time, and not everyone was taking to it well. Thankfully, his uncle's strongest supporters had either defected or were remaining silent.

The biggest grumblings were about his choice to aid the witches against the Crown and about letting the orcesses return to the horde. Vidorak knew not everyone would support this decision, but he was the one in charge now. The clan would be run how he saw fit, but it wouldn't be in the tyrannical way of his uncle. Those opposed could make their voices heard without severe punishment, but only when it was appropriate.

"Any updates, Grushag?"

"No," the raspy-voiced orc replied.

Grushag was leaning against the wall in the corner, always on the out-skirts of the group even when he was forced to be present.

Vidorak worried about him, and that's why he had chosen him to be in charge of the lateral flank of the horde rather than the charismatic Nazghor. Grushag needed to decide whether he was going to be part of the clan or not. Living it the shadows was no way to live.

Too soon it became evening, and the smell of food permeated the air. An elderly woman named Paola ran the kitchens, and she wasn't shy about directing whoever came into her eyesight. She was currently ordering one of his orc warriors to place a large pot of stew on the table. Given the space, meals were eaten in whatever room was available.

"She said to move it inward or it will spill." One of the orcesses, Nakia, translated for his warrior. About half the clan didn't speak the common tongue, which resulted in occasional difficulties. Nakia, having been the guard for the human women at the mountain, was one of the more advanced speakers.

Satisfied that the warrior was following her direction, Nakia continued marching toward them. "Jarl Grushag, I finished scouting the woods and found an area with good coverage."

The eagerness of the orcesses to fight for the clan reaffirmed to Vidorak that this was the right decision, no matter what some of the dissenting male orcs thought.

"I'm not a jarl," Grushag growled before storming off with her. "Let's go."

Vidorak was discussing things with his warriors, making sure the channels of communication were clear when he felt Calypso nearby.

Even without seeing her, his body was attuned to hers on an invisible level. He felt her when she was close and ached for her when she was absent.

After he finished speaking, she walked up to him and handed him a bowl of food. "You haven't eaten all day."

"Have you?" he asked, waiting to eat until she nodded.

She had little appetite since the lake a few days back. While she hadn't cried again, there was a sullen, quiet air around her. It was as if all her energy had been released at once, and she was empty for a moment.

"I finished the resurrections. Forty in total."

He hadn't been thrilled with her suggestion to resurrect a small army of birds, but she had been adamant in doing so given the royal archers that were arriving with the army.

The bandage around her forearm, where she'd cut herself to perform her black magic, was coming undone, and he put his bowl aside to help re-wrap it. "How are you feeling?"

"Fine." Her answer was unsurprising to him.

Before they could speak further, booming laughter grabbed their attention. Nazghor entered with a wide grin as Astra came in red-faced but smiling.

"I take things went well?" Vidorak asked.

"It went great!" Nazghor responded, just as Astra said, "They stabbed him with a pitchfork."

Vidorak had sent both of them to discuss things with the local human militia. Their forces were negligible, but it was their town that was about to be occupied, and they deserved a seat at the table.

Nazghor shrugged. "They ultimately agreed, didn't they? Their leader, Angus, will be by shortly."

That was good because Vidorak didn't just plan to win; he planned to keep the town for the long haul. He'd meant what he'd said to Calypso—there would be no peace with the Crown while witches faced persecution.

It wasn't just about his feelings toward Calypso, though they did often overtake all his reason, but it was simply self-serving practicality. The nobility's dislike of all magical races meant that one day they would be next as well.

Nazghor's optimism proved correct when, an hour later, a burly man arrived at the estate. Vidorak had to give the man credit for joining, as most wouldn't enter an estate overflowing with orcs.

In addition to the militia leader, his elite warriors, several powerful witches, and the witch who would tend to the injured were present.

Having everyone's attention, Vidorak addressed the room. "On recent accounts, the king regent is less than a day's travel away, accompanied by an army of almost five hundred—a mix of soldiers and archers. He will probably seek to come straight to the estate, where the witches will remain. The horde will be stationed in the woods as three separate units, each with its own leader. There is one magical ward around the town, which will notify us when Davinger arrives, and a second, stronger ward around the manor, which will block airborne attacks. With the coven at the estate and my units attacking from the sides, the aim is to box in Davinger and overwhelm him despite his numbers."

"As for the coven," Astra began, briefly looking at each of the witch leaders. "Nyx will accompany the witches whose strength lies in archery and wind on the balcony. I will join the earthen and fire witches on the grounds. Those whose powers are not yet developed will help Marianna at the infirmary."

"Calypso?" He looked over at his mate.

"I will be where Davinger is, ideally slicing his throat," she commented, previously tired eyes now brimming with golden anger. "Until then, I will be on the balcony with Nyx to lead the birds."

Laid out like that, the plan sounded easy and straightforward, but Vidorak had seen enough war to know nothing ever went according to plan.

"Gemma wants to be stationed in the woods and cast a spell to shroud any sight of the horde," Nyx spoke up, but Vidorak could tell the silver-eyed woman wasn't happy about this.

"I will assign her a guard," he reassured her before turning toward the human militia leader. "Now we must discuss how to protect your people."

"Surely the king regent wouldn't attack the townspeople?" Angus asked, surprise coloring his features.

"It doesn't matter. An army of that size will be destructive, even if they aren't here for you."

That statement sat like that for a beat. The unspoken part being that this was only happening because the coven was there.

"Davinger is capable of anything, even razing the town if it serves him," answered Calypso. "Everyone should evacuate their families to the outskirts of town."

Angus relented in understanding. "We will get everyone out and barricade the businesses in town."

Talk persisted for several more hours after that as they discussed different strategies, trying to anticipate any possibility that Davinger might attempt.

"Okay, now let's run the scenario again if the forces come from the west." Astra concentrated on her maps.

As much as Vidorak wanted to remain and talk through things, Calypso's stifled yawn made him take action.

"You need rest." Vidorak tugged her up gently and knew how correct he was when she didn't resist.

Nyx stood as well. "I am going to bed to look through my spellbook." At Astra's look of betrayal, she added, "We won't stand a chance if we all pass out from exhaustion."

The blonde witch opened her mouth to argue, but Nazghor spoke first.

"Let the others go. I will stay and talk through your scenarios." Nazghor waved them away, looking more than content to stay with Astra.

They walked up the stairs in silence, thoughts heavy with what was to come.

"There is one thing we didn't discuss at the meeting." Vidorak watched her closely, eyeing the ruby amulet she continued to wear. It remained an unspoken barrier between them, each of them insistent on their perspective of the situation.

"Vidorak." She paused, as if deciding what to say next. "I will try not to use it. I *don't* want to use it. But things look dire . . ."

He knew that was the best he was going to get, and he hated that. "I see."

For the first time in days, her lips twitched. "You are thinking of ways to drag me back to the mountain, aren't you?"

He chose not to answer and just opened the door to let them in. They had barely entered the bedchamber when she threw herself at him. Her mouth on his, hands in his hair, tugging him closer. His hold tightened at her waist, and he tried resisting the urge to rub her against his erection.

Regrettably, he pulled back. "You need rest."

She leaned back and bit his lip before running her tongue over it. "I need you inside me."

Lust and yearning warred within him. He gripped her hair and brought her mouth back to his. The fear that he had almost lost her, that he might lose her still, was too raw.

He wanted her so badly it made him lose all sense of reason. She had pulled him from the darkness and given him a taste of love. But she had lied to him as well, lied to her own detriment. And Vidorak still felt angry at her for that.

He gripped her waist and pressed her back against the wall. Her arms went around his neck, and she melted into him, compliantly. He pulled her head back so that he could see her eyes.

"Are you sure, little witch? I don't think I can be gentle."

Her eyes lit up, and she whispered at his lips, "I want you to give me everything."

With a biting kiss, he stepped back, allowing her just an inch of space, then commanded, "Undress."

With the way lust pounded through his veins, if he tried to help her, he'd end up tearing another one of her dresses.

She unbuttoned her dress, eyes not leaving his, and let it pool at her feet. Her naked breasts swayed as she pushed down her undergarments. Her hard nipples grazed his chest when she stood back up.

Then her hands went to his trousers, rubbing down the length of his erection. "Should I undress you too?"

Without waiting for an answer, she undid his trousers, springing free his hard cock. She squeezed him, running her hand over his length twice before he grabbed her wrist and stopped her.

"Turn around."

She complied, turning to face the wall. Hand between her shoulder blades, he pushed to bend her forward. He caressed the curve of her back, relishing the softness.

When he got to her bottom, he gave it a stinging smack, causing her to jump in surprise. He doubted his powerful witch had ever received a spanking.

Caressing where he had spanked her, he leaned to her ear. "Never lie to me again about things that put you at risk."

She actually pouted at that. "I didn't lie. I omitted information that wasn't for you to know."

That was the wrong answer.

He gave another, harder spank to her backside. Then he growled, "Everything that has to do with you is my right to know."

Her eyes widened, and her mouth opened, most likely to argue, but she closed it after a second.

"Good girl," he praised. "Now I want to hear you say it."

She hesitated for one too many seconds, and he gave her another swat.

"Fine. I won't lie to you."

He rubbed her slightly reddened bottom. "Good."

Then he pushed apart her legs and kneeled. He ran his tongue over her glistening sex. She tasted like perfection. She tasted like his.

He licked and sucked at her until she squirmed in his hold. Then he thrust his tongue into her tight core, wanting to swallow every drop of her. He pinched her clit, drawing more moans from her throat. He didn't let up in his ravishing, continuing to lick and rub at her until she was trembling around him.

He didn't give her a second to recover and turned her while her legs were still unsteady. With a smooth motion, he picked her up and pushed her back against the wall as her legs encircled him.

True to what he said earlier, he entered her hard and unapologetically. She gasped at his sudden intrusion but tightened her hold on him. He pounded into her mercilessly, devoid of any control. With each stroke, he poured the emotions of the recent days. The need, the heartache, the anger—all of it. He slammed into her until she was the only thing imprinted on his soul.

When he felt her clench around him, his own release followed, his seed filling her completely. He closed his eyes and caught his breath, still buried deep inside her.

Regrettably, he lifted her off him, then carried her toward her bed. He grabbed a washcloth to clean them both up.

He was wiping her thighs when she grabbed his wrist. Looking up, he found her staring at him with half-lidded eyes.

"I love you, orc. For so long my world only contained anger and pain. Happiness wasn't just a liability, it was an impossibility. But then there you were." Her hands skimmed his face, light as feathers. "You protected me, healed me, loved me. But you know what cut me the most?"

She said the last part quietly, as if she were letting him in on a secret. "You never looked away. No matter what evil, bloody parts of me I showed you. You never looked away." She gave him a slight smile before removing her hand. "The mate bond definitely knows what it is doing."

How she managed to utterly take his breath away at the most unexpected times, he didn't know. Her freely given truth, laced with such vulnerability, was the most precious gift to him.

"My little witch, I didn't fall in love with you because of the bond. I fell in love because you have awakened me. You feel too much, but I spent years feeling nothing. I thought it was what I wanted, but I was a fool. How can I go back to blindness now that I can see? You, my fiercely powerful mate, bring color to my life. There is not a part of you that I am not completely and utterly in love with. Especially your wild and stubborn nature."

Wordlessly, she sat up and touched her lips to his. Their kiss was soft and sweet, cementing the words that had passed between them.

When he got into bed, she curled into him with her head on his chest and their legs intertwined. He couldn't see her eyes, but could tell she was still very much awake. After their conversation, he wasn't sure how easily he would be able to sleep. Their words were sweet, but dangerous circumstances still loomed above them.

He was moving his hand up and down her back when she suddenly reached for her head in pain. Vidorak held her, unsure of how to help, feeling useless while she groaned in pain.

"The town wards," she said with a pained breath. "He's crossed it."

CHAPTER THIRTY-FIVE

CALYPSO

Reality shattered the illusions of their planning and preparation. An alarm bell rang through the estate, warning them of the oncoming army.

Accustomed to warfare, Vidorak sprung into action, commanding his orcs with practiced ease. He wore metal plates on his shoulders and leather wraps on his hands and wrists. His axe was strapped to his back and his daggers secured at his hip. He remained bare-chested rather than get bogged down by additional heavy armor.

His appearance was a weapon in itself. With his looming height, muscular strength, and hard expression on his face, he was every bit a vicious orc that sparked nightmares.

She worried about the repercussions of his help, but was also incredibly grateful for his presence.

Even while shouting commands, Vidorak did not forget to pull her into a crushing kiss. "Stay safe, my love."

"You too," she answered, gripping the dagger that he'd pushed into her hand.

Without further delay, she rushed to the open balcony off the highest floor. Here, the air witches could manipulate their magic with line of sight of the approaching troops. With her bow at her back, Nyx directed the women. Above them, the moon was in full glow, as if it had come out to witness this event.

Having readied the witches, Nyx came to stand by Calypso, their shoulders just grazing a touch. Familiar with her sister, that touch was not an accident but a gesture of comfort.

"Any regrets?" Calypso asked her silver-eyed sister. She knew Nyx burned with a need to kill Ker Beck, and by confronting Davinger now, there was a risk that she would never get that chance.

That thought suffocated Calypso, and she couldn't fully form her question.

But Nyx knew what she referred to. "I would never regret the chance of ending an evil man." Her eyes softened a fraction when she turned toward Calypso. "I meant what I said. Ker Beck will die by my hand. This changes nothing, it's simply an unexpected delay."

So strange, seeing her stoic and pragmatic sister be the overconfident one. Instead of certainty, Calypso sensed impending doom. Not for her, she'd made peace with her death long ago, but for all the others that had gathered to fight this war. Part of her considered ripping out the amulet and completing the second part of the spell, unleashing the dragon at Davinger's army.

But she had promised to trust in their plan, so instead she asked, "Is everything in place?"

"Somehow, yes. The orcs are safely veiled in the woods. Astra is on the grounds with the earthen witches."

"Now we wait."

Like a rising wave, the royal soldiers appeared in the distance, marching ever closer. It took her breath to see exactly how much space such an army took. Even if they didn't attack the town, the destruction caused by their presence alone would demolish it.

Once in view, Nyx quietly commanded, "Release the first wave of arrows."

Without any hesitation, the witches released a string of arrows, guided by air magic into the first line of soldiers. Most hit, but it was a drop in the bucket of how many were here.

The soldiers released their own barrage of arrows, but they all fell uselessly once they hit the dome of magical protection around the manor.

Calypso sighed with relief, seeing that the barrier was working.

"Again," Nyx commanded.

Another set of arrows flew, but this time the soldiers were prepared and blocked with metal shields. Less died.

The soldiers moved as one, shields high, closer toward the dome, only to find it physically prevented them from entering.

There was a brief pause as they awaited their next set of orders. Nyx held off on shooting more arrows, not wanting to waste what they had.

A dark caravan pushed its way toward the front of the line, and a hooded figure emerged. The face remained hidden, but Calypso sensed it was Davinger. The irrational, bloodthirsty part of her wanted to rush at him, bypassing all the other pesky parts of the battle.

Davinger stepped up to the magic dome and put out a hand to caress it. The protective barrier shattered in an instant, crumbling away into the night faster than they'd ever anticipated.

Blocked no longer, the royal archers raised their bows and let loose a string of arrows. Some aimed for the balcony, intending to take lives. Others were lit with fire and aimed at the fields, intending to cause destruction.

One of the air witches chanted an incantation, which summoned a slicing gale to deflect the arrows as they fell.

Calypso opened her palms, feeling the tug of each resurrected bird vibrate upon her skin. Gaze fixed on the royal army, she commanded, "Take their eyes."

Flocks of undead birds rose behind her and ascended upon the army like daggers. Confusion rippled through the army, and then cries pierced the air as beaks and claws tore at the soldiers.

The army's arrows changed course, and instead of aiming for the manor, they aimed for the birds. One by one, her winged troops dropped to the ground. Each sacrifice from her undead army caused a slicing pain through her body. Calypso had reanimated each of the creatures and felt every connection as it severed.

The advantage they had given them was brief, but enough to allow time for the orcs to descend upon the army from the woods.

Like dark beasts emerging from the depths of hell, they came at the soldiers in a rage. From the balcony, she could see the size difference, and even their royal training would not be enough to ease the fear of that sight.

The water witches called upon their magic to quell the fire spreading toward the manor. Astra and her earthen witches charged from the front. Grasping roots sprang from the ground, tripping and shackling the soldiers.

For a moment, it seemed things were in their favor. But that hope was incredibly short-lived. Even with their magic and strength, the overwhelming force of their numbers was drowning them. For every kill, multiple soldiers took their place. One orc would fight three or four soldiers at a time. There was never a breath of reprieve. Only attack after attack.

Seeing the scene from above, Calypso realized a hard truth.

They would die. They would all die.

Vidorak

The army was so great that the outer flanks were in the fields and the back lines weren't even on the estate property. Dread sank deep within him, knowing this night would end in a slaughter. Ironically enough, his uncle would've loved such an event, though he never would've agreed to fight alongside others during it.

Vidorak saw a robed figure step out of the caravan at the front and walk up to the magical barrier Astra had placed. With a brief touch, the entire magical dome shattered into nothing. Although Vidorak didn't expect this would be easy, witnessing the mage's power highlighted the gravity of their situation.

Unhindered, the hooded figure barked out a command and disappeared into his caravan. The archers drew back their bows and let loose a spray of arrows. Chaos spread as magical winds pushed the arrows aside and resurrected birds descended in attack.

His body was primed, ready to rush the grounds, but Vidorak controlled himself and let the smoke from the grass fires build. Their orc eyesight could overcome it, and it would only serve as an advantage.

The air became hazy with smoke, shrouding the estate in a thick cloud. Most of the troops were now on the grounds, approaching the manor.

"Now!" Vidorak bellowed and rampaged forward, his warriors close behind.

The second unit would follow from across the way, and the third would go around back, picking off the soldiers from behind. That group faced the greatest risk of becoming isolated from help, but it was necessary to overcome the significant numbers advantage the Crown held.

He swung his axe brutally at the soldiers in front, taking two down with just a single swing. He fought like a beast unleashed, roaring through the spray of blood. If it weren't for the bond keeping him somewhat sane, he would've sworn this was berserker frenzy.

Even on the goriest of days, he'd never caused bloodshed such as this. He fought as if their very existence depended on it, because it did.

From a distance, he saw the earthen witches on the grounds getting overwhelmed and pushed through the soldiers, chopping limbs and spines as he went. Before he could reach them, a group of five soldiers surrounded him.

The initial confusion was over, and the soldiers now realized orcs were in their midst. They changed strategy, attacking in groups.

"Don't be intimidated by his size! He can't do anything if we all attack at once," one soldier yelled. The royal army didn't hold back regarding the quality of its armor. The soldiers wore chain-mail protecting their chests and vital organs, sturdy iron helmets, and their metal gauntlets gripped undamaged swords.

The northern guard had worn less armor, but they were more practiced from Captain Von Ahlen's training and the repeated battles with Urim throughout the years. Although the royal army had received expert training, most of the soldiers had yet to see deployment. For all their sturdy armor, there was no accounting for experience and knowledge of exactly where the weak points of these protections lay.

Before they could decide what sort of attack to conduct, Vidorak sprang forward, grabbing the heads of two soldiers with his large hands and slamming them together. They crumbled to the ground before even realizing what had happened.

He kicked at the chest of a soldier coming at him, sending him flying back. The remaining two charged with their swords forward. One sword bounced off his metal shoulder plate while the other managed to slice his forearm.

The soldier who had struck had been the largest of the group and quickly maneuvered to face him again. The man was unwavering and charged without fear.

Vidorak grabbed the other soldier and spun him to his front, using him like a shield. The other soldier was forced to adjust his attack, looking for another openings to strike at Vidorak.

In the distance, he could see Astra struggling to hold her own. She struck with spiked branches from the ground but was shaky on her feet as blood dripped from the side of her head.

Not wasting any time, Vidorak grabbed his dagger and plunged it into the exposed area of the soldier's neck, then shoved him toward the other soldier.

As they crashed onto the ground, Vidorak headed toward the blonde witch. He got only several steps ahead when another group of fighters surrounded him.

"Got you now!" The shout came from the soldier who was fighting Astra, his hands around her neck.

Vidorak growled at the delay, sensing the noose closing around them. Did he use his axe to smash through the enemies in front, or did he hurl it toward the man choking Astra?

Just as he reached for his axe to send it flying, Nazghor barreled into the soldier holding the witch. He beat the soldier's face with his bare fists. The soldier's helmet bent from the impact, and Nazghor didn't stop even as his fists bled.

With that, Vidorak was able to handle the group in front of him easily. Momentarily, he felt things might swing in their favor.

But then the ground shook, and he heard the familiar growl of demon hounds. They sprang from the earth like the undead creatures they were and charged into the fray, their red eyes glowing ominously.

The salt traps that the witches had placed captured a few, but Davinger had released so many that it didn't make a difference.

"Decapitate them!" Vidorak bellowed in reminder as his warriors brutally slashed at the demons, only to find them still attacking.

A sick realization set in as the tide turned. As strong as his horde was, this was a massive disadvantage, one that they wouldn't overcome even with magic.

This was a scenario that he knew was possible and had planned for. May his mate forgive him, but he could not stay and watch her burn with them all. He had spoken with Grushag privately and told him that if they were losing, Grushag was to knock Calypso out and flee with her in tow.

Vidorak planned to stay and die with the rest of his horde and the witches. As deceitful and selfish as it was, his bond would not permit him to so easily accept her death.

In a sudden explosion of fire, his mate hurled from the air onto the grounds. She landed several paces away with a sickening thud, and he feared she had become injured. But she stood without difficulty, her eyes completely flooded in that golden glow when she was at her maddest.

Chapter Thirty-Six

CALYPSO

Everything degraded into flashes of horror. Snarls radiated around her, and the smell of rotten flesh permeated the air. She slid on blackened blood that soaked the ground as the demon hounds persisted in their assault. Nearby, a witch's scream abruptly cut short as the hound mauled her neck.

Gold flooded Calypso's eyes as she went to that place of bloodlust and rage. She became a creature of fire, incinerating the hounds. Truthfully, she was no different from the beasts in this state.

Her fire struck at every threat, hound or human. Burning flesh stung her nostrils, and streams of blood blocked her vision. She felt no remorse for taking the lives of the soldiers. She would do it repeatedly until death finally satiated the darkest part of her soul.

One of the demon hounds slammed into her from the side, knocking her to the ground. She held it back as it snapped its maw above her, its enormous jaw containing multiple rows of sharp teeth. She was struggling to get the upper hand when an arrow pierced the demon's skull, ending its awareness. Black substance coated Calypso's fallen body as the creature disintegrated.

Seeing the arrow, she looked back at the manor to find it burning faster than the water witches could stop it. Nyx was now the only witch on the balcony, shooting arrows at an unbelievable speed.

Calypso searched the chaos for Astra, finding her alive but in an equally precarious position. Then her eyes found her mate. Vidorak was slicing through the soldiers, but so many kept flooding relentlessly.

This was her limit. She was certain that if the situation continued, they would all perish. There was no guarantee that the amulet would save them, but she needed to try.

Calypso snapped the amulet off her neck in a savage pull. Her grip was so tight the ruby dug into her palm, and without further hesitation, she spoke the words she had memorized long ago.

The amulet awakened, glowing with her lifeblood, and waiting for the final part of the spell.

Nails at her left eye, she braced to claw out her organ when a slice of pain tore through her other hand. She dropped the amulet, and in its place was embedded a throwing knife.

"Very close, Calypso," reverberated the low voice of her enemy.

She looked up to see Davinger stride forward and pick up the amulet. He stood tall and self-assured in his long charcoal-colored robe. While he had lost weight since she last saw him, the strong features of his face remained. His hair was still that distinctive icy blond, but his perceptive dark blue eyes now looked almost black.

"Nice of you to spare me the trouble of hunting you down," Calypso said as she yanked out the knife from her hand.

"It's amusing that you think you have influenced anything that's occurred," Davinger talked down to her. "I have known everything you've done since fleeing the capital."

"I'm flattered by your interest." Her response was dry as she assessed him. "Though I would've preferred to end this years ago."

"You are a great bloodhound, and I needed you to bring me the Eye of Azara." He slipped the ruby amulet over his neck. "Part of me is tempted to chain you and keep you in my court."

She laughed at his threat. "You learn how to cast a couple of spells and all the sudden you think you are unbeatable. I am made of magic, just like my mother. Your magic is child's play compared to ours."

"Seraphina never opened her eyes to what her magic could become. I'm glad to see you are not of the same opinion." He slipped off his robe and revealed the dozens of runes embedded in his arms and chest. The inky marks of black magic swirled upon his body, similar to hers. The mutilation he'd done to himself staggered her.

Sick at the sight and at the knowledge she had done similar, she blasted a ball of fire at him, which he easily avoided.

"Why?" Calypso yelled. "Why kill her after all she did to help you?"

"I do whatever I want because I *can*," he spat out the last part. "The runes revealed who I truly am. And no one, especially not Seraphina Galanis, was going to stop me."

The confirmation of what she had suspected brought no comfort to Calypso. Instead, the tragedy of knowing her dear mother's life had been the price of his lust for power, caused a sharp pain in her chest.

She had nothing else to say to him, had no desire to hear him speak any further. All she desired was his death. Flames swirled up her arms like snakes, and she rushed at him.

Rage consumed her as she lashed out at Davinger, striking in any way she could. He met her blow for blow, his magic sending tendrils of shock up her arms. Pain shook her body, but she didn't dare stop.

Davinger swept her leg, knocking her to the ground, then stomped her chest, keeping her pinned. No matter how much fire she sent his way, his skin remained unharmed, shielded by the runes.

"I expected more from the mad witch." He took out a blade. "Pity."

Before he could stab her, a gust of wind suddenly sent Davinger flying back. Astra rushed over, helping her stand up. Calypso saw Nyx approach, sweat over her face as she focused in the direction she'd sent Davinger.

"I cannot hold him for long," Nyx said through gritted teeth.

"He has the amulet," Calypso told them. "Go before he returns."

"You should know better than to ask that," Astra responded, and Nyx gave her a hard look.

There was no further discussion to be had. Loving her sisters meant not only keeping them safe but trusting them to keep her safe as well. Calypso's attempts to separate them from her hardships had only brought them all more pain.

Too soon, Davinger returned, flanked by two large soldiers. She caught the unmistakable red glow in the soldier's eyes. Despite her use of black magic, the idea of reanimating a human repulsed her.

"It's nice to see you again, Astra." Davinger's eyes held a longing gaze toward her sister.

Astra stiffened by her side, though remained unwavering in her stance. Calypso rushed at him simply to take his covetous stare away from her.

Nyx and Astra jumped into action, focusing on the undead soldiers at his side. Astra dug her fingers into the earth, sending poisonous vines to wrap around one of the soldiers. He slashed himself free, but not before Nyx sent two arrows into his red eyes. Blinded, the soldier collapsed to the ground and became trapped in the quicksand Astra conjured.

"Be careful!" Calypso called out toward Nyx as the other undead soldier lunged in her direction.

He attacked Nyx with unforgiving swings of his sword. She defended, but her body became peppered with bloody slashes, her pale skin staining red. The soldier kicked her chest, sending her tumbling onto her back.

Calypso encased the soldier in flames, heating the metal until it glowed yellow-white. The soldier's movements became sluggish as she incinerated him inside his own armor. Within seconds he slowed to a stop.

Despite her wounds, Nyx moved without pain as she stood from the ground. Her gaze filled with terror as she focused behind Calypso. Nyx swiftly nocked a fresh arrow to her bow, aiming with unwavering concentration. Calypso turned to find out what had frightened her sister.

"Astra, I could have given you everything," Davinger snarled as he held Astra by her throat. "We could've *been* everything, but you denied me."

Astra clawed at his hand as she went pale.

"Nyx, guide me," Calypso yelled out, trusting her friend understood her meaning as she unleashed her fire. His skin may not burn, but that didn't mean his insides were safe. Nyx aided the stream of fire into Davinger's nostrils, attempting to burn him from the inside out.

That worked, and he released Astra, sending her crashing to the ground. Davinger yelled in pain and stumbled backward, disappearing behind a shield of his soldiers.

Nyx and Calypso rushed to help Astra, but she put up a hand and coughed. "I'm fine. He will return soon."

Staring in the direction Davinger hid behind his guard, Calypso shouted, "Give it up. We both know you'd never sacrifice yourself to use the amulet."

"You are correct."

The soldiers parted to reveal a young man being dragged over to Davinger. It took Calypso a moment to place him, as she hadn't laid eyes on Prince Isaac in ten years.

Davinger's hand gently caressed the prince's face before tugging his hair back harshly.

"What are you doing?" Calypso's voice was laced with disbelief at the sight before her.

"You've done such a marvelous job of infusing the amulet, it'd be a pity not to use it. All it requires is the last step after all." With a swift jab of his knife, he carved out Prince Isaac's eye and slammed the ruby inside.

The prince collapsed, his body shaking so severely she couldn't imagine it'd end in anything other than death. After what felt like an eternity, the shaking subsided, and he stilled. Then, like an illusion, his skin began to ripple. Limbs stretched and grew scales, slowly at first, then they picked up speed.

Horror seeped into her heart as what was once a human body transformed like molded clay. The transition wasn't beautiful, but was uneven and scattered. One side held the start of a wing, while the other was still a fully formed human hand. Scales were plastered on haphazardly, shining like emeralds. Sharp predator teeth grew from a jaw that hadn't caught up in enlarging.

Her stomach heaved when she saw him move, trying to make sense of what was happening. Compared to this, death would be a mercy.

Terror overtook his features, and he thrashed around. Nothing calmed him, as he was blind and deaf to the world. His panic seemed to slow the transition, and Prince Isaac was stuck in this grotesque form between human and beast.

"Transform!" bellowed Davinger, and a shock spread through the prince's body. He completely stilled, not of his own accord, but ordered by something magical. The transition sped up, faster than before, more painful than before.

The excruciation human scream from the prince morphed into a dragon's roar that shook the ground. The dragon was the size of the manor, its wingspan so great it blocked the light of the moon. All fighting halted as everyone took in the ancient monster before them. It seemed impossible that anyone could conquer such a creature, let alone rid all of its kind from the realm.

As everyone watched the dragon, Calypso looked over to see Davinger's bright eyes manically take in his new pet. The runes over his heart glowed eerily.

If the runes were protecting Davinger, then Calypso needed to relinquish him of them. Without further thought, she rushed at him and dug her sharp nails around the glowing rune at the center of his chest. Hearing the squelch of his tissue tearing was satisfying, and she persisted even as her arm throbbed in pain.

Rune grasped, she tore it from his body. Davinger screamed, clutching at the gash on his chest, which exposed the muscles and bones beneath.

Connection severed, the dragon unleashed a fiery breath across the army, triggering a cacophony of cries and sending the soldiers fleeing. Then, the dragon took off into the sky and disappeared behind the clouds.

"How dare you!" Davinger screamed and made to come at her but stumbled. "Soldiers, retreat!"

Immediately, a group of soldiers closed around Davinger, and what remained of his army began to withdraw from the grounds.

"We need to go after him," Calypso told Astra and Nyx. "We may not get another chance."

Nyx responded, but Calypso couldn't make out what she said. Everything became blurry, and pain blossomed in her abdomen. She looked down to see her dress soaked in blood.

The last thing she heard as she crumbled to the ground was her mate's savage roar.

CHAPTER THIRTY-SEVEN

CALYPSO

The afterlife smelled of rosemary and lemon. Her nose twitched at the potent scent. How strange that even in death she had a sense of her body parts. She always thought death would be an endless void, without emotion or sensation, not a place where she could breathe or feel the need to urinate.

She frowned. That couldn't be right. Her bladder felt very full, and she needed to relieve herself immensely.

As she opened her eyes, searing bright light flooded in, prompting a headache. She blinked a few times, adjusting to the sudden and confusing pull to reality.

Ignoring her protesting muscles, she frantically scanned the room. "Vidorak?"

Her orc mate was nowhere to be found. Instead, she saw she was in the infirmary surrounded by buckets filled to the brim with rosemary and lemons. It was such an odd sight that it made her question whether she was actually awake.

"You're awake," Marianna answered her unspoken question. She stepped away from the workbench, putting down the tincture she had been holding. "And the orc chieftain is alive."

The relief that flooded her was overwhelming. As was the pressure from her bladder.

"Chamber pot." The words came out raspy from her dry throat.

Without hesitation, Marianna helped her to the washroom connected to the infirmary. Once she had completed her business, the medicinal witch led her back to the bed with a strength that was surprisingly sturdy for her short stature.

Marianna handed her a glass of water, which she quickly drank to ease her dry throat. Then Calypso raised a questioning eyebrow at the scene around the room.

Catching her meaning, Marianna explained, "Rosemary and lemon help to bring back those in deep slumber. They are not in season here, so the orc chieftain traveled south to gather this."

"Where is he now?" Even though she knew he was alive, she needed to see for herself.

"In town with his clan." Marianna handed her a bowl of porridge and then sat on the edge of the bed. "He wasn't happy to leave your side, but there were pressing matters to address."

Before she could eat, Calypso needed to know the answer to her burning question. "How many died?"

Marianna hesitated but then answered, "Eleven witches and six orcs died. More than a dozen were injured but have since recovered. You have been unresponsive for a fortnight."

They lost almost a third of the witches who had put their trust in them. They'd fought for change, but whether that goal was achieved was something she felt too scared to ask.

Recalling her injury, she touched her abdomen and felt a dull ache.

"The wound has healed, but it took some time because his dagger was tipped with poison," Marianna explained.

Having had a taste of food, her body remembered it hadn't eaten in days and demanded she stuff herself.

"Slow down!" Marianna put out a hand. "You'll get sick eating so fast. Pause while I get Nyx and Astra. They'll have my head if I don't tell them you've awakened."

Memories from the battle flashed in her mind in a disjointed and jagged manner. One thing she recalled clearly was the end with Davinger and the dragon. It was difficult to accept what had occurred to Prince Isaac. He may be a royal, but he was also a victim of Davinger's political ambitions.

The door swung open, and her sisters ran in. Astra burst inside and threw herself onto the bed while Nyx strolled swiftly behind her.

"Not happy to see me?" Calypso teased her silver-eyed sister.

"I am still furious with you for jumping off the balcony. You could have broken your legs."

Seeing the demon hounds slaughter their troops had enraged Calypso to the point where she'd jumped from the balcony after instructing Nyx to blunt her fall with her wind magic.

Calypso chuckled. "I have full faith in your abilities."

Nyx was not amused and remained stiff-backed at the foot of the bed. "You forced me to remember a spell I hadn't chanted in years."

"I am glad there's at least one person who isn't furious with me." Calypso looked at Astra, who was embracing her tightly.

"I was angry for a week, but then it turned to worry. Then back to anger. Lucky for you, I went back to worry yesterday." After another squeeze, she let go. "You are insane, but I am glad you are alive."

"I am too." Nyx relaxed her pose and came over to give her own light embrace. "If for no other reason than Astra and your orc will stop sniping at each other."

"Is there trouble between you and Vidorak?"

"They were competing to see who could hover over you more. Marianna banned them both for a few days until she took pity upon Vidorak's despondent appearance."

Her heart squeezed thinking about what he must've gone through. She was sure that in his place she'd be just as distraught and likely very destructive.

"I want to see him." Calypso suddenly felt an overwhelming need to lay eyes on him.

"He should be back soon. I told Marianna to send a messenger to fetch him," Astra said while pushing the bowl of porridge back into her hands. "Now eat."

"Only if you talk." Her stomach growled, exposing the lie. "Tell me what happened after I lost consciousness."

"The prince's fire devastated the royal army," Astra began. "I think he was trying to help us before flying off."

Nyx shook her head in disagreement. "I saw the eyes. There was no prince anymore. It was all dragon."

From Astra's stiff posture, Calypso could tell she didn't agree with that assessment. "Regardless, what remained of the army retreated quickly after that. Davinger has been in hiding since. It is possible he succumbed to his wounds."

That would be too good to be true. While Calypso had certainly damaged him severely by ripping out his rune, she didn't doubt he was alive and planning his next move.

"And the royal court? Who sits on the throne with the prince and regent king gone?"

"A coalition has formed between the top noble families while the incident is investigated. They call themselves the Shalimar Alliance," Nyx answered. "We are still waiting for our sources at the court to write back. Information has been slow, unsurprisingly."

Her mind was spinning as she considered the implications of this. The nobility likely had their own agenda that they could now put into action without the king's oversight. Perhaps that could be to their advantage, but they would need to act fast.

"If they can form an alliance, so can we. The Witch-Orc Alliance of the North." Calypso liked the sound of that. "There will be no persecution of witchkind in this district. Or of any other magical races."

"There will be plenty of time to discuss that after you rest," Astra said, but her eyes were bright with agreement.

"I've rested plenty. It's vital we speak the truth before the nobility spreads their own version."

Before she could speak further, the door slammed open, and Vidorak rushed in, his dark eyes immediately finding hers. He stared in disbelief that she was actually awake.

"We should go," Nyx said softly, and she and Astra stood. They embraced Calypso once more before leaving.

His eyes never left hers as he approached, crouching by the side of the bed and placing his hand on her cheek. "You are truly awake."

From the dark circles under his eyes and his loose, unbraided hair, she could tell that he was exhausted. Between her and the responsibilities of his clan, he was running himself into the ground. Unable to resist touching him, she ran her fingers through his silky black hair.

"I owe it all to your collection." She indicated toward the buckets of rosemary and lemons. "When was the last time you slept?"

He grunted, "There will be time for that. Too many things need done."

"Marianna mentioned you were in town. Is everything okay?"

He gathered her up in his arms and laid behind her in the bed. The furniture wasn't made to hold his large frame, let alone both of them, but she wouldn't have it any other way. "The army destroyed several town businesses, and the clan is helping to rebuild."

She looked at him incredulously. "Your orcs were agreeable to that?"

"The objectors came around when we also added several future orc homes," he said with a mischievous grin.

"That is the plan? To move the clan to Taybe?" she asked, resting her head on his chest.

"It will not be a fast move, but I would like to work on it."

Her mate may have challenged Urim from a sense of responsibility to his clan, but he was always meant to be a leader. He'd barely held the role of chieftain and already accomplished more for the clan than his uncle had in years.

"It's what your father wanted." She wondered if perhaps the past attempt at a colony worried him.

"It is what's best for the clan. We can't stay at the mountain forever."

She was in awe of her mate and his ability to build toward a future. For so long, her view of the future was quite narrow. Nothing else had mattered outside of the pact.

"Davinger is still alive." She felt him stiffen at her words.

For the first time, that statement didn't make her want to track him down and peel his skin off. Oh, she still wished for his demise and planned on being there to see it happen. But she also wished to stay here with her sisters and her mate. She wanted to help Vidorak establish a new orc colony out of the mountains, to formalize the Witch-Orc Alliance, and to make this an actual sanctuary for witchkind.

She put her hand on his cheek reassuringly. "I won't stop seeking to avenge my mother, but you've helped me see I could do more. I plan to petition to lift Davinger's decree and reinstate the first coven."

"We will do it together." His voice softened before becoming strict again. "Now, your only task is to heal. The problems can wait once you are strong enough to leave the bed."

She hated to admit it, but he was right. "Fine. Though as long as you're in bed with me, my incentive to leave is low."

He chuckled and continued to massage her arms and shoulders. She wanted to say so much more, but the movement was so soothing that she eventually fell asleep.

The next several days were spent primarily in bed, though not in the way Calypso would've preferred. Between Vidorak and her sisters, she was being fussed over like a helpless chicken. On the third day, she snuck into the gardens to help replant and feel productive again. The task exhausted her, and she earned an extensive scolding from Vidorak, who insisted on carrying her back to the infirmary.

It wasn't the smartest decision to hurry her healing, but she was impatient to progress toward their goals. They had written up a petition to retract the decree, but there were already reports the Shalimar Alliance would blame their illegal coven on the prince's disappearance.

When Nyx came to the evening meal with a proposal, Calypso saw she wasn't the only impatient one.

"I want to go to the capital in disguise."

"No," Astra shut that down immediately.

Nyx glared and continued. "Messages aren't going through. There is clearly a block of some sort, and we need information on the alliance."

"It is too dangerous. If you become stuck, we may not even know or be able to help you."

"It is more dangerous to allow the Alliance to spread lies. We cannot afford to lose the opportunity to make our case known."

Calypso understood her point, but sensed something else. "Is that all?"

Nyx hesitated, catching her meaning. "Yes, but if I get a chance at Ker Beck, I will take it."

Astra unhappily relented. "You need to send word every week or I will go after you."

In the following days, Nyx readied and left with Gemma. Despite her worry, Astra's attention was busy with the influx of witches coming to the stronghold seeking refuge. Calypso thought the recent fight would've scared them away, but many saw it as a sign of strength. The manor was overflowing before, but now was impossible to house so many.

"We need to return to the Vestrahorn mountain," Calypso told Vidorak during one of their afternoon walks.

"I can do my work from here," he reassured her, but she was aware of how much he'd sacrificed to be with her.

She shook her head. "I am grateful for your support, but you've spent more days out of the mountain than in it as chieftain." Then she added, "Besides, we have a mating ceremony to complete."

"Don't tease me, little witch." His eyes searched hers for confirmation, and she noticed the joy reflected there.

Smiling widely, she jumped into his arms. "I wouldn't dare."

They informed the others and, not long after, set out to return to the mountain. She wasn't naïve to think things between them would always be simple, but she was certain that he was worth the effort. They would figure out what their happiness would look like for them. For once, Calypso would choose happiness over revenge.

CALYPSO

"We don't have to do this," her mate grumbled. He'd been in a foul mood since the start of the festivities.

"Why not? Don't you want to show off your attractive mate?" Calypso teased him.

His eyes blazed. "I have changed my mind. We are canceling the ceremony at the lake. Rhunga can say the prayers in the throne room instead. Where we will be fully clothed."

"You can't do that. It is tradition."

"I am the chieftain. I decide what is tradition."

Calypso grinned at her adorably possessive mate before leaving comforting kisses along his jaw. "That's too bad. I was looking forward to showing off my wonderful, sexy mate and how well he touches me."

After a few more kisses, he relented. "We can proceed. Though I can't promise not to snarl at anyone staring too close at you."

She shook her head, amused. "Okay, now leave. You are not supposed to be here."

"I am supposed to be wherever you are."

With another kiss and swat on her behind, her fearsome mate retreated from the room. Now that his anxieties were quelled, and she was finally alone, Calypso took out the dress she'd brought with her to the mountain. The dress shimmered like a diamond and flowed smoothly over her body.

"Ow!" She faced the crow tugging her hair for attention. "What do you want?"

The undead crow dropped a pearl hairpin into her hand. The bird continued to bewilder her, but she was growing quite fond of it. It acted unlike any other resurrected creature and had survived far longer than normal.

"Thank you." She pinned a loose lock of hair back.

Observing herself in the mirror, Calypso realized she was smiling. This newfound sense of happiness had become her norm over the past several weeks.

Things were far from over. Davinger was still in hiding, licking his wounds, and biding his time like the snake he was. The Shalimar Alliance was still an unpredictable entity. There were also no further sightings of the dragon.

While problems remained, there was a steady comfort in knowing she would face whatever came with her family by her side. It wasn't just about building a future where they could survive, but one in which they could prosper.

Satisfied with the final touches, Calypso left her chambers and found Mor waiting nearby.

"You look beautiful," Mor said, looking her over. "I wanted to give you something before the ceremony."

Calypso took the bundle Mor handed her and carefully removed the cloth, seeing the shine of a dagger underneath.

"It is customary to give a gift to the new couple. I made it, though normally Ushnar would have forged this."

Calypso ran her thumb over Vidorak's family crest on the handle. "Thank you so much."

"Turn it around."

On the other side were etched the familiar alchemical signs for mercury and fire.

"Those were your mother's marks, weren't they?"

The truth was, her mother held two alchemical marks. Everyone knew of her mark for fire, but the one for mercury, which had given her the ability to sway, had been a secret.

"How did you know?" Calypso asked, overwhelmed with emotion.

"I met your mother many years ago," Mor said with a smile. "She was pregnant with you at the time and traveled in secret. Ushnar had just become chieftain, and she came to meet us. She encouraged him about the settlements, though that didn't happen until a few years later."

Her mother had often traveled the realm in an effort to build relationships with the different magical communities. Calypso had childhood memories of these visits, but they had lessened as she'd grown older.

"This means a lot." She never got to have a keepsake of her mother after fleeing Sanograd.

"It was a brief meeting, but I remember her being genuine and kind," Mor gently said. "I believe she would be happy her daughter found a mate."

Calypso blinked back tears. "Excuse me for a moment."

Upon reentering the bedchamber to store the dagger, Calypso saw a familiar face in the corner. It was the clear image of her mother, red hair pinned back in a bun, eyes warm and radiating love. Even after everything, the hallucinations and voices persisted but became less frequent. Instead of the typical gruesome scene, her mother appeared at peace.

"You would have liked him, Mother," Calypso whispered before composing herself and returning to the hallway.

Mor took her hand, and together they traversed the tunnels toward the lake. The northernmost mountain range formed the basin of the sacred lake and was accessible only through a single tunnel. The travel took over an hour, and she passed many clan members heading to witness the ceremony. No one complained about traversing the steep tunnel and instead, walked along merrily singing or engrossed in excited conversation. The celebrations had begun earlier in the day, and a good number of the clan had already indulged in the mead.

"How does it feel to see your son become chieftain?" Calypso asked the women, not having had much of a chance to speak in all the events of late.

"It is a mix of pride and worry. Chieftain is not an easy position to hold, and I see how seriously he takes it." Mor wore a solemn look on her face. "But I see happiness in him as well, something I thought he'd lost long ago."

"I want to help him keep that." She truly meant that. Her mate may claim that she had opened his eyes, but he had done exact same to her. He deserved so much happiness and love and she aimed to give that to him. Along with some frustration, but she had a feeling he enjoyed that too.

They exited the tunnels onto the flat basin to see that most of the clan had gathered. The mountain peaks surrounding the basin resembled stone giants, shielding them from the rest of the realm. The lake sat in the middle of the basin, and the water shimmered an iridescent blue-green beneath the moonlight glow.

She understood why the clan considered it sacred and had embarked on the journey without complaint.

As they approached the water, Mor stopped and faced her. "With all the ugliness of our world, you two have found each other and made it more beautiful. I am thrilled for you both." Mor gave her hands a squeeze before letting go. "I will stay for Rhunga's prayer, but then I will leave. The rest a mother doesn't need to see."

With that, Mor went to join the crowd and left Calypso to take the final steps alone. Across the way, the crowd cleared, and she saw her mate step forward. His long black hair flowed down his back in a braid. His chest was bare, showing off his achingly delicious ropes of muscle. She wondered if she'd ever stop feeling that rush of heat whenever her eyes landed on him.

The comforting tug in her chest, which she attributed to the bond, reminded her she wasn't alone. Eagerly, she stepped into the lake and felt the tingle of magic within the waters. She was happy to do his Orcish ceremony, but knowing magic flowed through here too made the connection even deeper.

Vidorak's eyes didn't leave hers as they closed the distance, stopping an arm's reach away. Rhunga stood at the edge of the lake, his hair full of beads and chest colored in paint.

"You come together as individuals, but you leave the springs as one, forever bound." He handed each of them a thin golden bracelet. "Once the bracelet is clasped, it cannot be removed."

Calypso reached for Vidorak first, closing the golden bracelet around his left wrist, feeling the final click as the circle became whole.

He took her wrist but didn't put it on right away. His thumb rubbed the inside of her wrist, and he asked, "Are you sure?"

She knew he was hesitant given their history with the shackles. "It seems apt in a way. It's how we started things after all."

He searched her eyes for another moment before slipping it on her and clicking it closed. A slight shock went up her wrist, and she ran her fingers over the new lifelong jewelry. Luckily, gold happened to be her color.

Satisfied with how they had completed their task, Rhunga switched to speaking in Orcish. Calypso recognized a few words Vidorak had taught her, but mostly she just looked into her mate's dark eyes and followed the timber of the shaman's voice.

After a couple of minutes, Rhunga stopped and nodded. "It is done."

Without any further flair, he grunted and walked away.

"That's it?" she asked, feeling the whole thing seemed a bit anticlimactic.

"That's it for the prayer." Vidorak tugged her forward, bringing her chest to his. His lips went to her ear, sending shivers down her spine. "Are you sure you want to do this? I can kick everyone out right now."

"Shut up and take me, my orc," Calypso responded with a laugh.

"Your wish is my command, my little witch." He picked her up, crushing her body to his.

Her legs went around his waist, and he held her up with one hand while the other gripped her hair and angled her mouth to his. This time his kisses were not gentle but domineering. He plunged his tongue into her mouth, taking over space he thought of as his.

She felt utterly and completely his. Felt his desire for her but also his love and devotion. The bond between them had opened her eyes and peeled away the darkness. There was something utterly touching in knowing that he accepted every flawed, annoying, mad part of her.

Right now, there was one part of her that ached to its core for him. He kissed her so thoroughly that any thoughts of onlookers completely melted away. Only her strong, sexy mate was before her, and she needed him inside her immediately.

As if sensing her maddening desires, he pulled away, his hand releasing her hair and moving down to tug up the ends of her dress. Calypso smiled as she kissed his neck, aware that the only thing stopping her passionate mate from ripping her dress, as he often did, was to avoid exposing her to his clan.

Her smile turned to a gasp when, in one quick motion, he entered fully inside. Her head arched back in a moan. She loved it when he entered her hard, not giving her time to adjust. That edge of pain left her desperate for more.

Vidorak's mouth quickly swallowed her moans. He moved her along his cock fast and hard, taking her quickly and breathlessly. Her fingers dug into his shoulders as her pleasure slammed into her. Waves crashed along the edge of the lake with each thrust.

He released her mouth and bit at the curve of neck, hard enough to mark. The feeling of his bite caused her to clench around him further. Her body was still quivering with her release when she felt the warm spill of his seed.

With a kiss at where he bit her, he released her slowly back into the water. The clan cheered and started to dissipate, eager to get back to their drinking and celebrating.

Calypso paid no mind to anyone else other than her mate. Her hand went to his cheek. "I love you, my strong, perfect mate."

He grabbed her hand and brought it to his lips. "I love you too. You are my heart and my light. I will protect you, cherish you, and support you till my last breath."

"Yours was better." She smiled. "Let's go get drunk on orc mead. We will leave our problems for tomorrow and keep tonight for us."

"As long as we are together."

Hand in hand, they left the magical waters with hearts finally at peace.

Acknowledgements

Thank you for reading Calypso and Vidorak's story!

This book was a process to say the least. Many times it became a process I didn't think would have an end in sight. It would not have ultimately come together without the help of many people very dear to me.

Most importantly, I am very grateful to my husband, who served at beta reader/editor/idea bouncer/motivator/and Kleenex bringer (when the hopes were particularly low).

I am also incredibly thankful to the rest of my other beta readers, Ioni and Krisi, who helped me talk through every small detail and question that popped up in my mind. It is a miracle my number wasn't blocked my number by the end of it.

I'm also so very thankful to fayspeaker and her wonderful talent. I am still in awe over the cover.

Thank you, reader, for taking a chance on their story and giving your time to them.

Best,

Victoria Dove

About the Author

Victoria Palumbo is a steamy fantasy romance author who loves to write about complex heroines and their devoted mates who love them. When not writing, she is trying to survive the toddler phase supported by her own devoted mate and an endless amount of coffee.

See more about what she's up to on her website at www.authorvictoriadove.com